TALES FROM THE CRYPT®

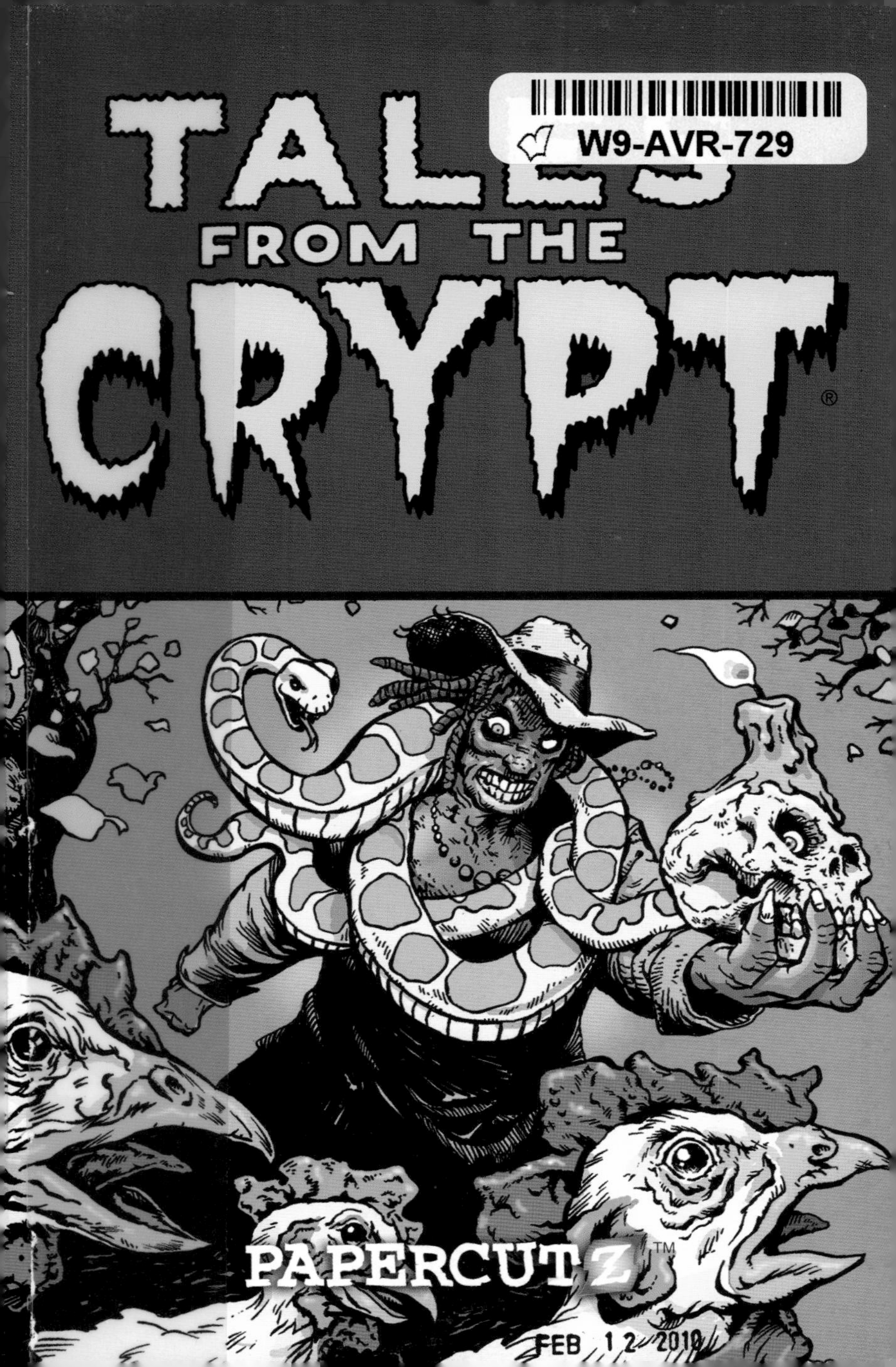

PAPERCUTZ™

TALES FROM THE CRYPT ®

NO. 6 – *YOU TOOMB*

JOHN L. LANSDALE
ROB VOLLMAR
GREG FARSHTEY
JIM SALICRUP
Writers

JAMES ROMBERGER &
MARGUERITE VAN COOK
TIM SMITH 3 &
LAURIE E. SMITH
MR. EXES
RICK PARKER
Artists

MR. EXES
Cover Artist

Based on the classic EC Comics series created by WILLIAM M. GAINES.

PAPERCUT Z ™
New York

"CHICKEN MAN"
JOHN L. LANSDALE – Writer
JAMES ROMBERGER &
MARGUERITE VAN COOK – Artists
MARK LERER – Letterer

"BRAIN FOOD"
ROB VOLLMAR – Writer
TIM SMITH 3 – Artist
LAURIE E. SMITH – Colorist
MARK LERER – Letterer

"LITTLE DARLIN'"
JOHN L. LANSDALE – Writer
JAMES ROMBERGER &
MARGUERITE VAN COOKE – Artists
JAMES ROMBERGER – Letterer

"MURDER M.A.I.D."
GREG FARSHTEY – Writer
MR. EXES – Artist
MARK LERER – Letterer

GHOULUNATIC SEQUENCES
JIM SALICRUP — Writer
RICK PARKER — Artist, Title Letterer, Colorist
MARK LERER – Letterer

CHRIS NELSON & SHELLY DUTCHAK
Production

MICHAEL PETRANEK
Editorial Assistant

JIM SALICRUP
Editor-in-Chief

ISBN-13: 978-1-59707-136-9 paperback edition
ISBN-10: 1-59707-136-6 paperback edition
ISBN-13: 978-1-59707-137-6 hardcover edition
ISBN-10: 1-59707-137-4 hardcover edition

3 8001 00091 2174

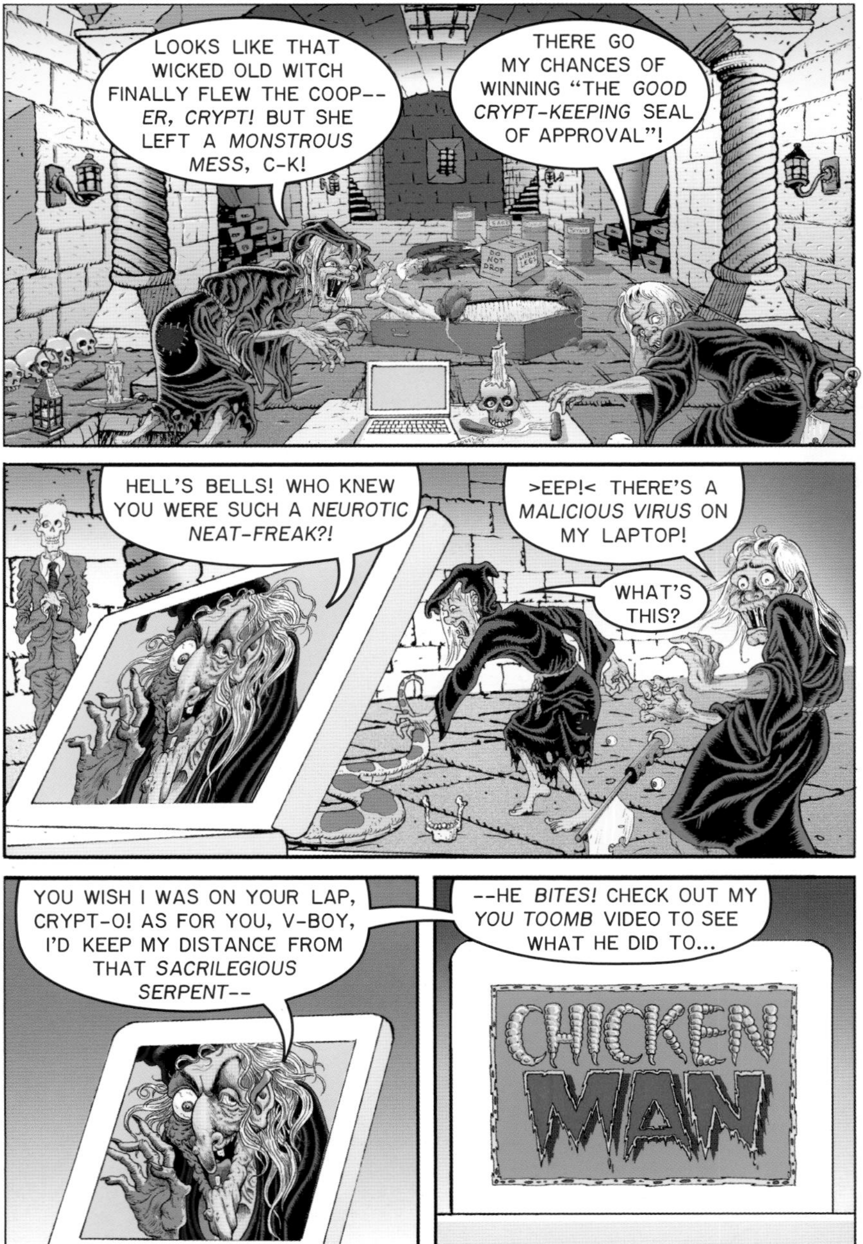
LOOKS LIKE THAT WICKED OLD WITCH FINALLY FLEW THE COOP-- *ER, CRYPT!* BUT SHE LEFT A *MONSTROUS MESS*, C-K!
THERE GO MY CHANCES OF WINNING "THE *GOOD CRYPT-KEEPING* SEAL OF APPROVAL"!
DO NOT DROP
HELL'S BELLS! WHO KNEW YOU WERE SUCH A *NEUROTIC NEAT-FREAK?!*
>EEP!< THERE'S A *MALICIOUS VIRUS* ON MY LAPTOP!
WHAT'S THIS?
YOU WISH I WAS ON YOUR LAP, CRYPT-O! AS FOR YOU, V-BOY, I'D KEEP MY DISTANCE FROM THAT *SACRILEGIOUS SERPENT*--
--HE *BITES!* CHECK OUT MY *YOU TOOMB* VIDEO TO SEE WHAT HE DID TO...
CHICKEN MAN

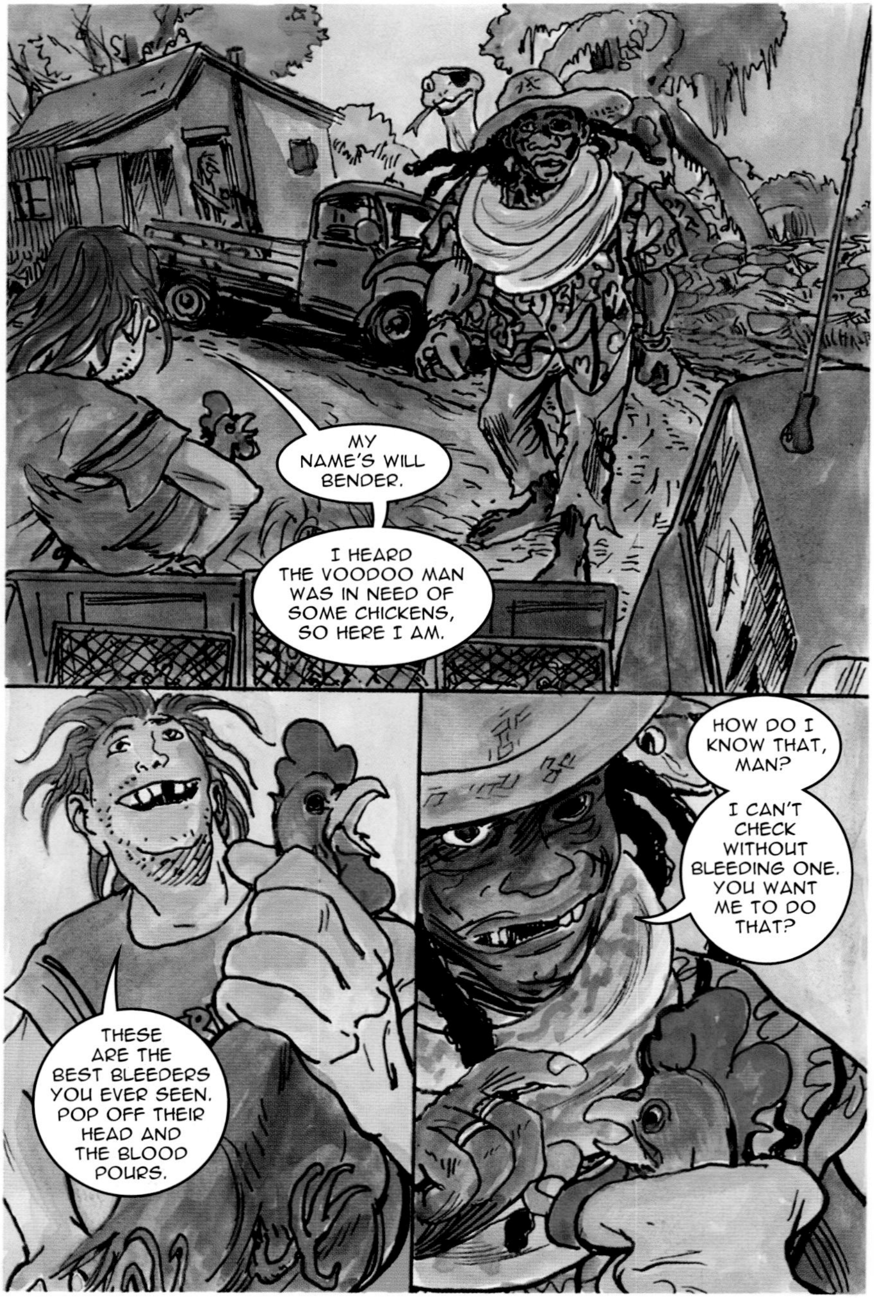
MY NAME'S WILL BENDER.
I HEARD THE VOODOO MAN WAS IN NEED OF SOME CHICKENS, SO HERE I AM.
THESE ARE THE BEST BLEEDERS YOU EVER SEEN. POP OFF THEIR HEAD AND THE BLOOD POURS.
HOW DO I KNOW THAT, MAN?
I CAN'T CHECK WITHOUT BLEEDING ONE. YOU WANT ME TO DO THAT?

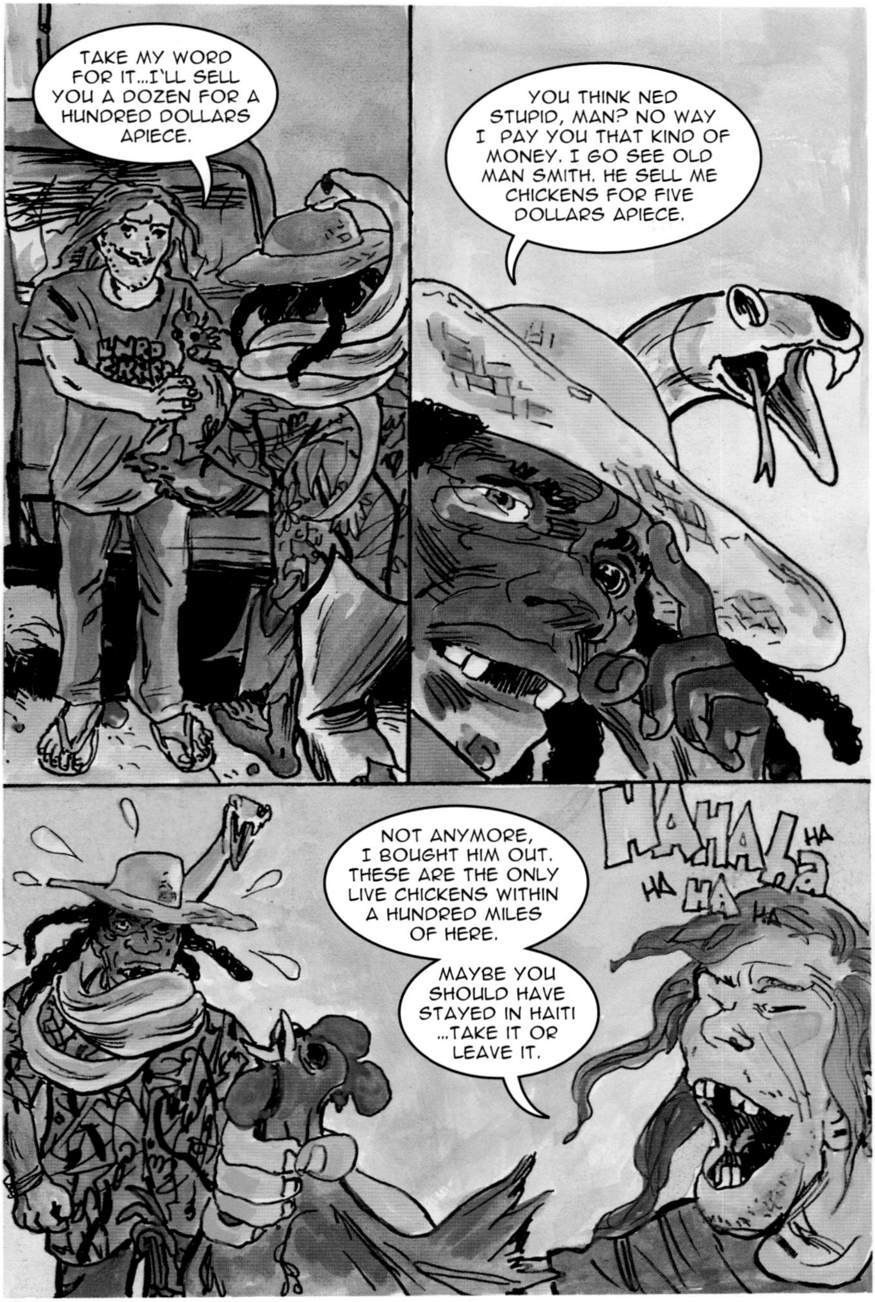
TAKE MY WORD FOR IT...I'LL SELL YOU A DOZEN FOR A HUNDRED DOLLARS APIECE.
YOU THINK NED STUPID, MAN? NO WAY I PAY YOU THAT KIND OF MONEY. I GO SEE OLD MAN SMITH. HE SELL ME CHICKENS FOR FIVE DOLLARS APIECE.
NOT ANYMORE, I BOUGHT HIM OUT. THESE ARE THE ONLY LIVE CHICKENS WITHIN A HUNDRED MILES OF HERE.
MAYBE YOU SHOULD HAVE STAYED IN HAITI ...TAKE IT OR LEAVE IT.
HAHAHa HA
HA HA HA

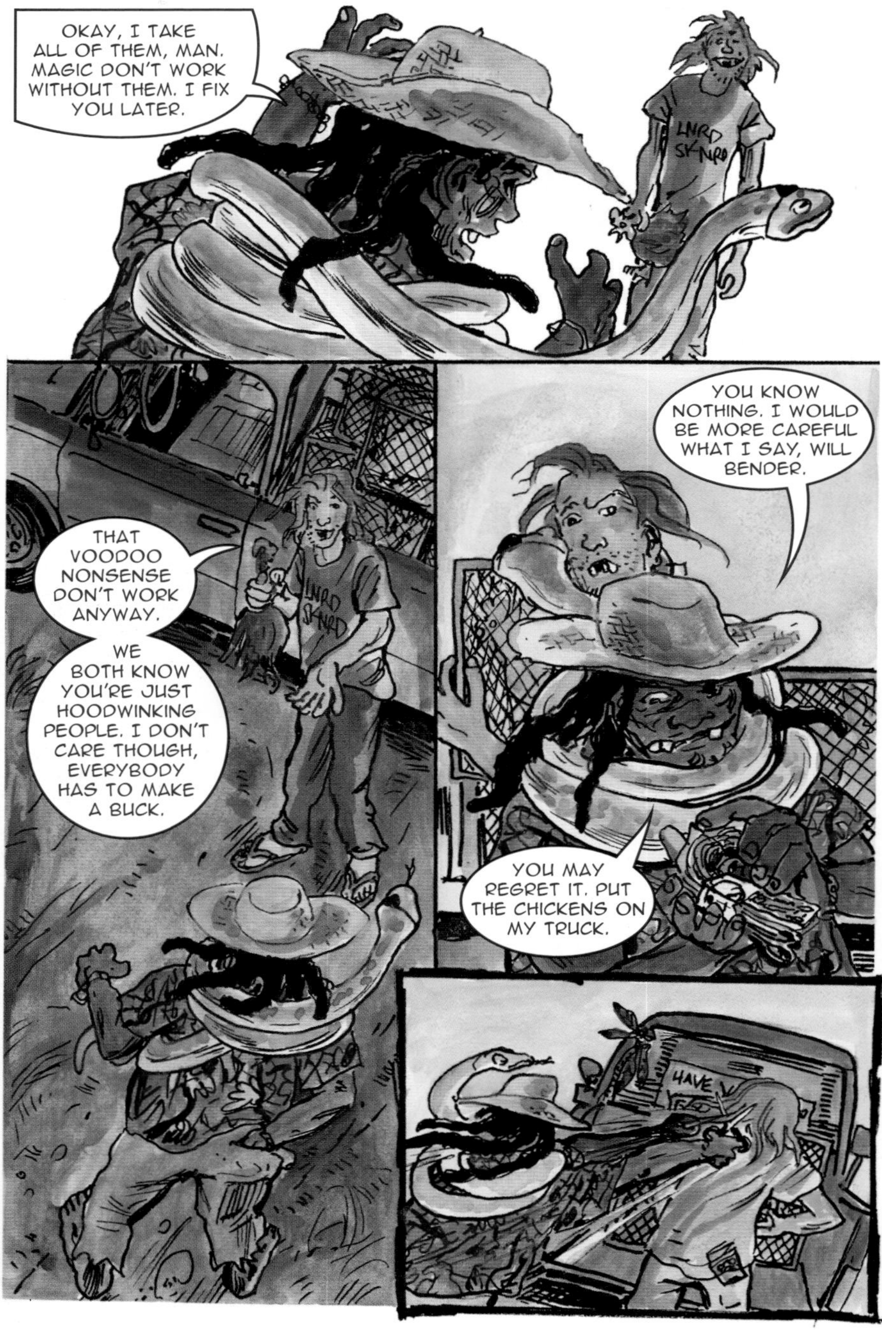
OKAY, I TAKE ALL OF THEM, MAN. MAGIC DON'T WORK WITHOUT THEM. I FIX YOU LATER.
LNRD SKNRD
THAT VOODOO NONSENSE DON'T WORK ANYWAY.
WE BOTH KNOW YOU'RE JUST HOODWINKING PEOPLE. I DON'T CARE THOUGH, EVERYBODY HAS TO MAKE A BUCK.
YOU KNOW NOTHING. I WOULD BE MORE CAREFUL WHAT I SAY, WILL BENDER.
YOU MAY REGRET IT. PUT THE CHICKENS ON MY TRUCK.
HAVE

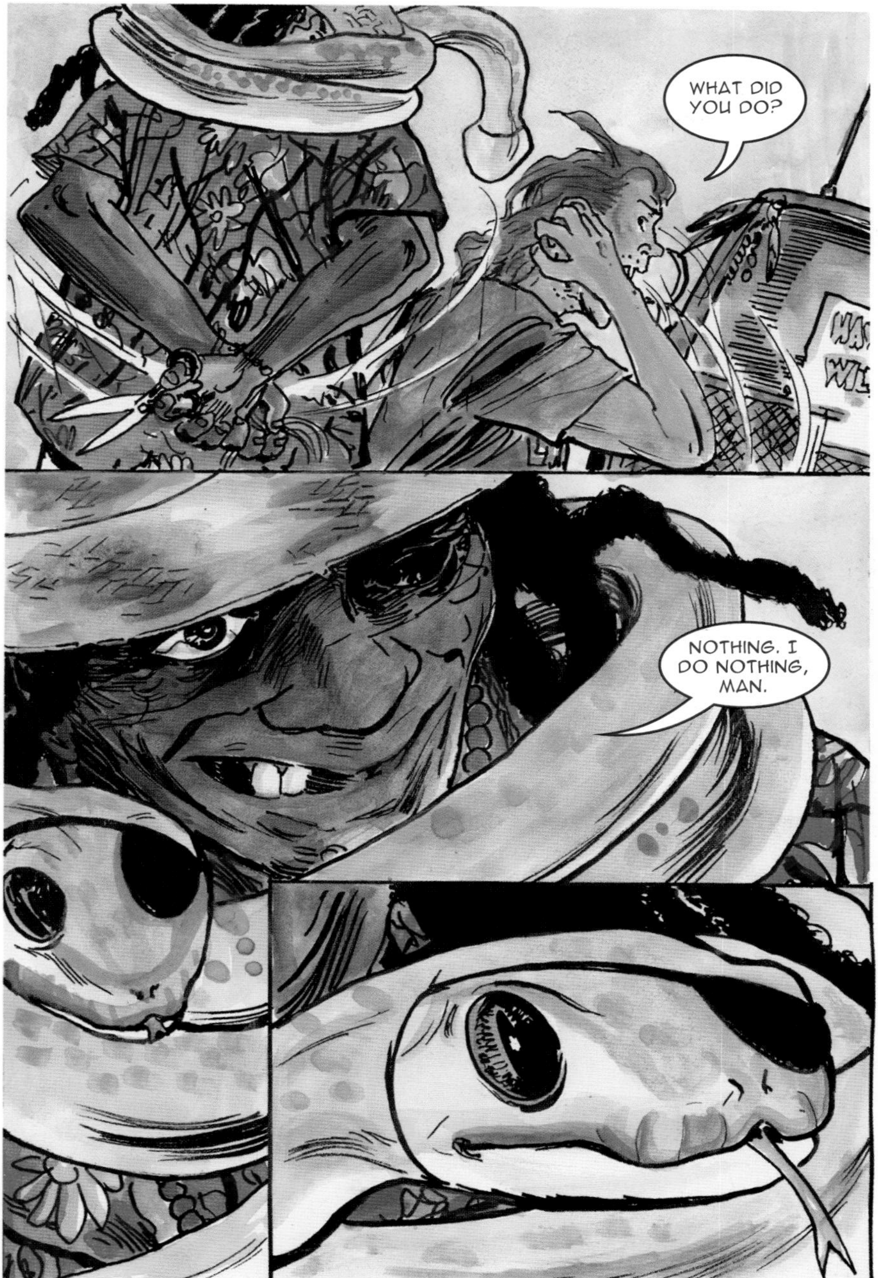
WHAT DID YOU DO?
NOTHING. I DO NOTHING, MAN.

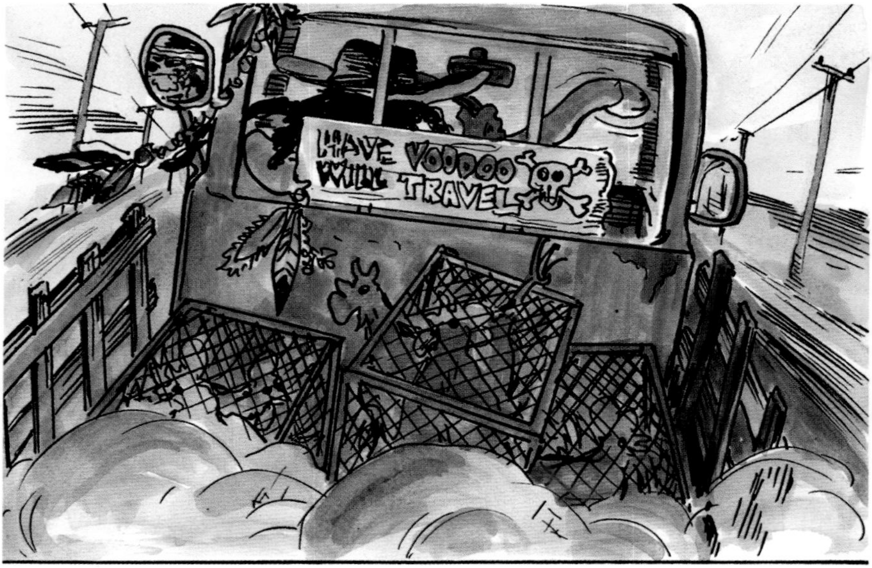
HAVE VOODOO
WILL TRAVEL

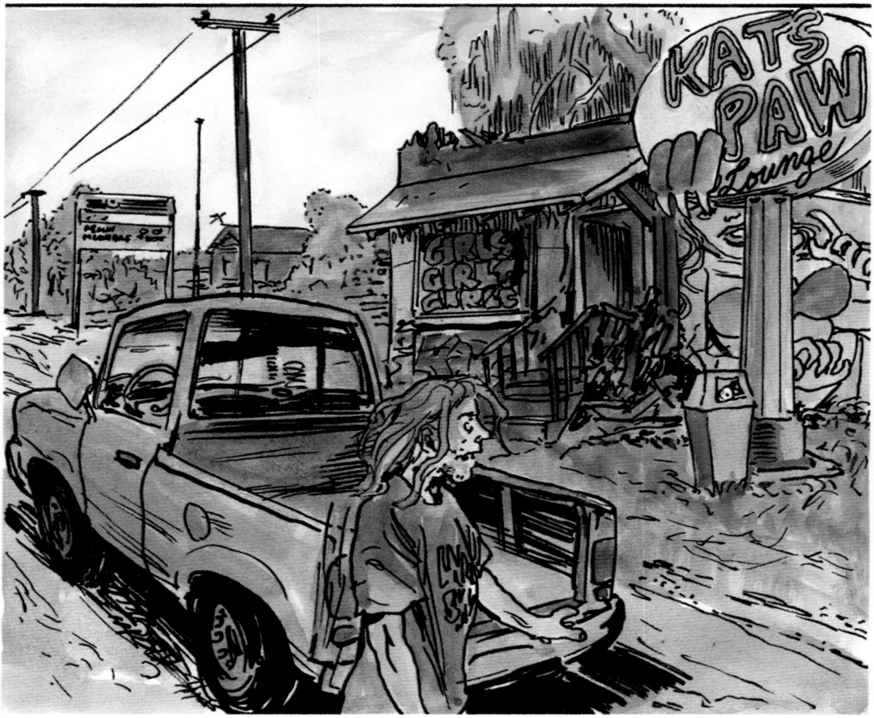
KATS PAW
Lounge

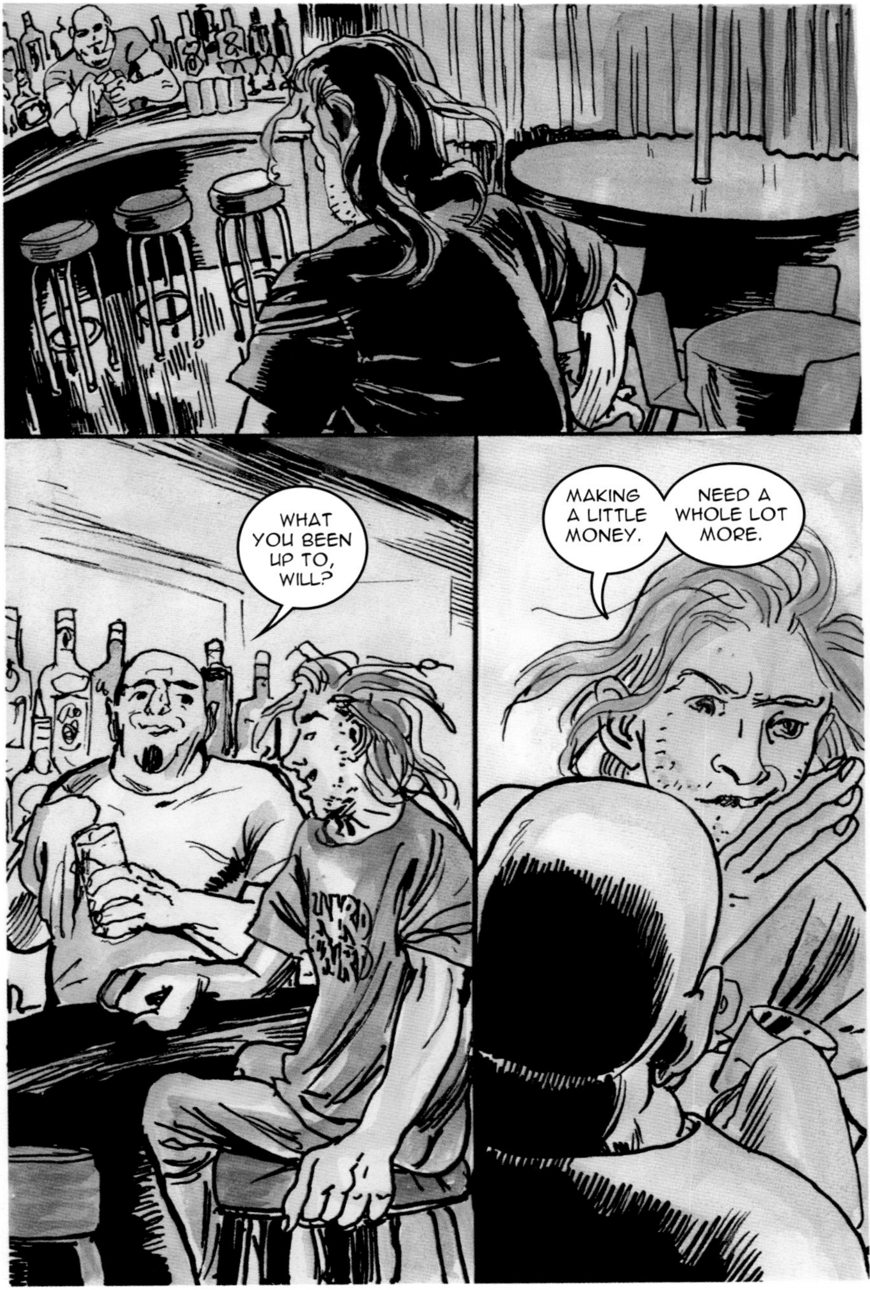
WHAT YOU BEEN UP TO, WILL?
MAKING A LITTLE MONEY.
NEED A WHOLE LOT MORE.

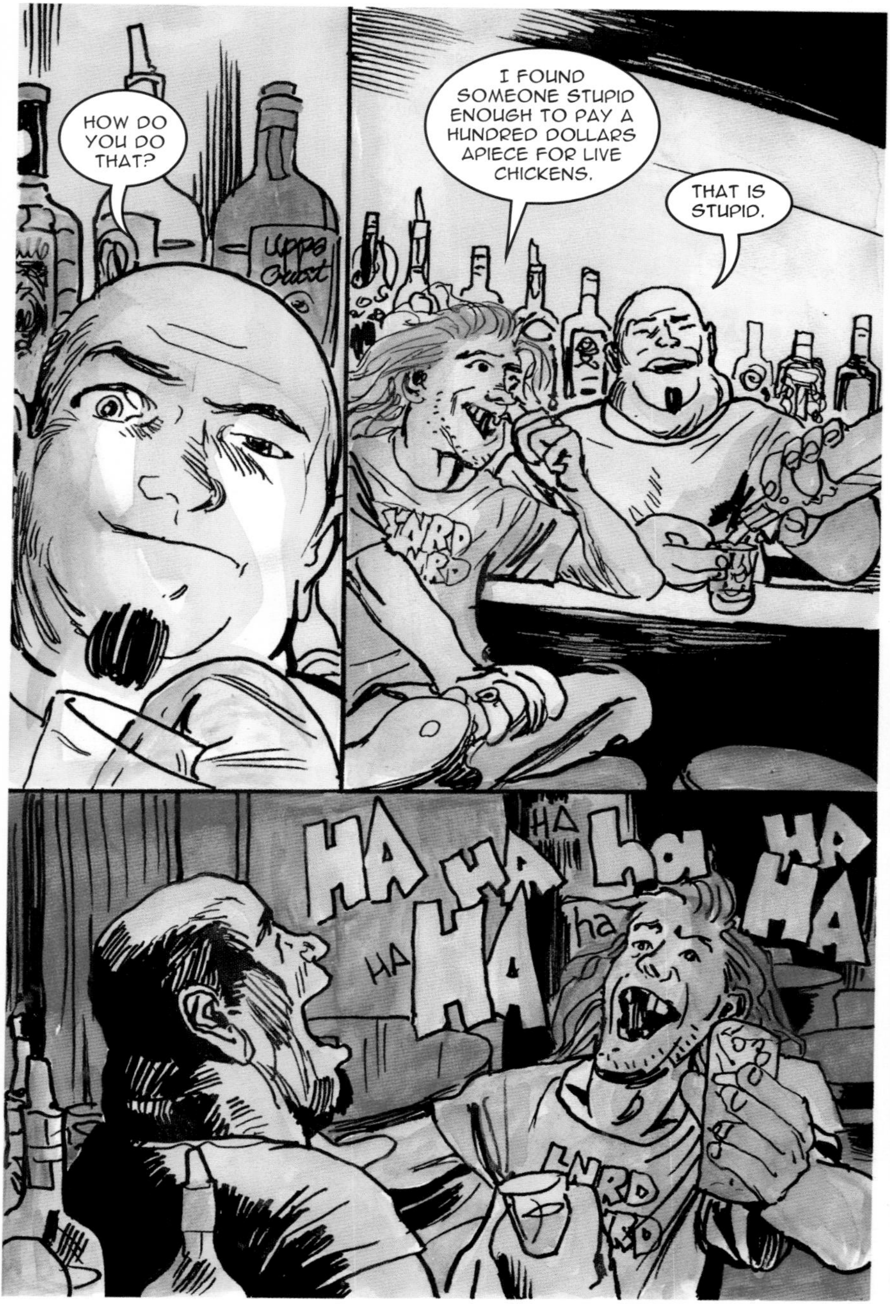
HOW DO YOU DO THAT?
I FOUND SOMEONE STUPID ENOUGH TO PAY A HUNDRED DOLLARS APIECE FOR LIVE CHICKENS.
THAT IS STUPID.
HA HA HA ha HA HA ha HA HA HA

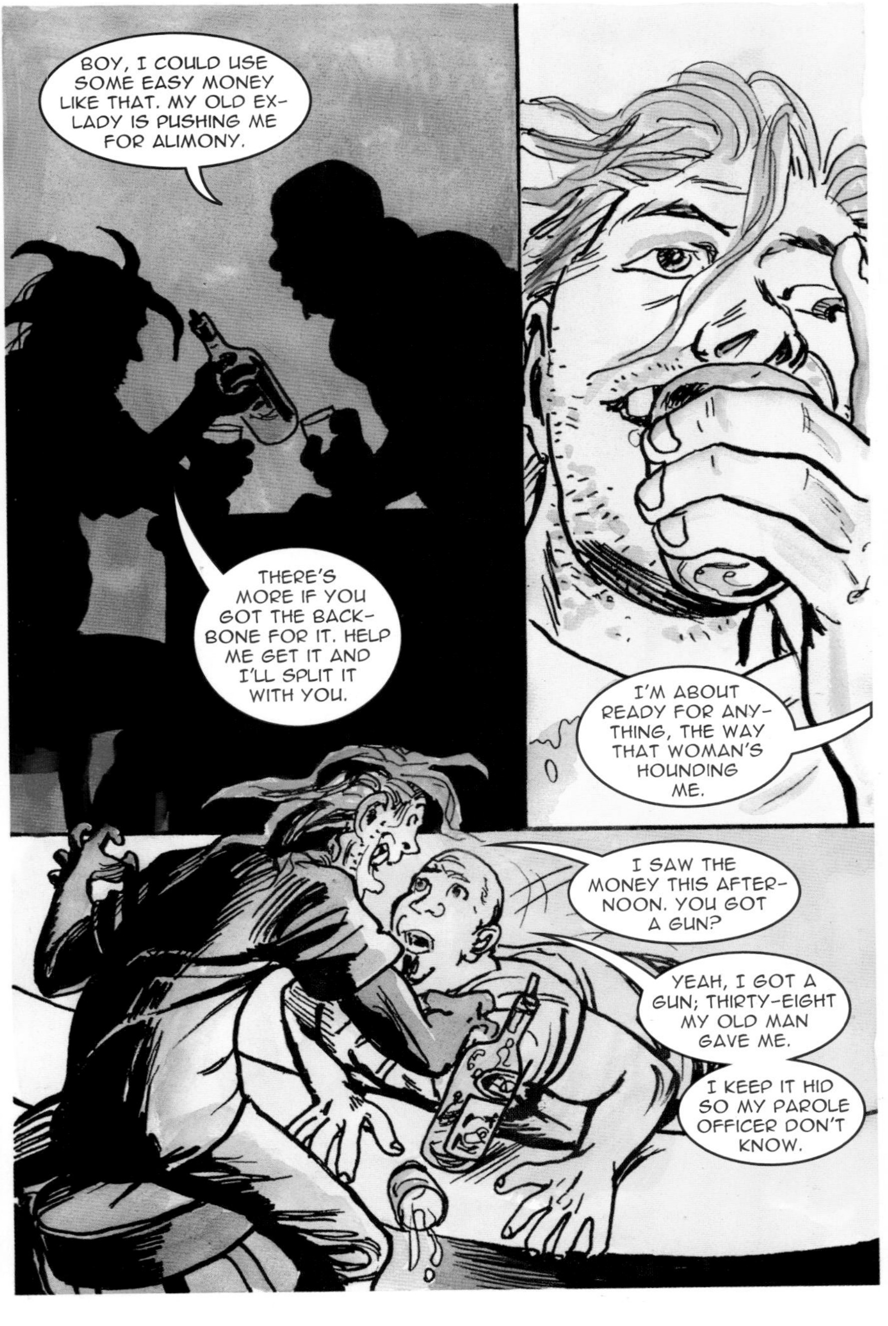
BOY, I COULD USE SOME EASY MONEY LIKE THAT. MY OLD EX-LADY IS PUSHING ME FOR ALIMONY.
THERE'S MORE IF YOU GOT THE BACK-BONE FOR IT. HELP ME GET IT AND I'LL SPLIT IT WITH YOU.
I'M ABOUT READY FOR ANY-THING, THE WAY THAT WOMAN'S HOUNDING ME.
I SAW THE MONEY THIS AFTER-NOON. YOU GOT A GUN?
YEAH, I GOT A GUN; THIRTY-EIGHT MY OLD MAN GAVE ME.
I KEEP IT HID SO MY PAROLE OFFICER DON'T KNOW.

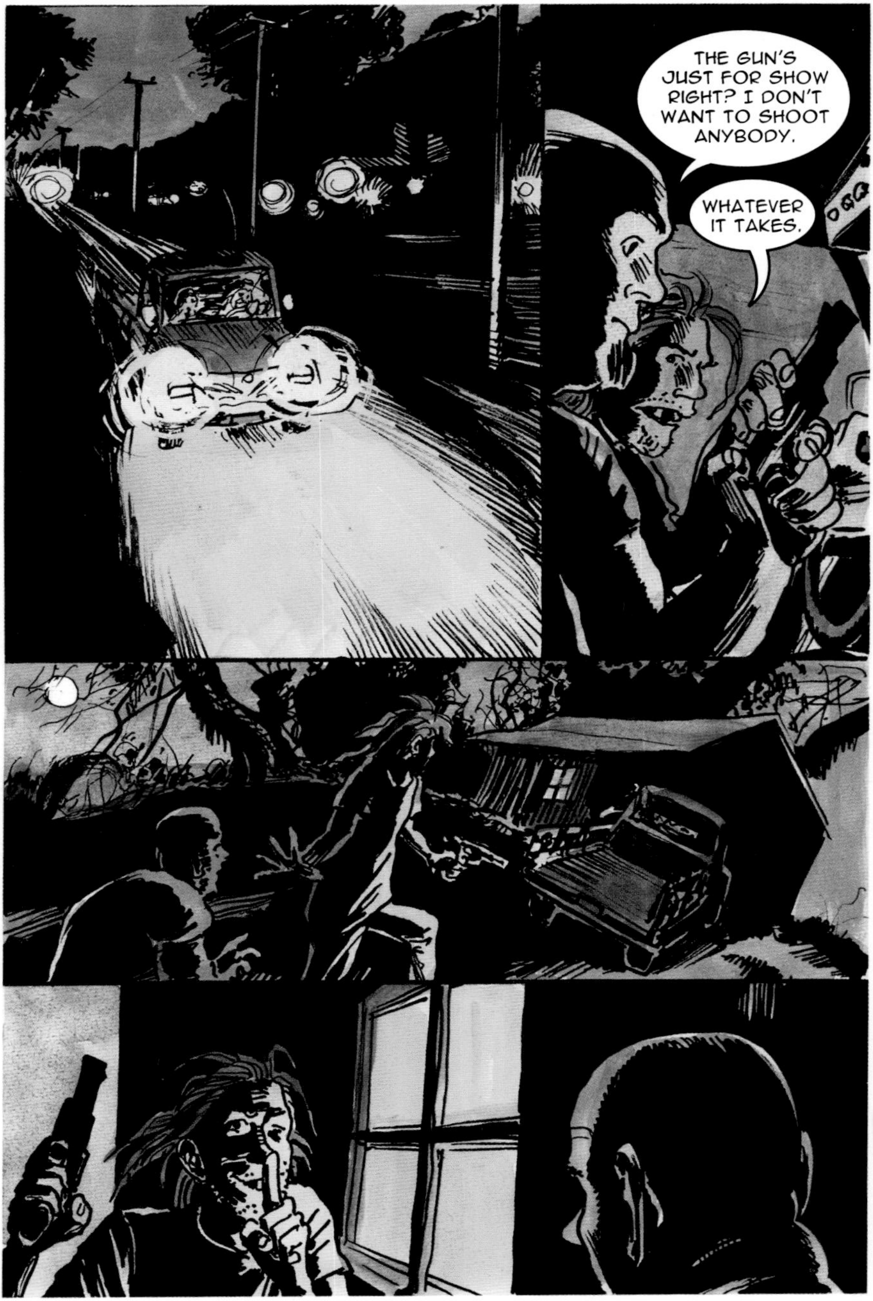
THE GUN'S JUST FOR SHOW RIGHT? I DON'T WANT TO SHOOT ANYBODY.
WHATEVER IT TAKES.

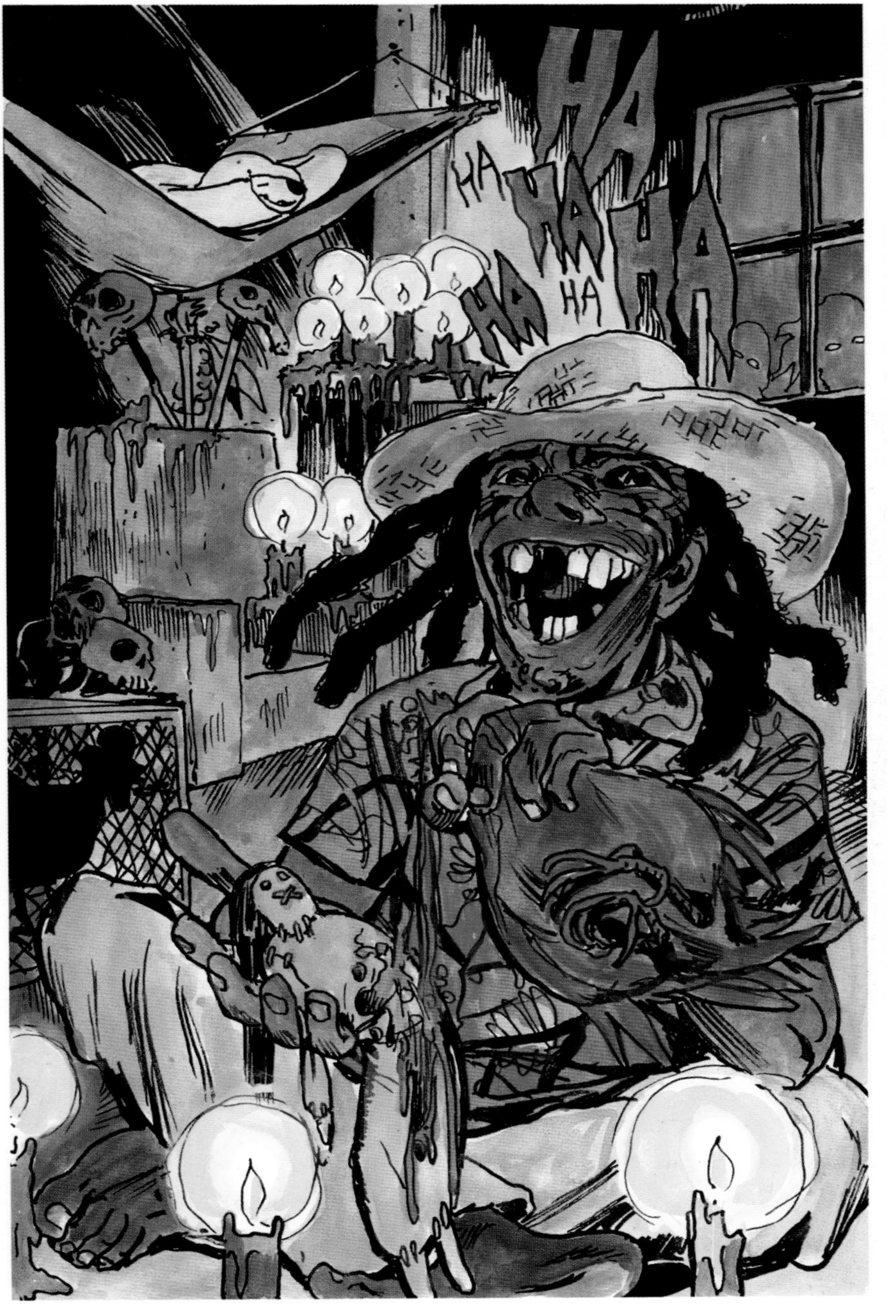

HA
HA
HA
HA
HA
HA
HA
HA

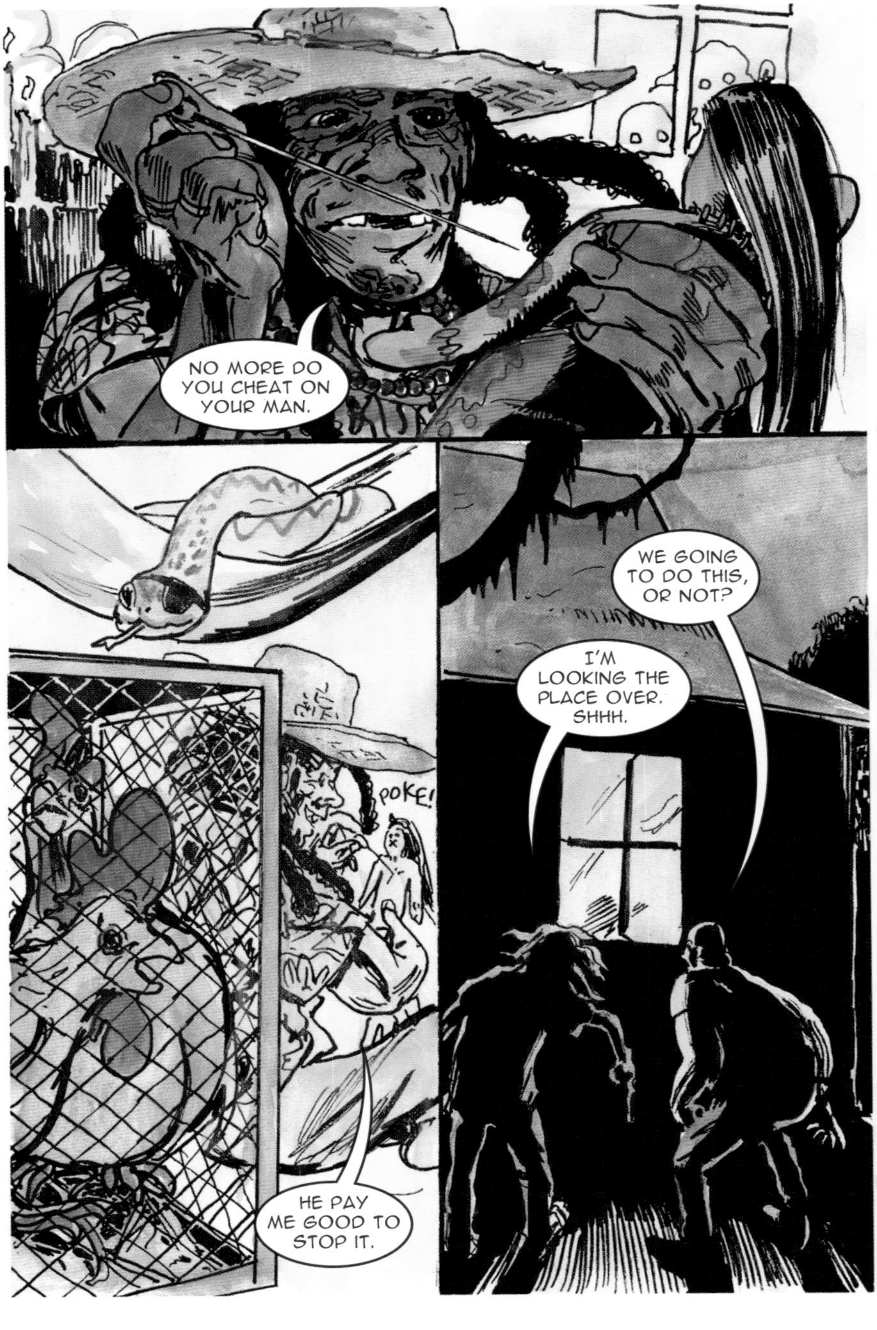
NO MORE DO YOU CHEAT ON YOUR MAN.
WE GOING TO DO THIS, OR NOT?
I'M LOOKING THE PLACE OVER. SHHH.
POKE!
HE PAY ME GOOD TO STOP IT.

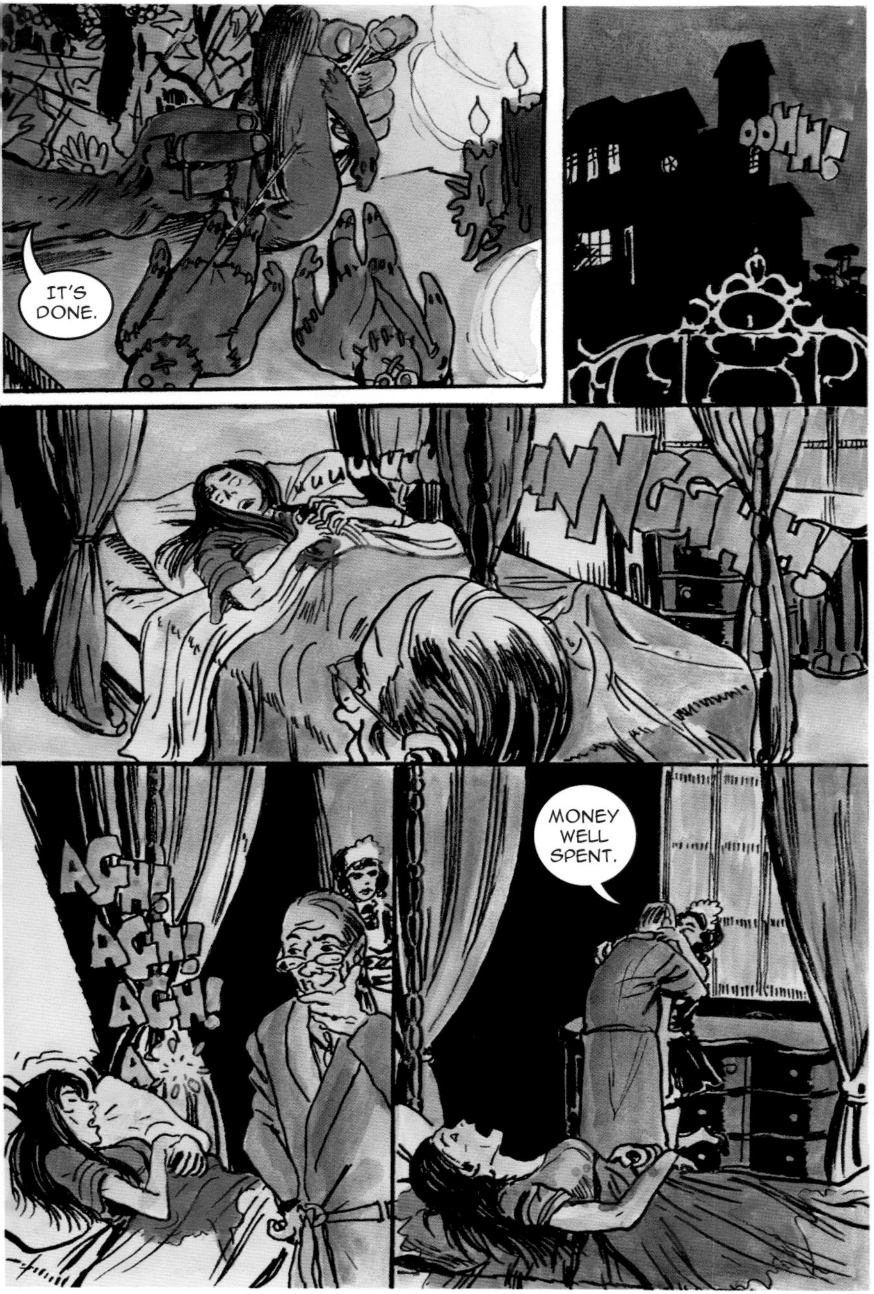
IT'S DONE.
OOHH!
NNGGHH!
ACH! ACH! ACH!
MONEY WELL SPENT.

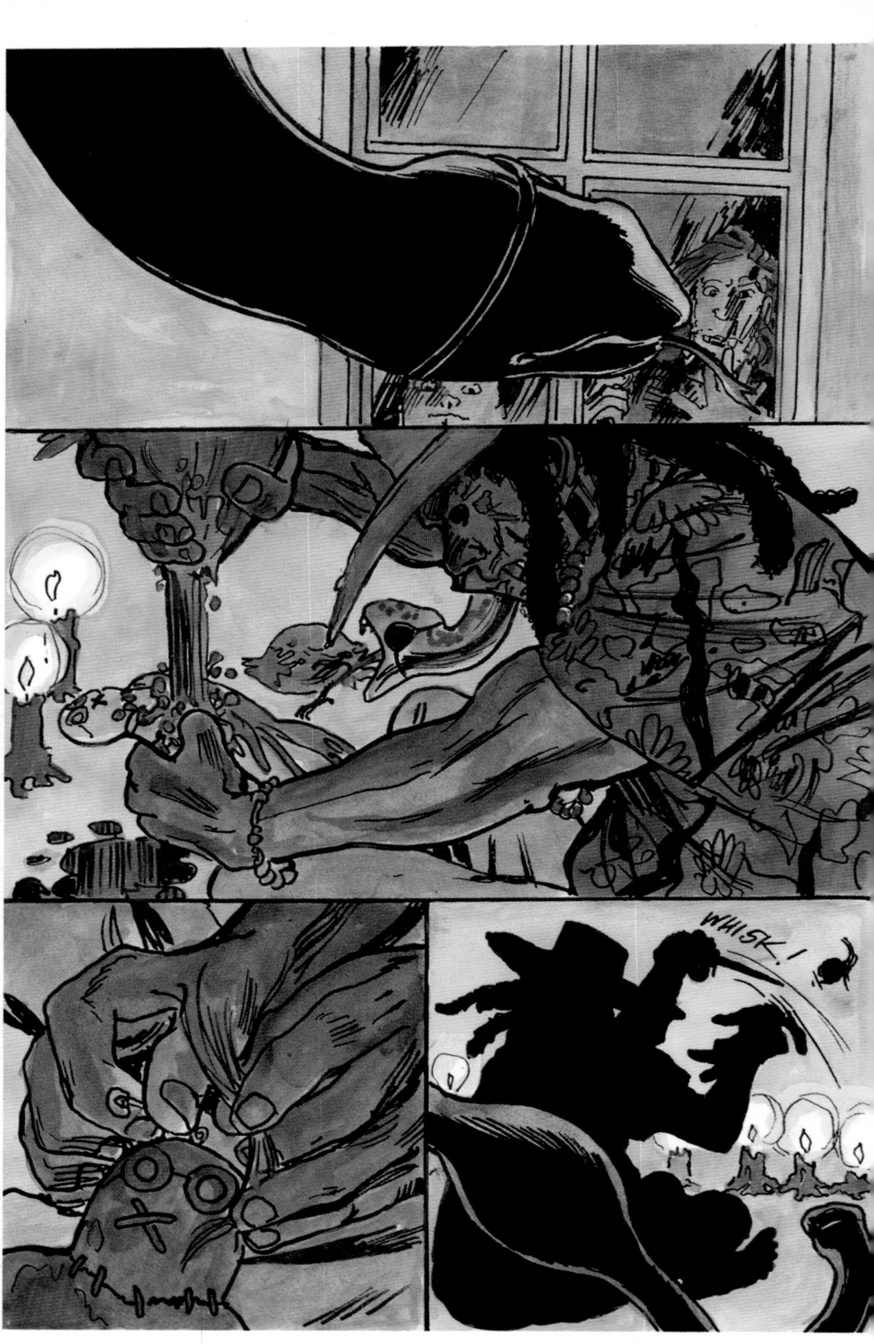
WHISK!

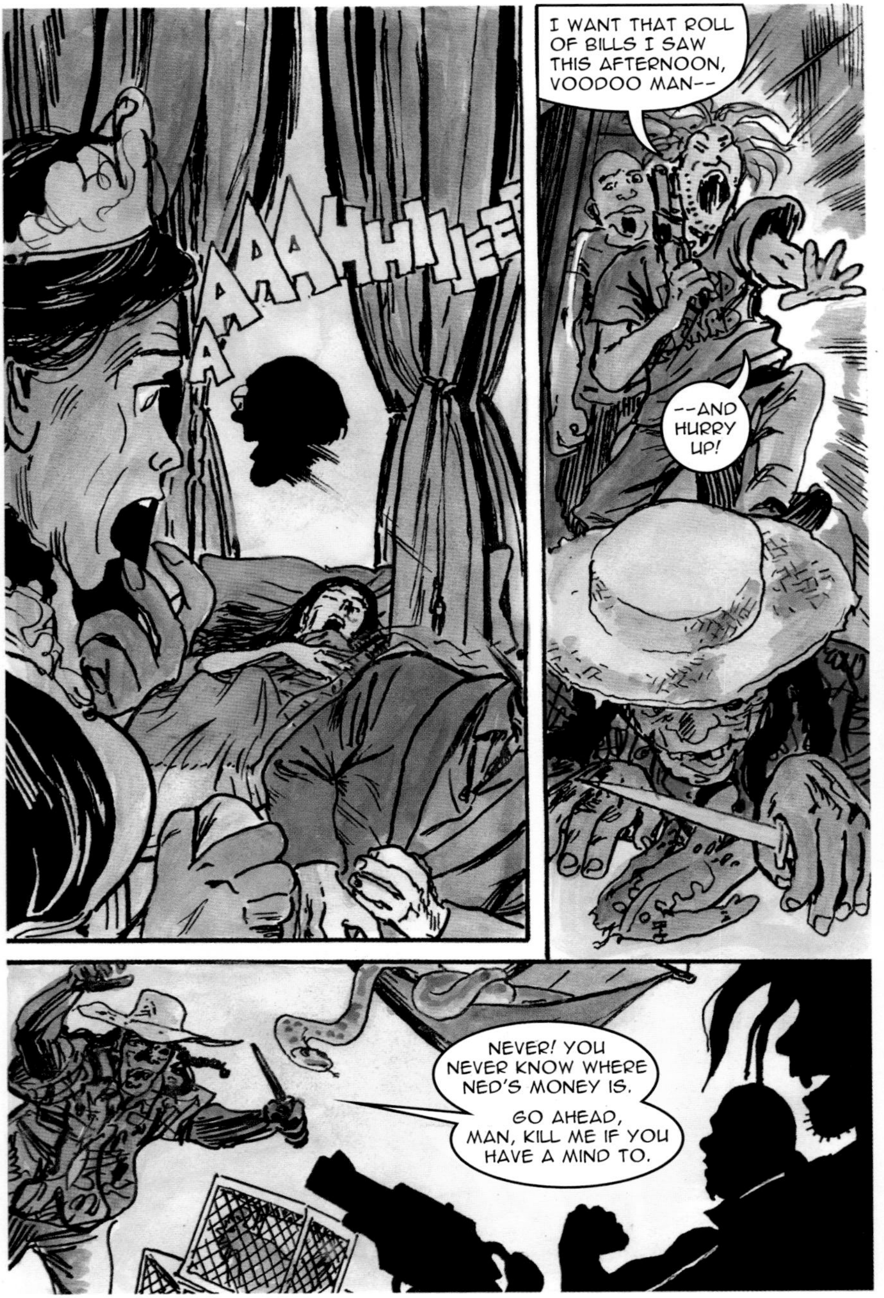
AAAAHHIIEE
I WANT THAT ROLL OF BILLS I SAW THIS AFTERNOON, VOODOO MAN--
--AND HURRY UP!
NEVER! YOU NEVER KNOW WHERE NED'S MONEY IS.
GO AHEAD, MAN, KILL ME IF YOU HAVE A MIND TO.

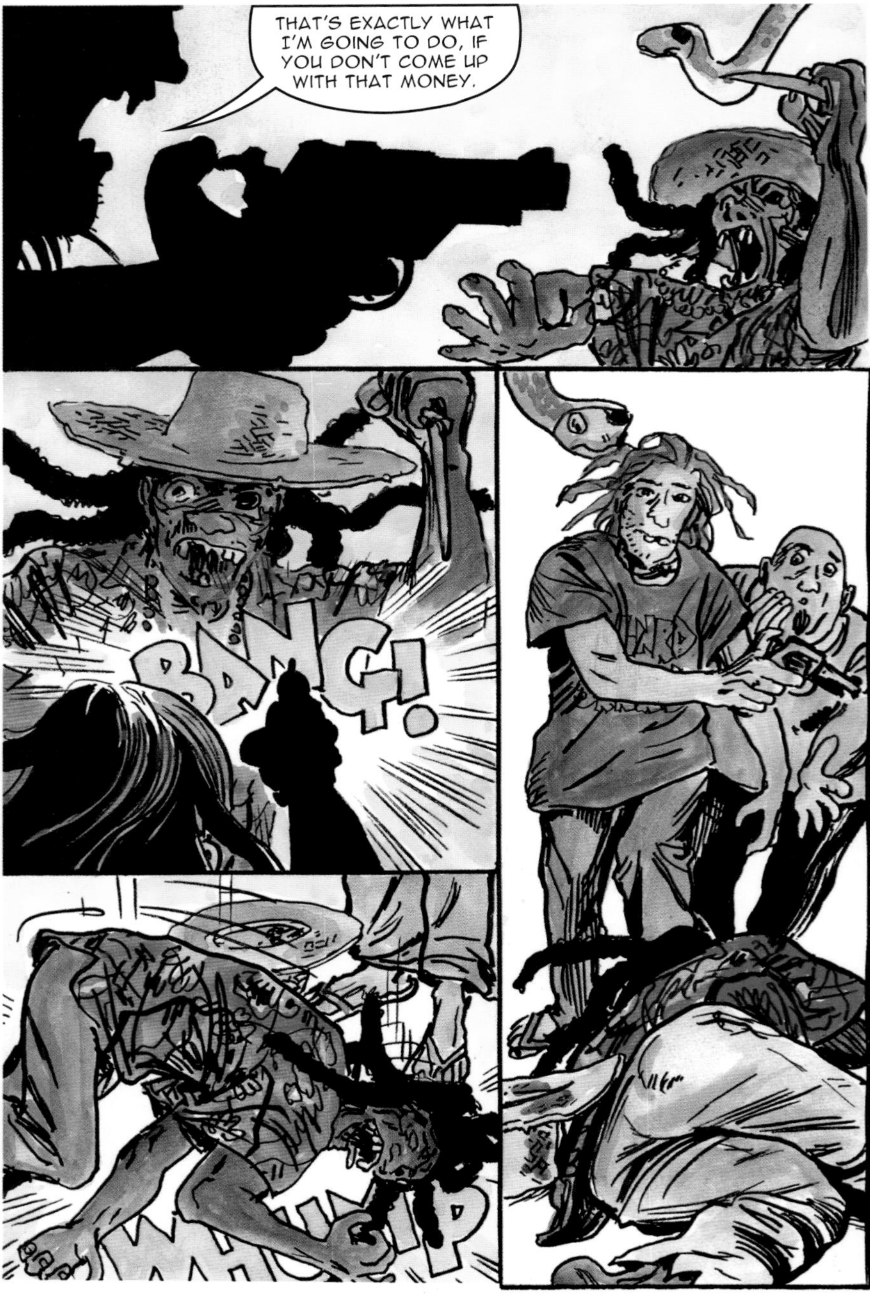
THAT'S EXACTLY WHAT I'M GOING TO DO, IF YOU DON'T COME UP WITH THAT MONEY.
BANG!

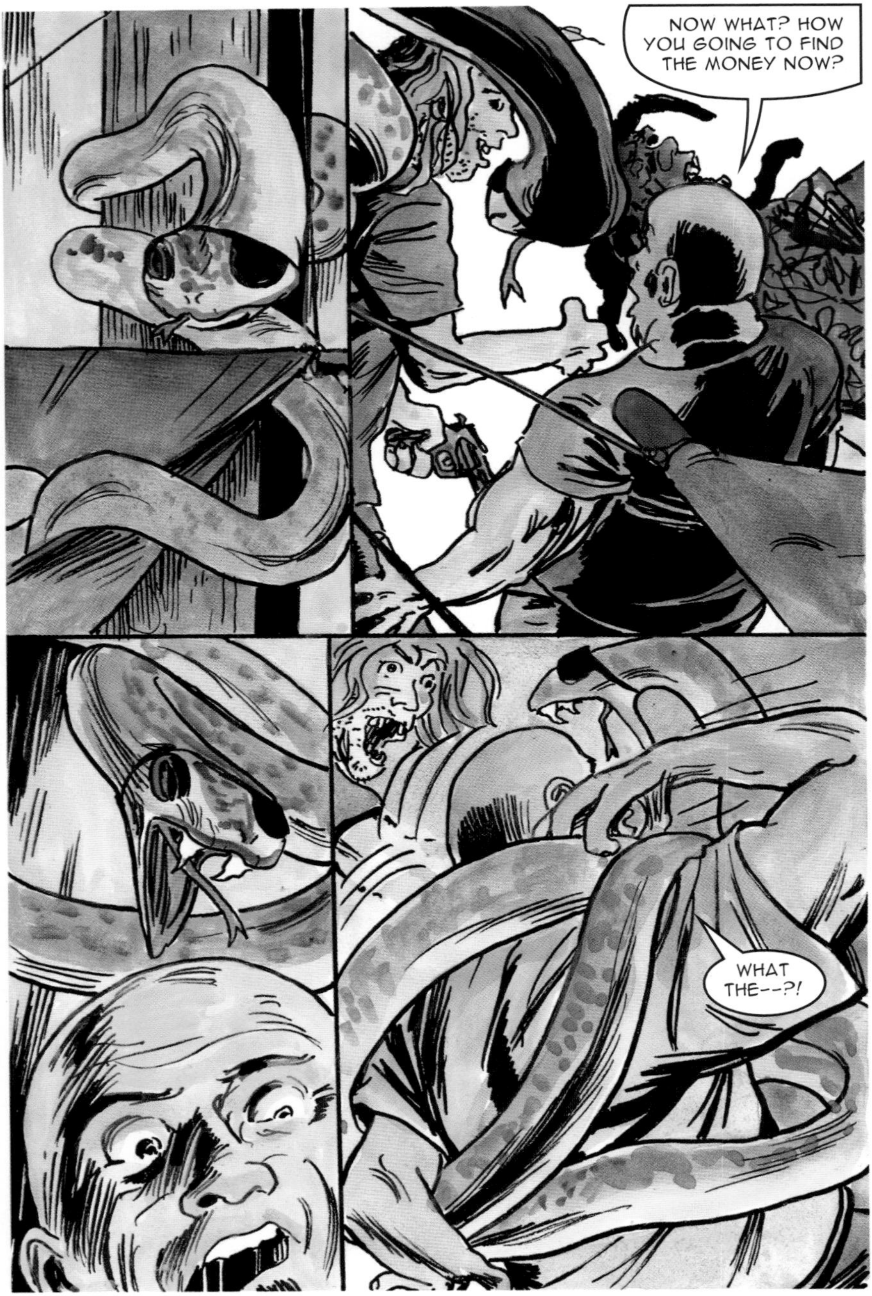
NOW WHAT? HOW YOU GOING TO FIND THE MONEY NOW?
WHAT THE--?!

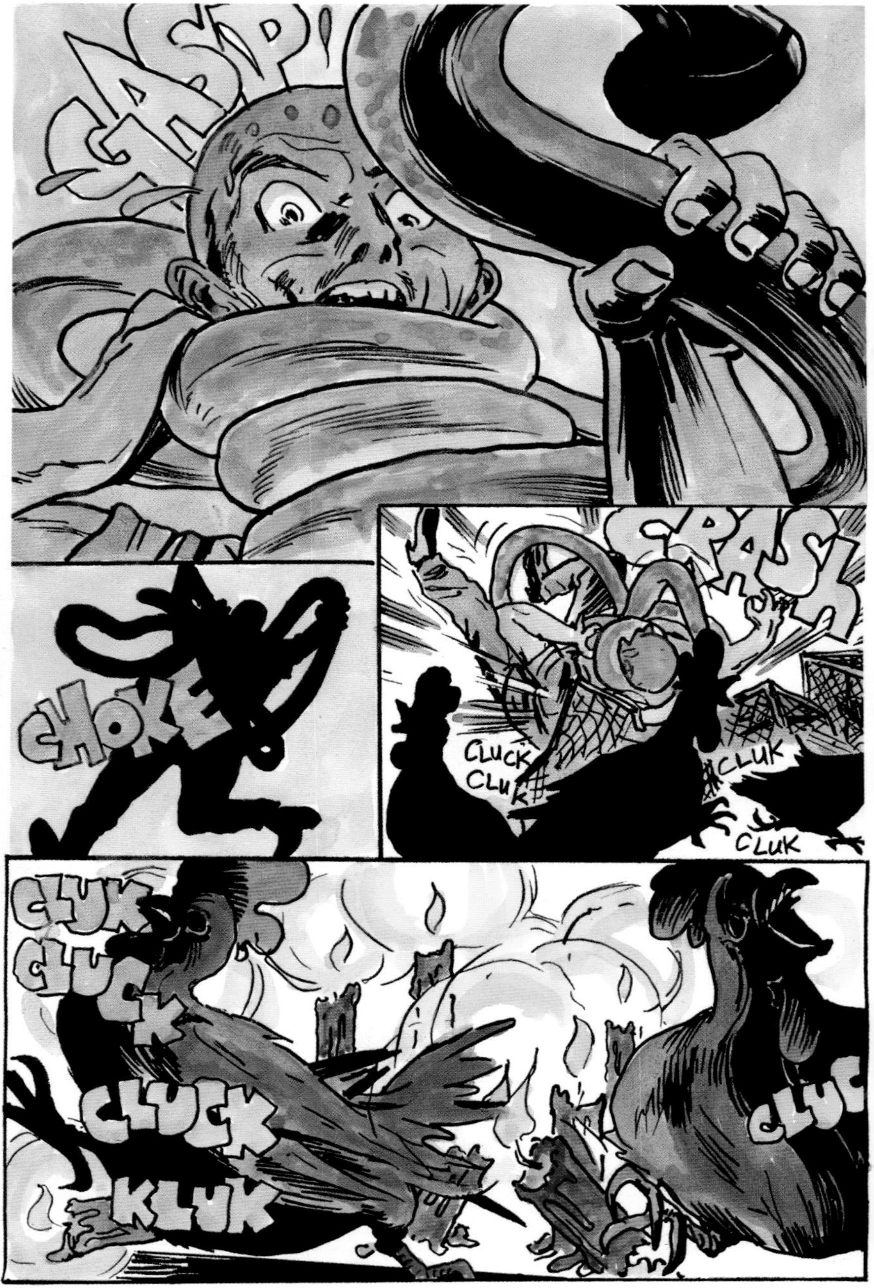
GASP!
CHOKE
CRASH
CLUCK
CLUK
CLUK
CLUK
CLUK
CLUCK
CLUCK
KLUK
CLUC

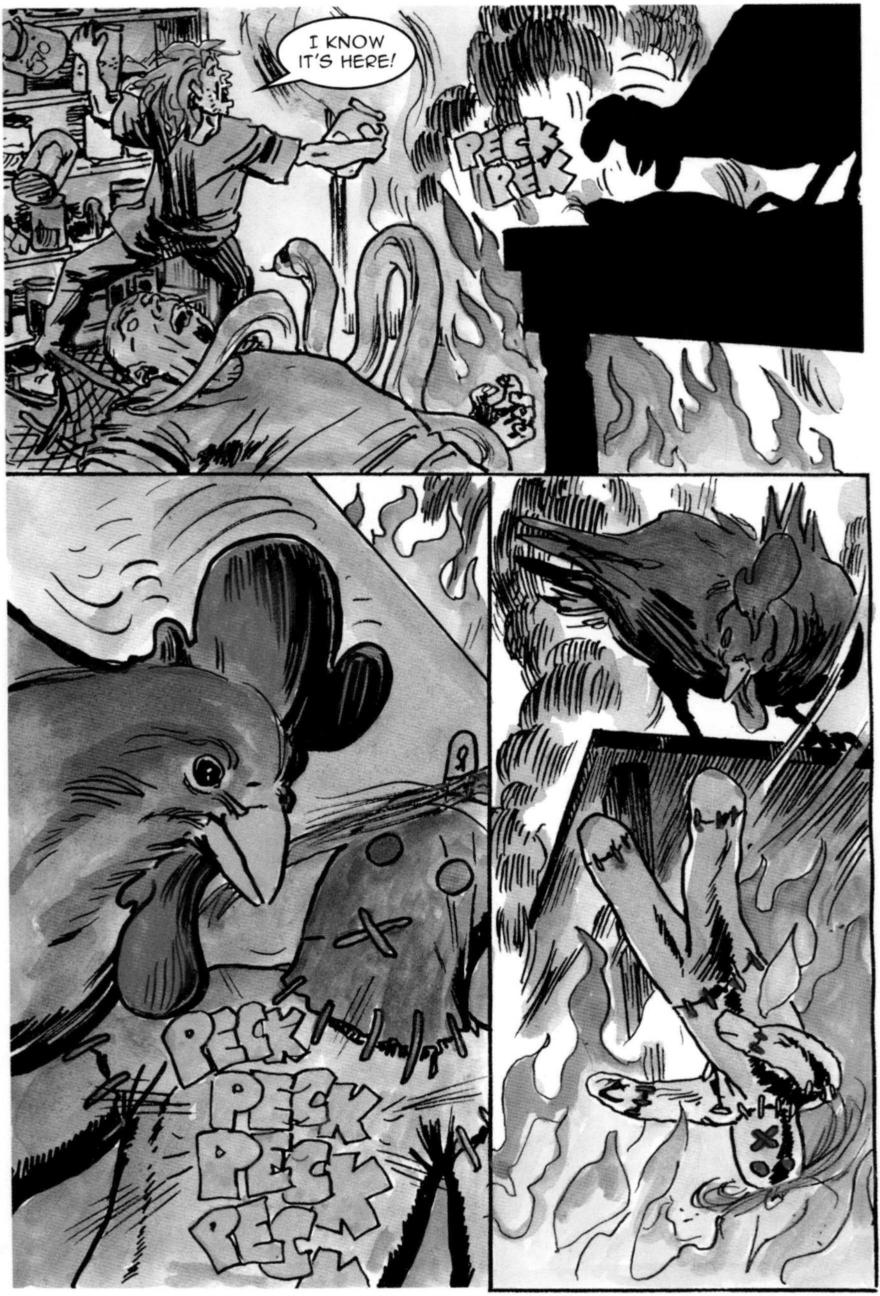

I KNOW IT'S HERE!
PECK PEK
PECK
PECK
PECK
PECK

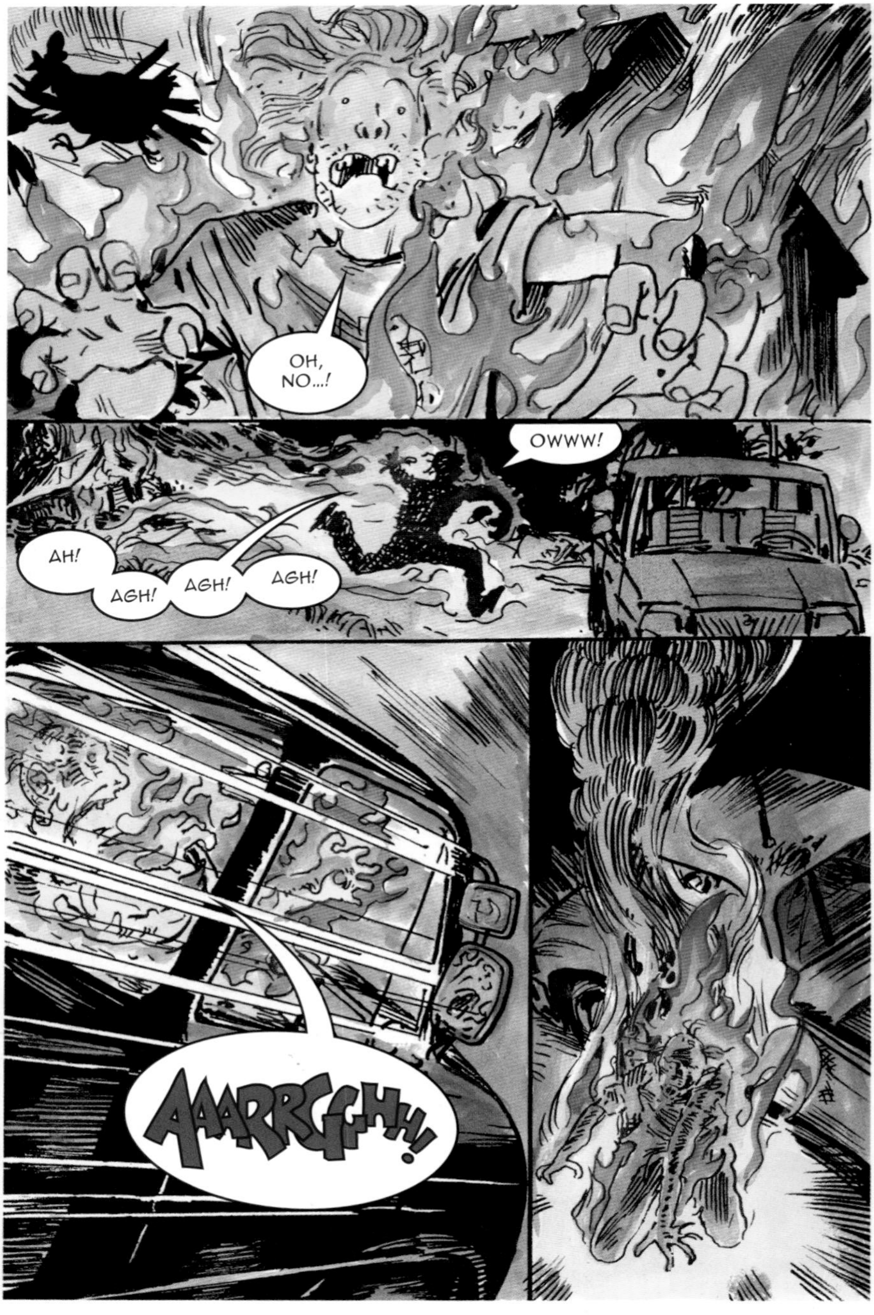
OH, NO...!
OWWW!
AH!
AGH!
AGH!
AGH!
AAARRGGHH!

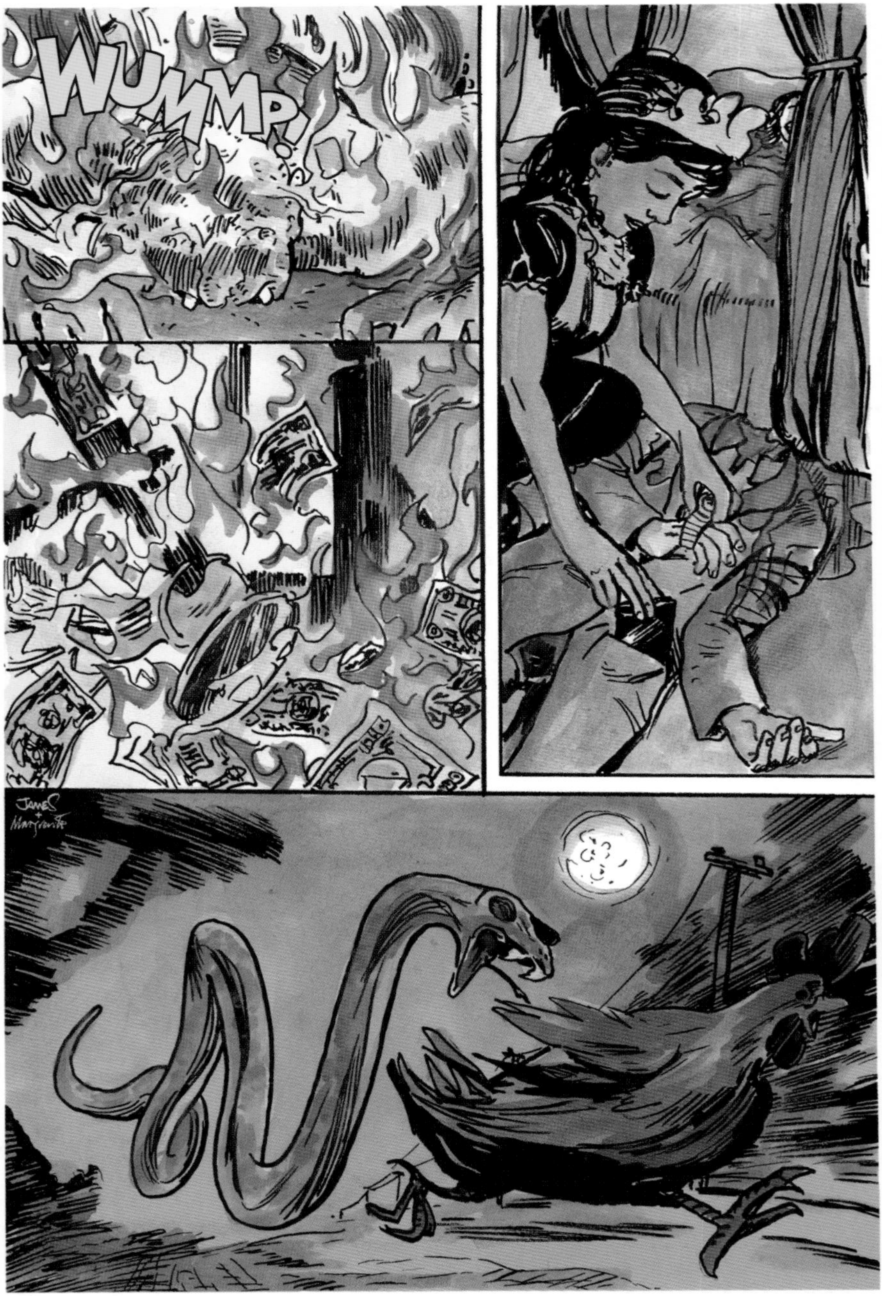
WUMMP!

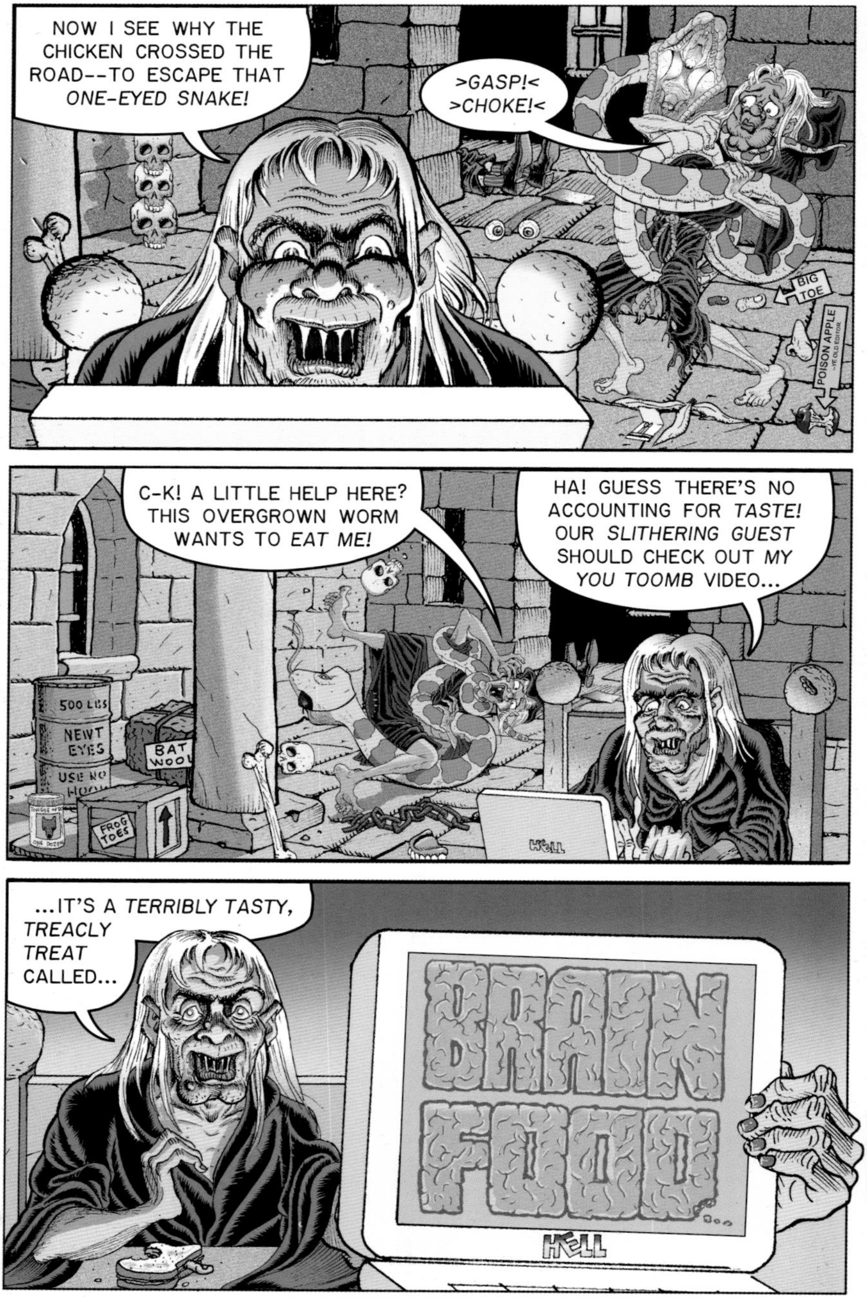
NOW I SEE WHY THE CHICKEN CROSSED THE ROAD--TO ESCAPE THAT *ONE-EYED SNAKE!*
>GASP!<
>CHOKE!<
BIG TOE
POISON APPLE
C-K! A LITTLE HELP HERE? THIS OVERGROWN WORM WANTS TO *EAT ME!*
HA! GUESS THERE'S NO ACCOUNTING FOR *TASTE!* OUR *SLITHERING GUEST* SHOULD CHECK OUT *MY YOU TOOMB* VIDEO...
500 LBS
NEWT EYES
BAT WOOL
FROG TOES
HELL
...IT'S A *TERRIBLY TASTY, TREACLY TREAT* CALLED...
BRAIN FOOD
HELL

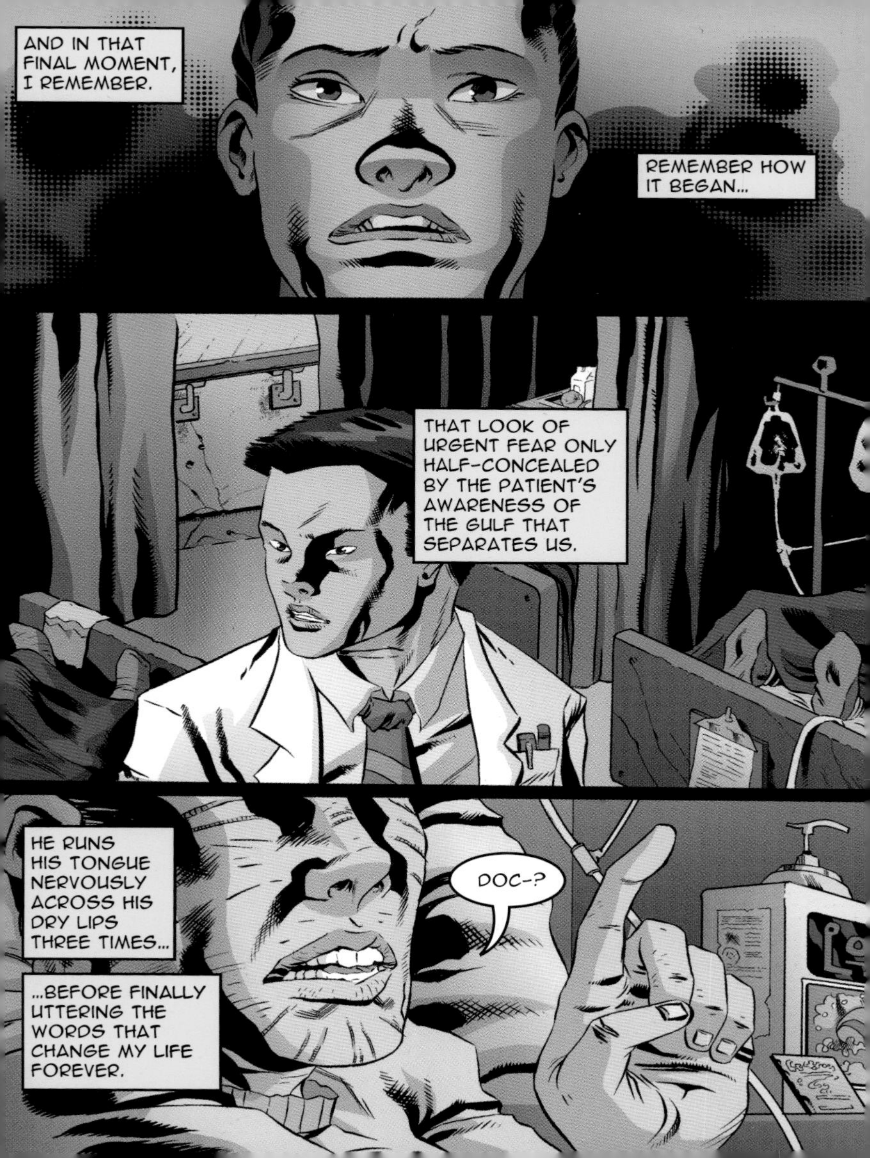
AND IN THAT FINAL MOMENT, I REMEMBER.
REMEMBER HOW IT BEGAN...
THAT LOOK OF URGENT FEAR ONLY HALF-CONCEALED BY THE PATIENT'S AWARENESS OF THE GULF THAT SEPARATES US.
HE RUNS HIS TONGUE NERVOUSLY ACROSS HIS DRY LIPS THREE TIMES...
...BEFORE FINALLY UTTERING THE WORDS THAT CHANGE MY LIFE FOREVER.
DOC-?

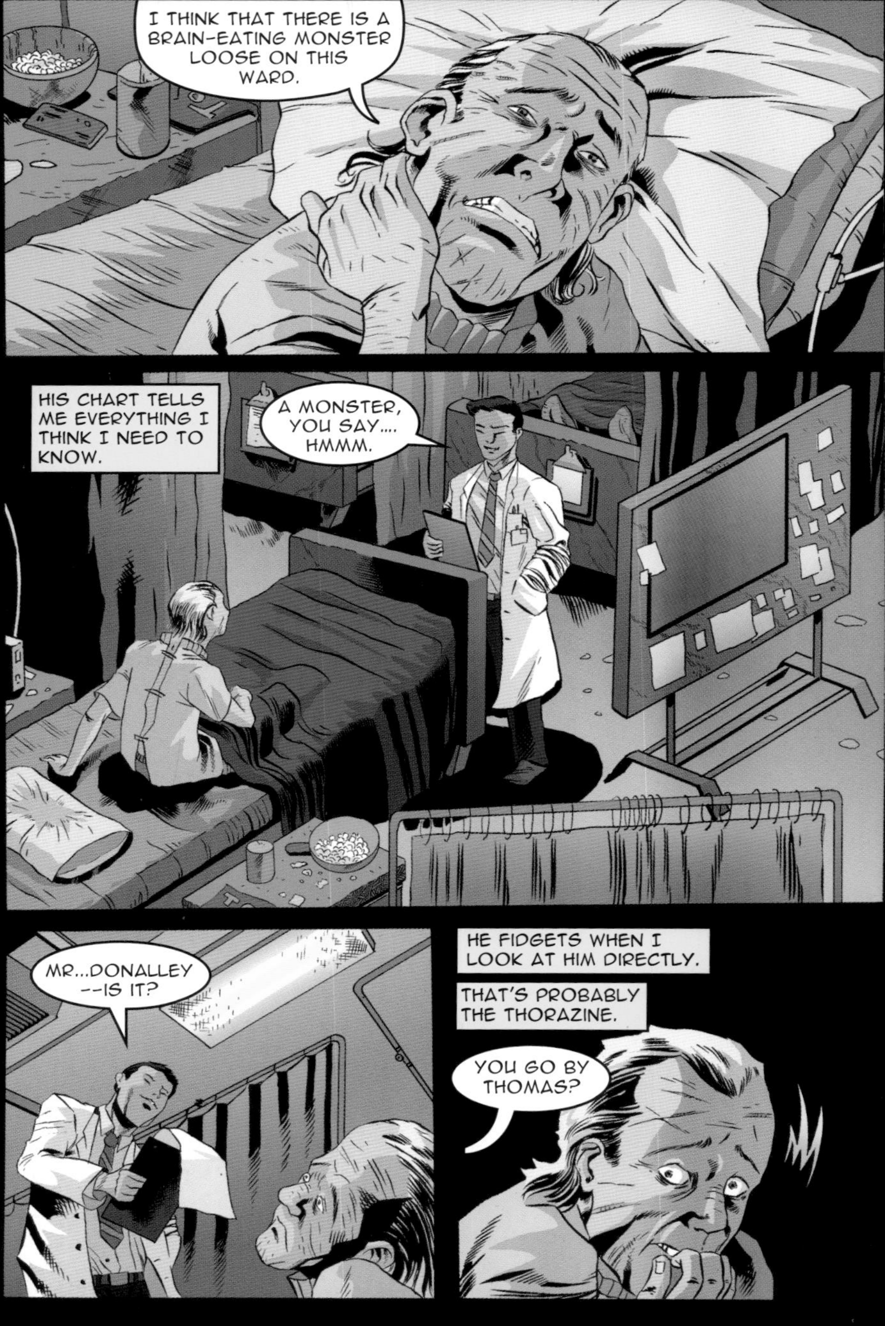
I THINK THAT THERE IS A BRAIN-EATING MONSTER LOOSE ON THIS WARD.
HIS CHART TELLS ME EVERYTHING I THINK I NEED TO KNOW.
A MONSTER, YOU SAY.... HMMM.
MR...DONALLEY --IS IT?
HE FIDGETS WHEN I LOOK AT HIM DIRECTLY.
THAT'S PROBABLY THE THORAZINE.
YOU GO BY THOMAS?

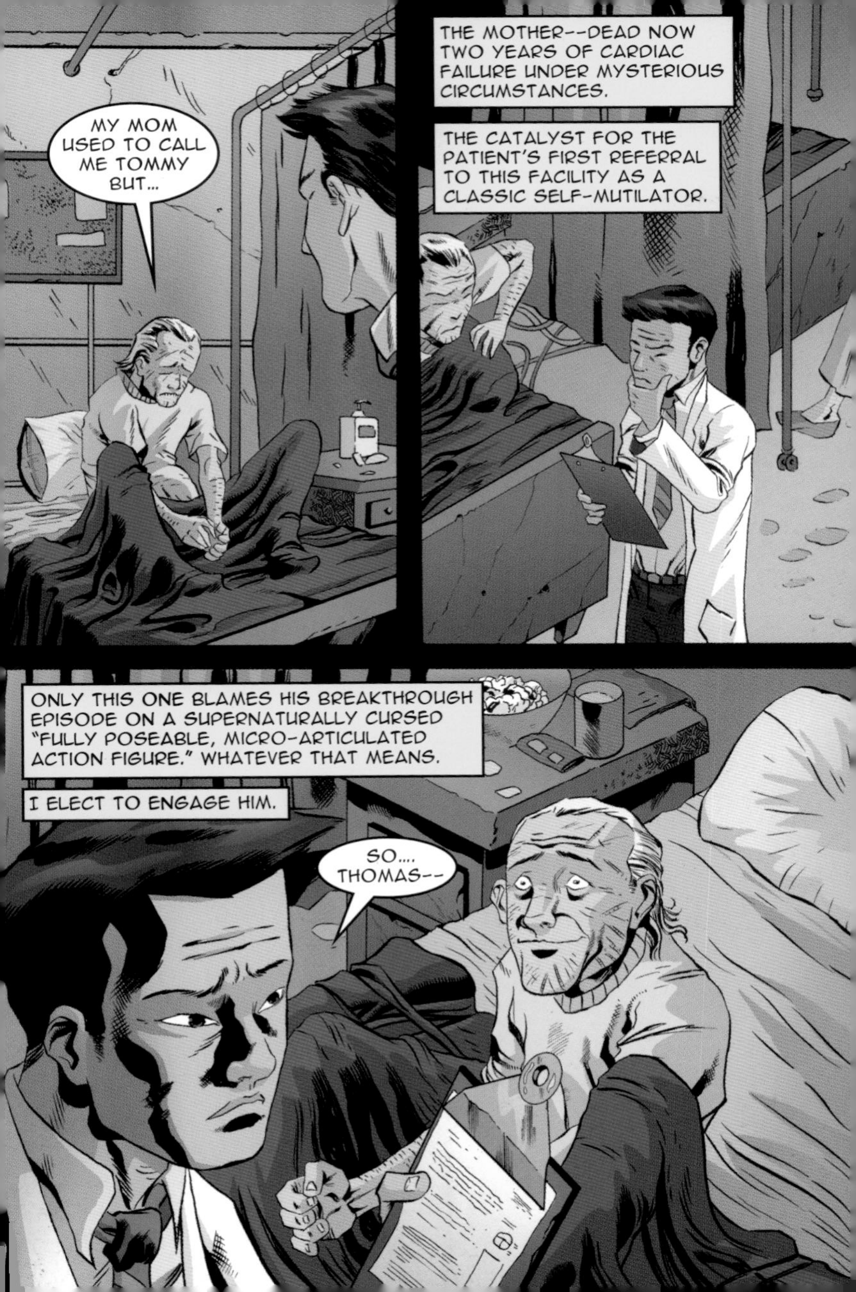
MY MOM USED TO CALL ME TOMMY BUT...
THE MOTHER--DEAD NOW TWO YEARS OF CARDIAC FAILURE UNDER MYSTERIOUS CIRCUMSTANCES.
THE CATALYST FOR THE PATIENT'S FIRST REFERRAL TO THIS FACILITY AS A CLASSIC SELF-MUTILATOR.
ONLY THIS ONE BLAMES HIS BREAKTHROUGH EPISODE ON A SUPERNATURALLY CURSED "FULLY POSEABLE, MICRO-ARTICULATED ACTION FIGURE." WHATEVER THAT MEANS.
I ELECT TO ENGAGE HIM.
SO.... THOMAS--

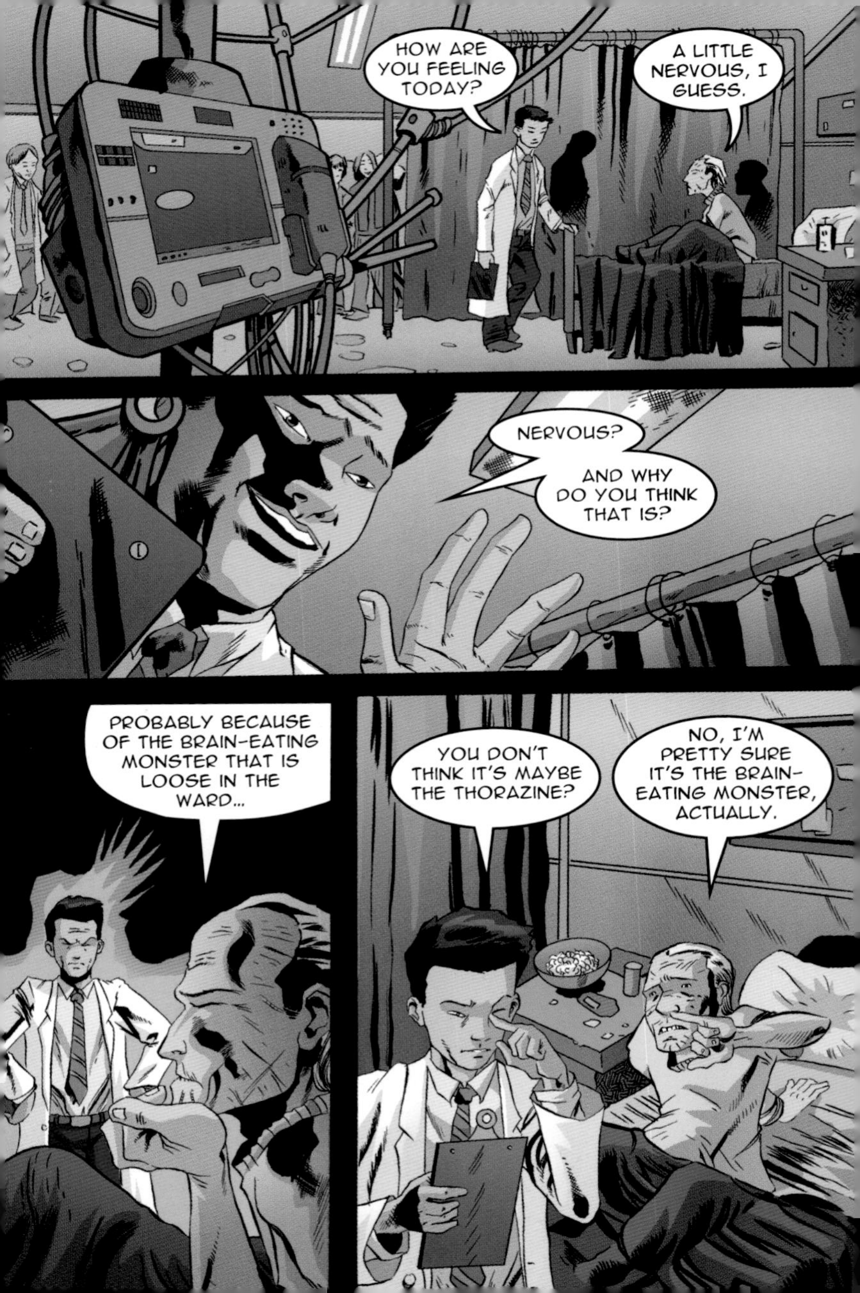
HOW ARE YOU FEELING TODAY?
A LITTLE NERVOUS, I GUESS.
NERVOUS?
AND WHY DO YOU THINK THAT IS?
PROBABLY BECAUSE OF THE BRAIN-EATING MONSTER THAT IS LOOSE IN THE WARD...
YOU DON'T THINK IT'S MAYBE THE THORAZINE?
NO, I'M PRETTY SURE IT'S THE BRAIN-EATING MONSTER, ACTUALLY.

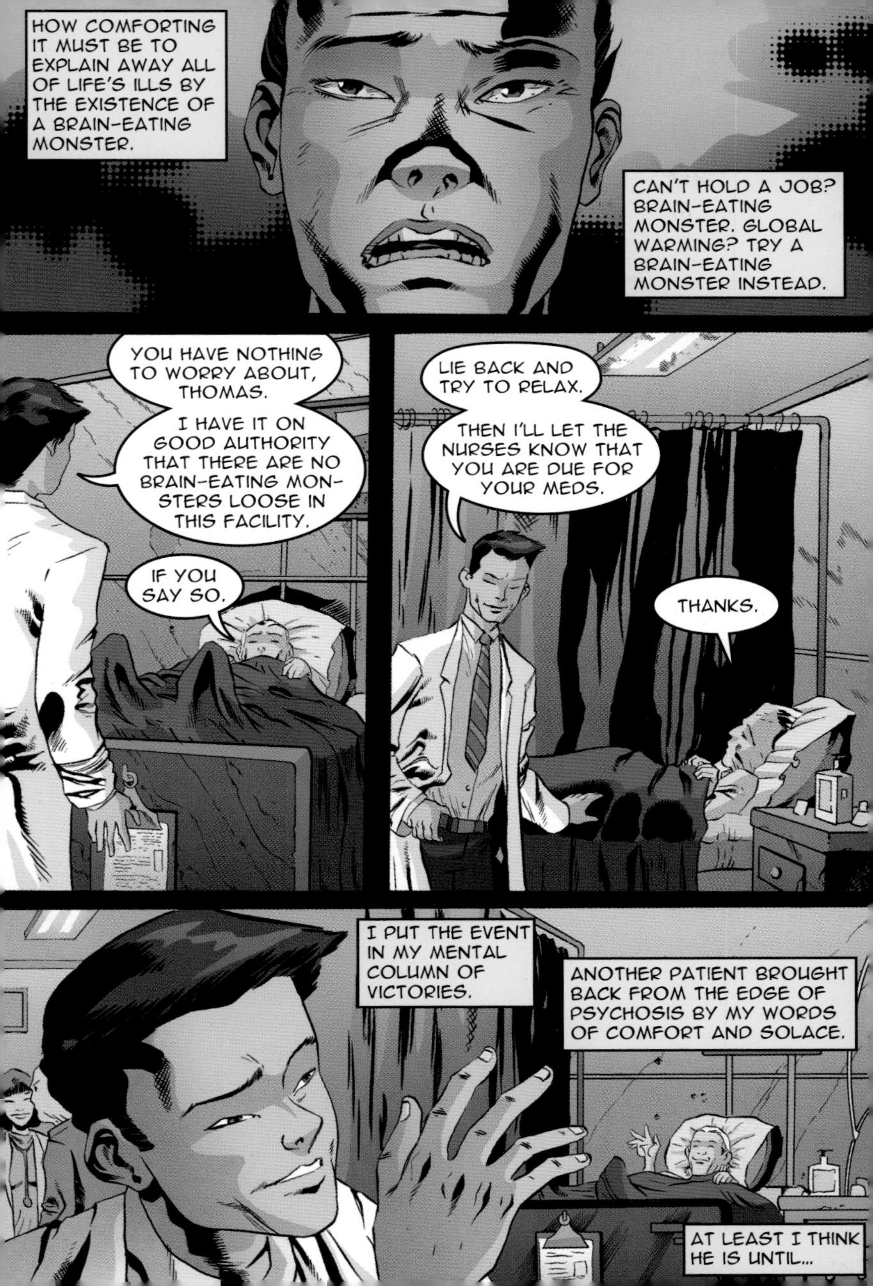
HOW COMFORTING IT MUST BE TO EXPLAIN AWAY ALL OF LIFE'S ILLS BY THE EXISTENCE OF A BRAIN-EATING MONSTER.
CAN'T HOLD A JOB? BRAIN-EATING MONSTER. GLOBAL WARMING? TRY A BRAIN-EATING MONSTER INSTEAD.
YOU HAVE NOTHING TO WORRY ABOUT, THOMAS.
I HAVE IT ON GOOD AUTHORITY THAT THERE ARE NO BRAIN-EATING MONSTERS LOOSE IN THIS FACILITY.
IF YOU SAY SO.
LIE BACK AND TRY TO RELAX.
THEN I'LL LET THE NURSES KNOW THAT YOU ARE DUE FOR YOUR MEDS.
THANKS.
I PUT THE EVENT IN MY MENTAL COLUMN OF VICTORIES.
ANOTHER PATIENT BROUGHT BACK FROM THE EDGE OF PSYCHOSIS BY MY WORDS OF COMFORT AND SOLACE.
AT LEAST I THINK HE IS UNTIL...

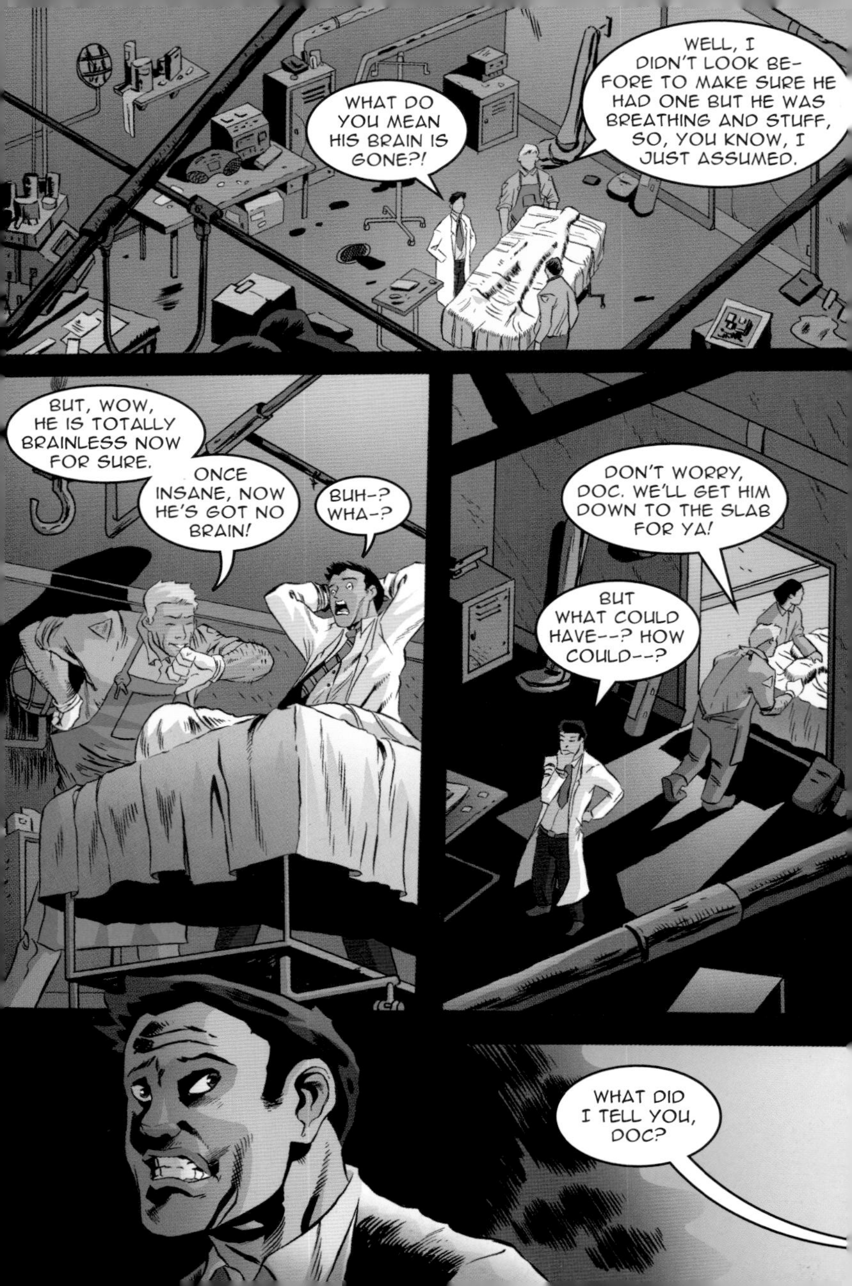
WHAT DO YOU MEAN HIS BRAIN IS GONE?!
WELL, I DIDN'T LOOK BEFORE TO MAKE SURE HE HAD ONE BUT HE WAS BREATHING AND STUFF, SO, YOU KNOW, I JUST ASSUMED.
BUT, WOW, HE IS TOTALLY BRAINLESS NOW FOR SURE.
ONCE INSANE, NOW HE'S GOT NO BRAIN!
BUH-? WHA-?
DON'T WORRY, DOC. WE'LL GET HIM DOWN TO THE SLAB FOR YA!
BUT WHAT COULD HAVE--? HOW COULD--?
WHAT DID I TELL YOU, DOC?

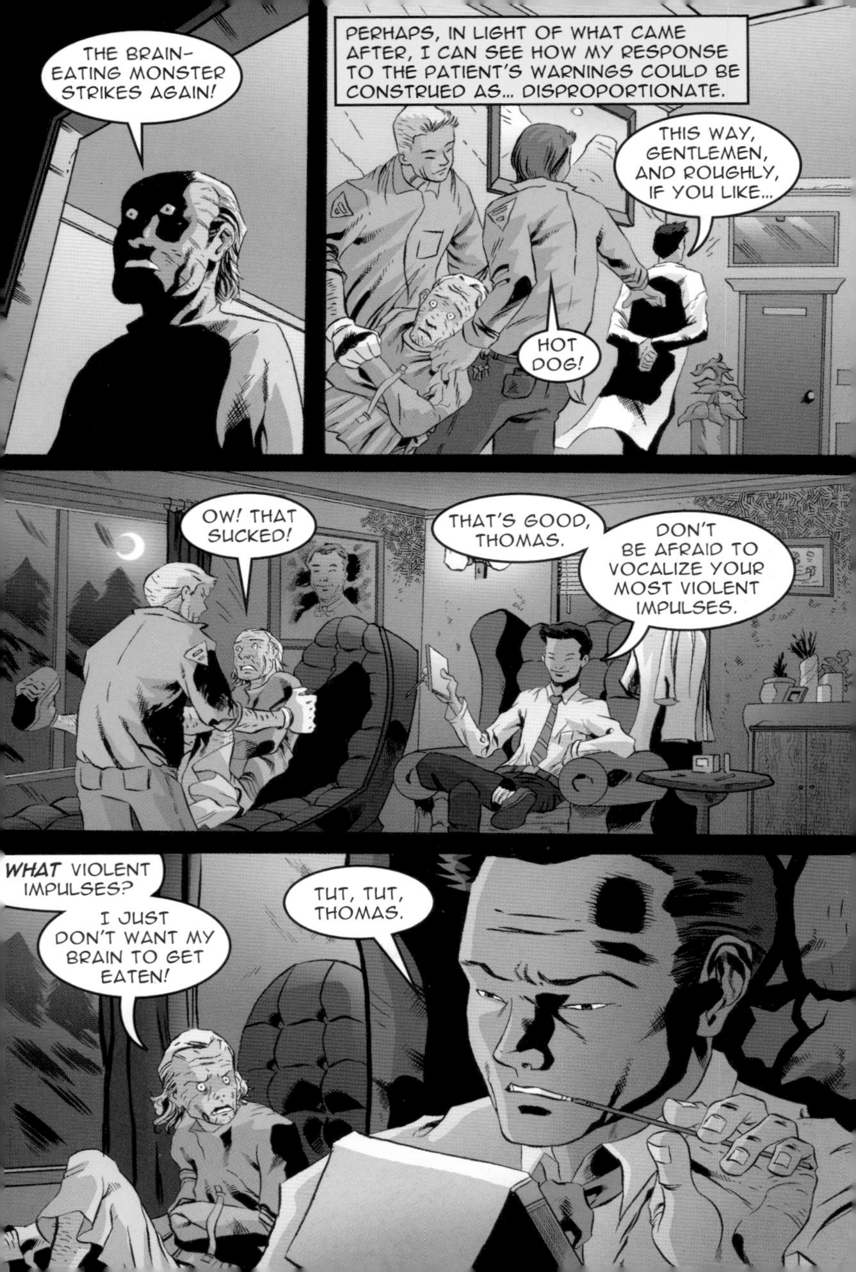
THE BRAIN-EATING MONSTER STRIKES AGAIN!
PERHAPS, IN LIGHT OF WHAT CAME AFTER, I CAN SEE HOW MY RESPONSE TO THE PATIENT'S WARNINGS COULD BE CONSTRUED AS... DISPROPORTIONATE.
THIS WAY, GENTLEMEN, AND ROUGHLY, IF YOU LIKE...
HOT DOG!
OW! THAT SUCKED!
THAT'S GOOD, THOMAS.
DON'T BE AFRAID TO VOCALIZE YOUR MOST VIOLENT IMPULSES.
WHAT VIOLENT IMPULSES?
I JUST DON'T WANT MY BRAIN TO GET EATEN!
TUT, TUT, THOMAS.

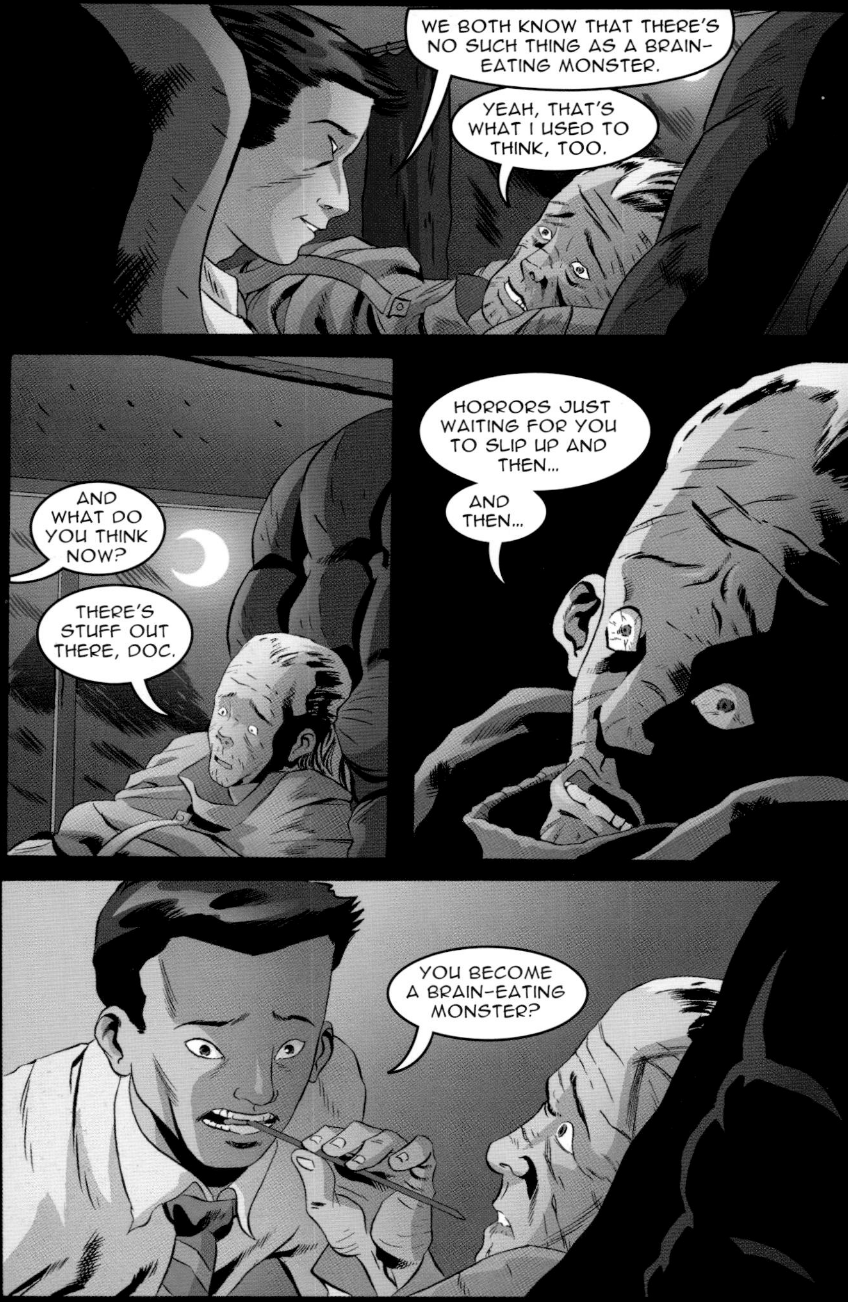
WE BOTH KNOW THAT THERE'S NO SUCH THING AS A BRAIN-EATING MONSTER.
YEAH, THAT'S WHAT I USED TO THINK, TOO.
AND WHAT DO YOU THINK NOW?
THERE'S STUFF OUT THERE, DOC.
HORRORS JUST WAITING FOR YOU TO SLIP UP AND THEN...
AND THEN...
YOU BECOME A BRAIN-EATING MONSTER?

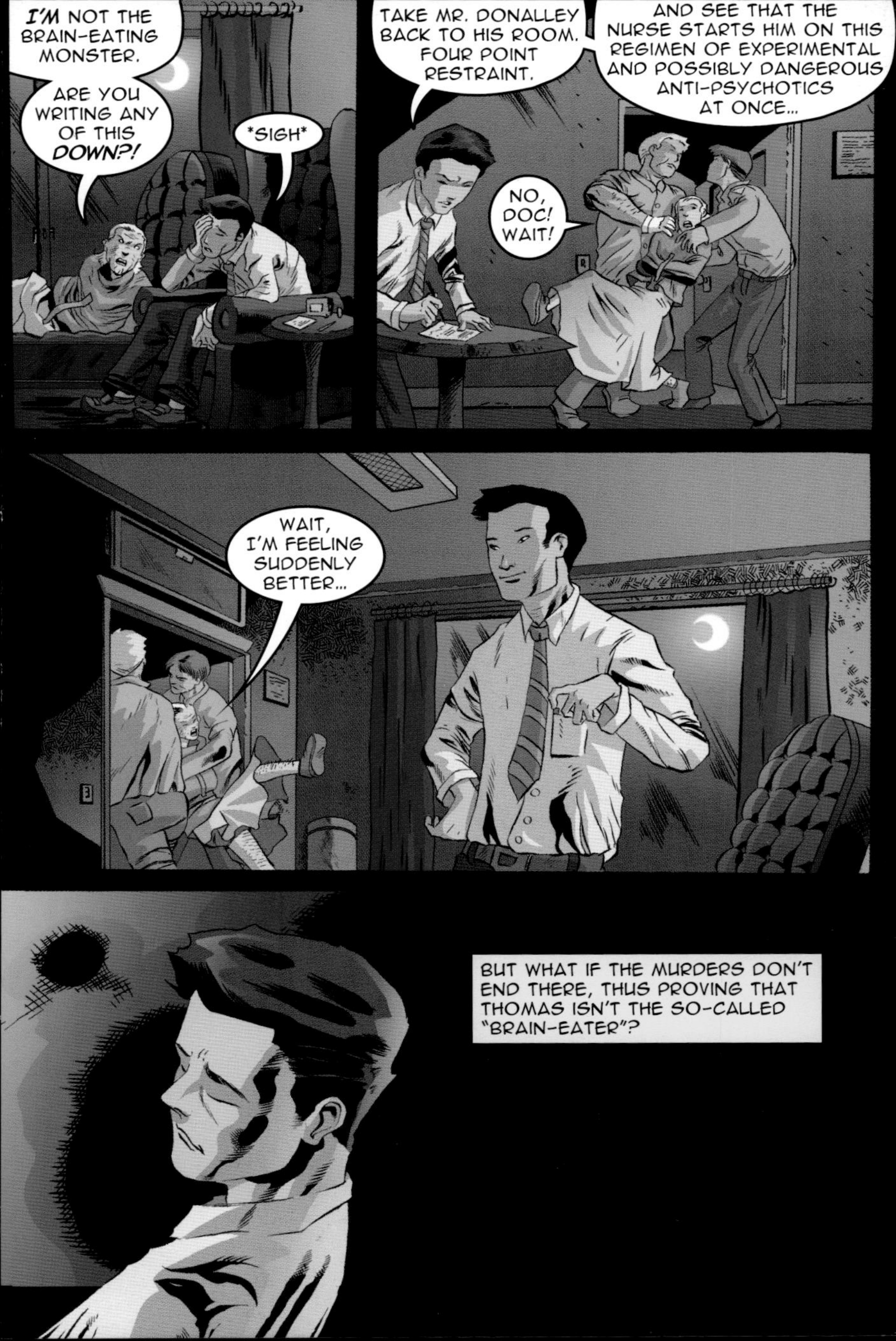
I'M NOT THE BRAIN-EATING MONSTER.
ARE YOU WRITING ANY OF THIS DOWN?!
SIGH
TAKE MR. DONALLEY BACK TO HIS ROOM. FOUR POINT RESTRAINT.
AND SEE THAT THE NURSE STARTS HIM ON THIS REGIMEN OF EXPERIMENTAL AND POSSIBLY DANGEROUS ANTI-PSYCHOTICS AT ONCE...
NO, DOC! WAIT!
WAIT, I'M FEELING SUDDENLY BETTER...
BUT WHAT IF THE MURDERS DON'T END THERE, THUS PROVING THAT THOMAS ISN'T THE SO-CALLED "BRAIN-EATER"?

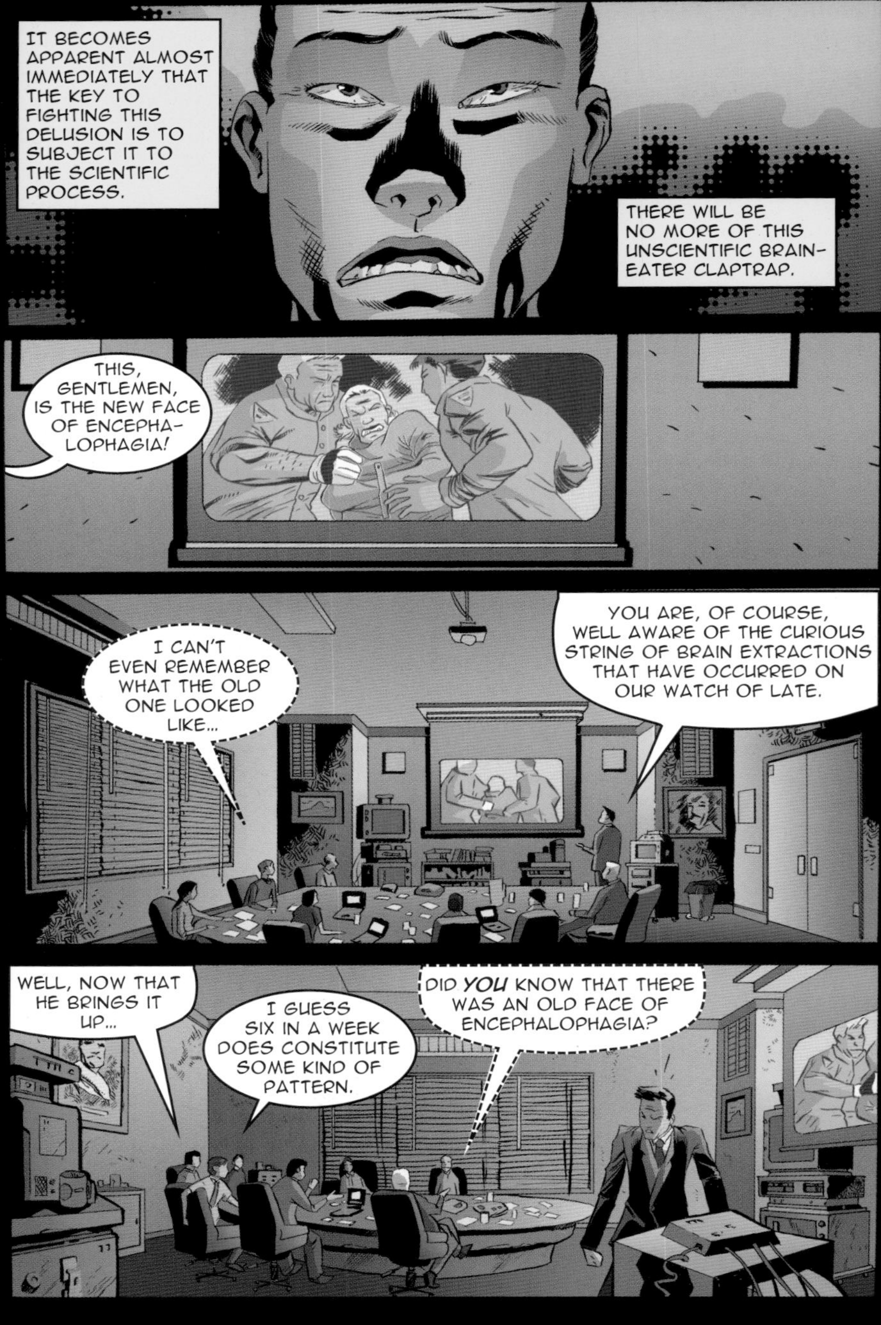
IT BECOMES APPARENT ALMOST IMMEDIATELY THAT THE KEY TO FIGHTING THIS DELUSION IS TO SUBJECT IT TO THE SCIENTIFIC PROCESS.
THERE WILL BE NO MORE OF THIS UNSCIENTIFIC BRAIN-EATER CLAPTRAP.
THIS, GENTLEMEN, IS THE NEW FACE OF ENCEPHA-LOPHAGIA!
I CAN'T EVEN REMEMBER WHAT THE OLD ONE LOOKED LIKE...
YOU ARE, OF COURSE, WELL AWARE OF THE CURIOUS STRING OF BRAIN EXTRACTIONS THAT HAVE OCCURRED ON OUR WATCH OF LATE.
WELL, NOW THAT HE BRINGS IT UP...
I GUESS SIX IN A WEEK DOES CONSTITUTE SOME KIND OF PATTERN.
DID *YOU* KNOW THAT THERE WAS AN OLD FACE OF ENCEPHALOPHAGIA?

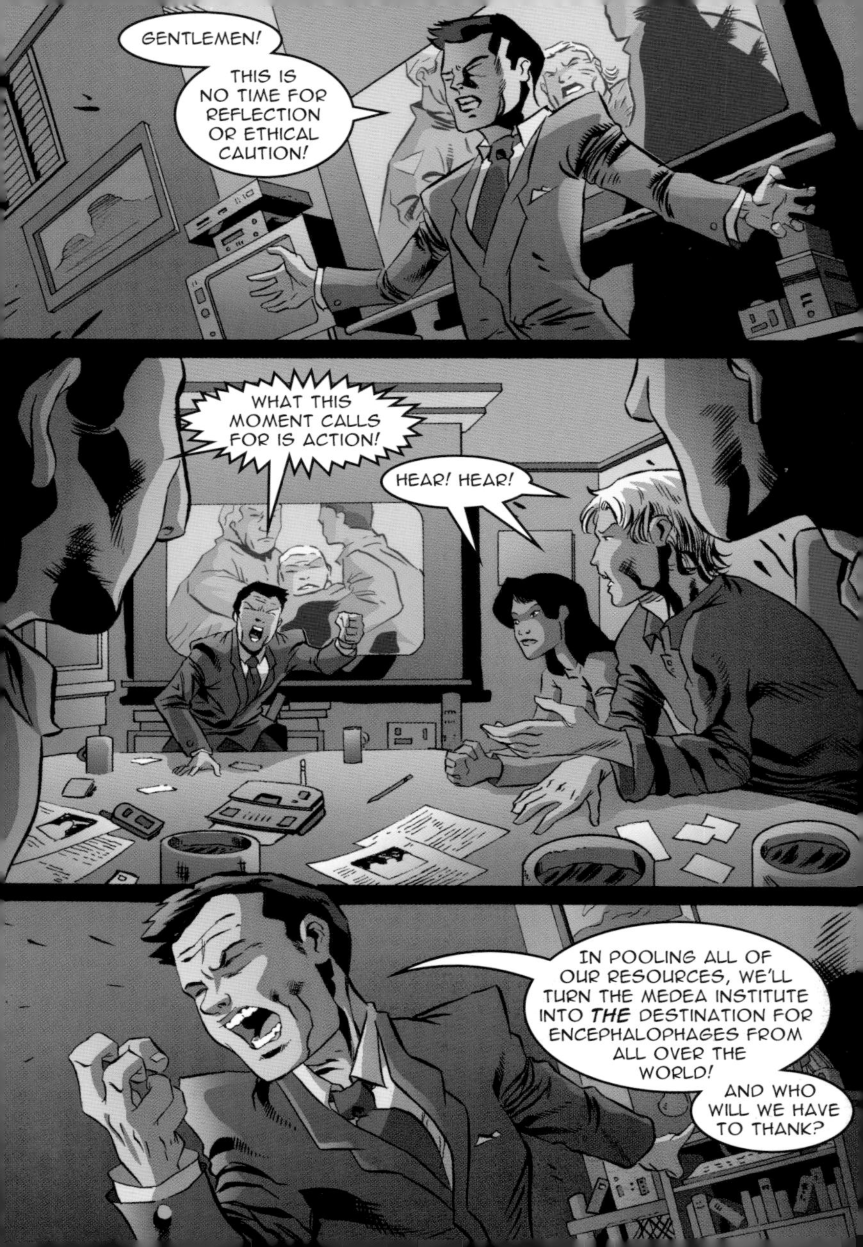
GENTLEMEN!
THIS IS NO TIME FOR REFLECTION OR ETHICAL CAUTION!
WHAT THIS MOMENT CALLS FOR IS ACTION!
HEAR! HEAR!
IN POOLING ALL OF OUR RESOURCES, WE'LL TURN THE MEDEA INSTITUTE INTO ***THE*** DESTINATION FOR ENCEPHALOPHAGES FROM ALL OVER THE WORLD!
AND WHO WILL WE HAVE TO THANK?

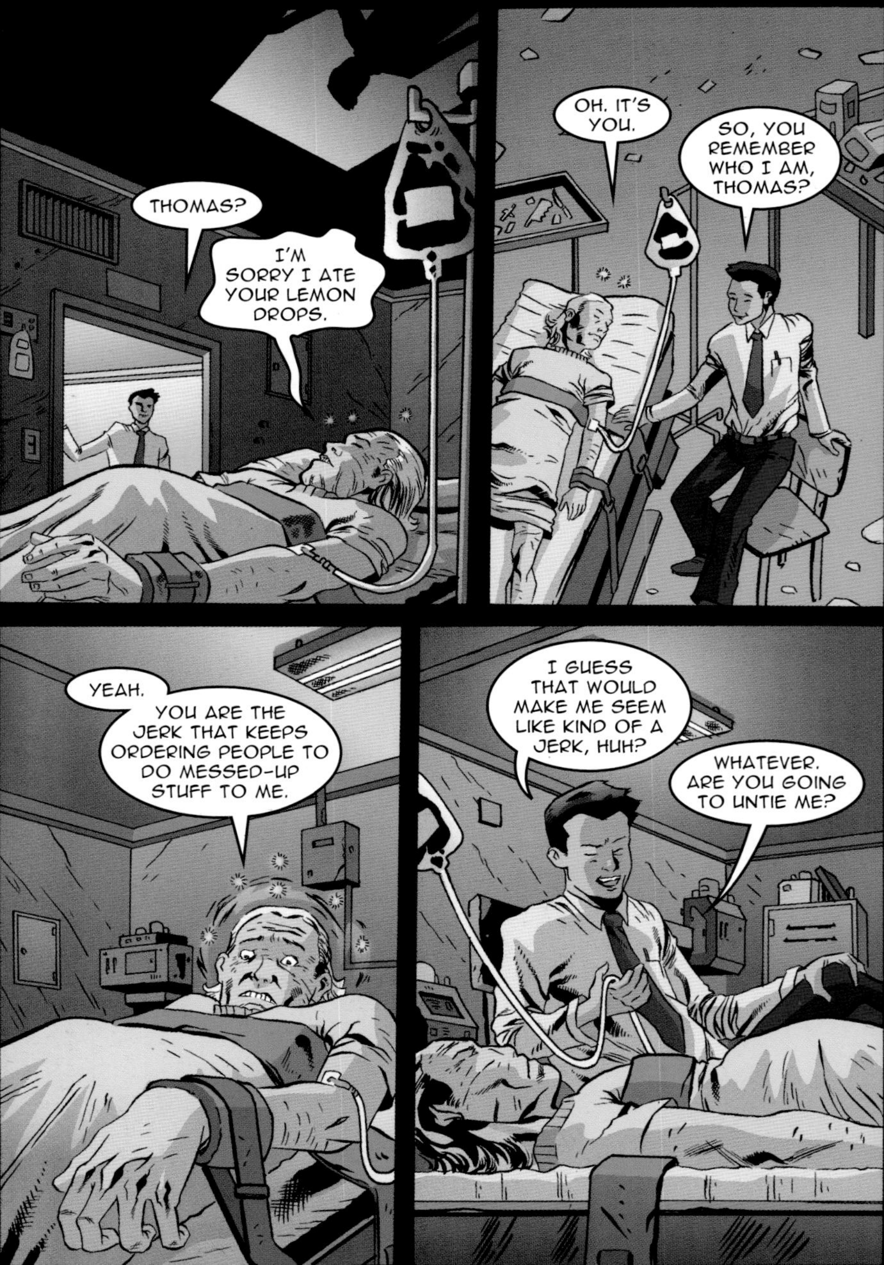
THOMAS?
I'M SORRY I ATE YOUR LEMON DROPS.
OH. IT'S YOU.
SO, YOU REMEMBER WHO I AM, THOMAS?
YEAH.
YOU ARE THE JERK THAT KEEPS ORDERING PEOPLE TO DO MESSED-UP STUFF TO ME.
I GUESS THAT WOULD MAKE ME SEEM LIKE KIND OF A JERK, HUH?
WHATEVER. ARE YOU GOING TO UNTIE ME?

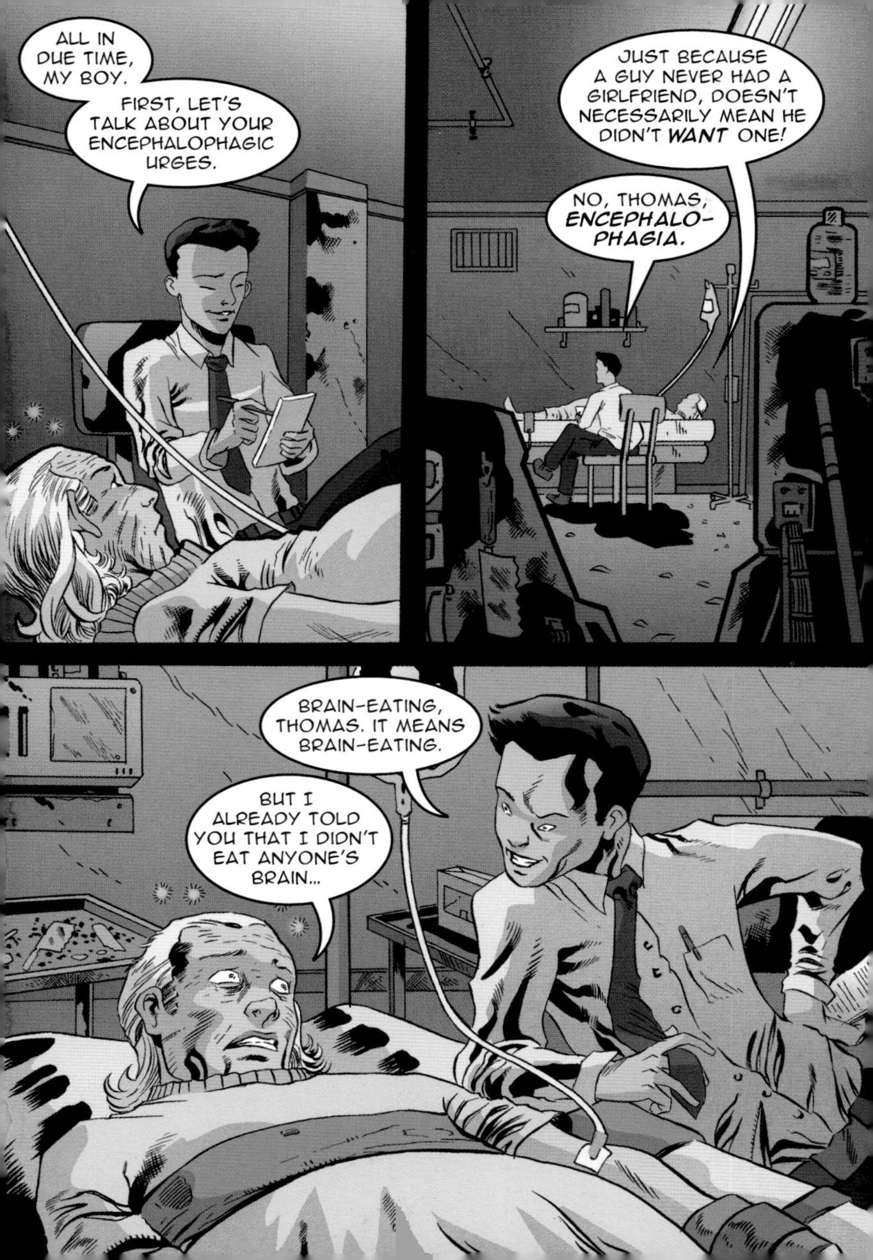
ALL IN DUE TIME, MY BOY.
FIRST, LET'S TALK ABOUT YOUR ENCEPHALOPHAGIC URGES.
JUST BECAUSE A GUY NEVER HAD A GIRLFRIEND, DOESN'T NECESSARILY MEAN HE DIDN'T ***WANT*** ONE!
NO, THOMAS, ***ENCEPHALO-PHAGIA.***
BRAIN-EATING, THOMAS. IT MEANS BRAIN-EATING.
BUT I ALREADY TOLD YOU THAT I DIDN'T EAT ANYONE'S BRAIN...

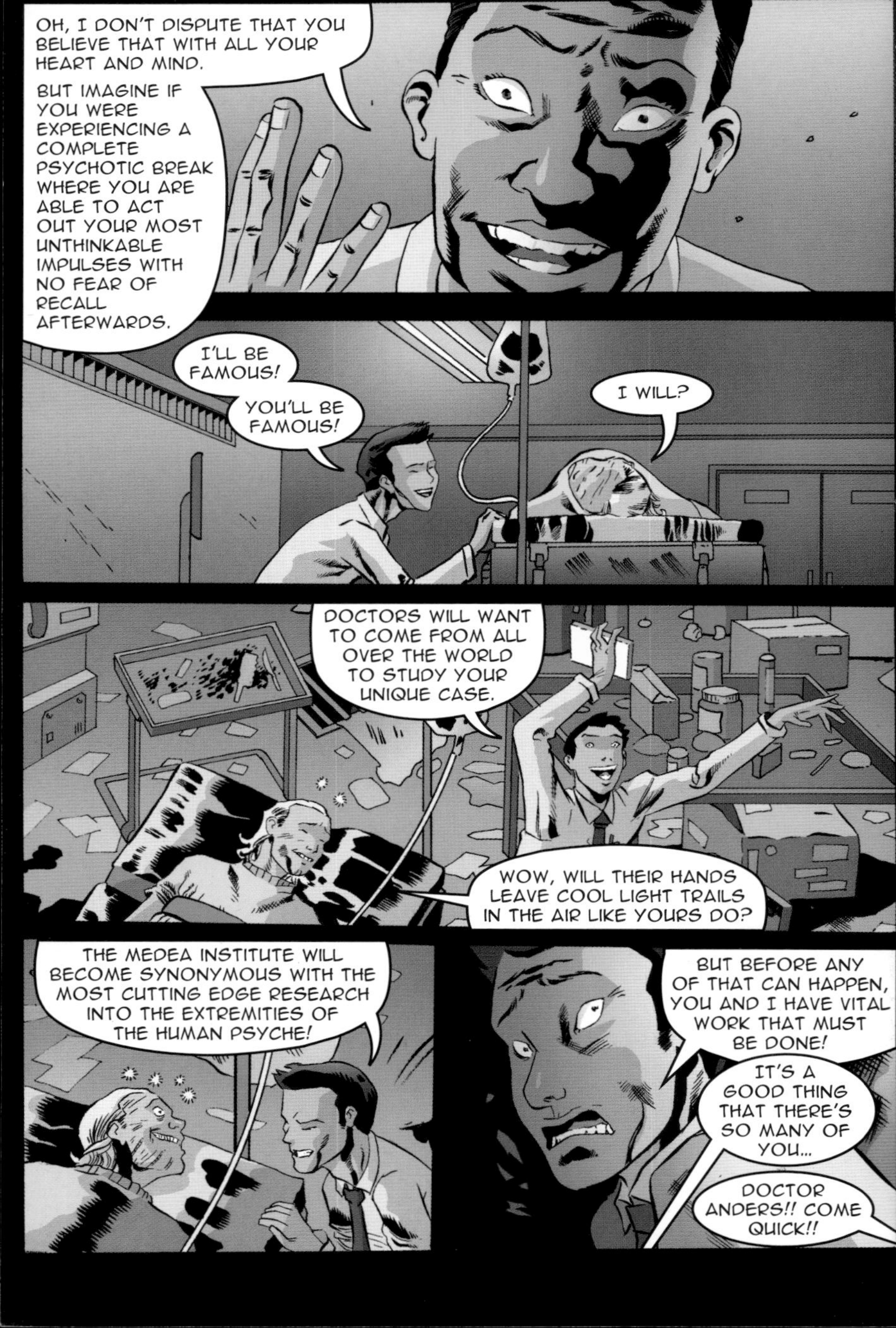
OH, I DON'T DISPUTE THAT YOU BELIEVE THAT WITH ALL YOUR HEART AND MIND.
BUT IMAGINE IF YOU WERE EXPERIENCING A COMPLETE PSYCHOTIC BREAK WHERE YOU ARE ABLE TO ACT OUT YOUR MOST UNTHINKABLE IMPULSES WITH NO FEAR OF RECALL AFTERWARDS.
I'LL BE FAMOUS!
YOU'LL BE FAMOUS!
I WILL?
DOCTORS WILL WANT TO COME FROM ALL OVER THE WORLD TO STUDY YOUR UNIQUE CASE.
WOW, WILL THEIR HANDS LEAVE COOL LIGHT TRAILS IN THE AIR LIKE YOURS DO?
THE MEDEA INSTITUTE WILL BECOME SYNONYMOUS WITH THE MOST CUTTING EDGE RESEARCH INTO THE EXTREMITIES OF THE HUMAN PSYCHE!
BUT BEFORE ANY OF THAT CAN HAPPEN, YOU AND I HAVE VITAL WORK THAT MUST BE DONE!
IT'S A GOOD THING THAT THERE'S SO MANY OF YOU...
DOCTOR ANDERS!! COME QUICK!!

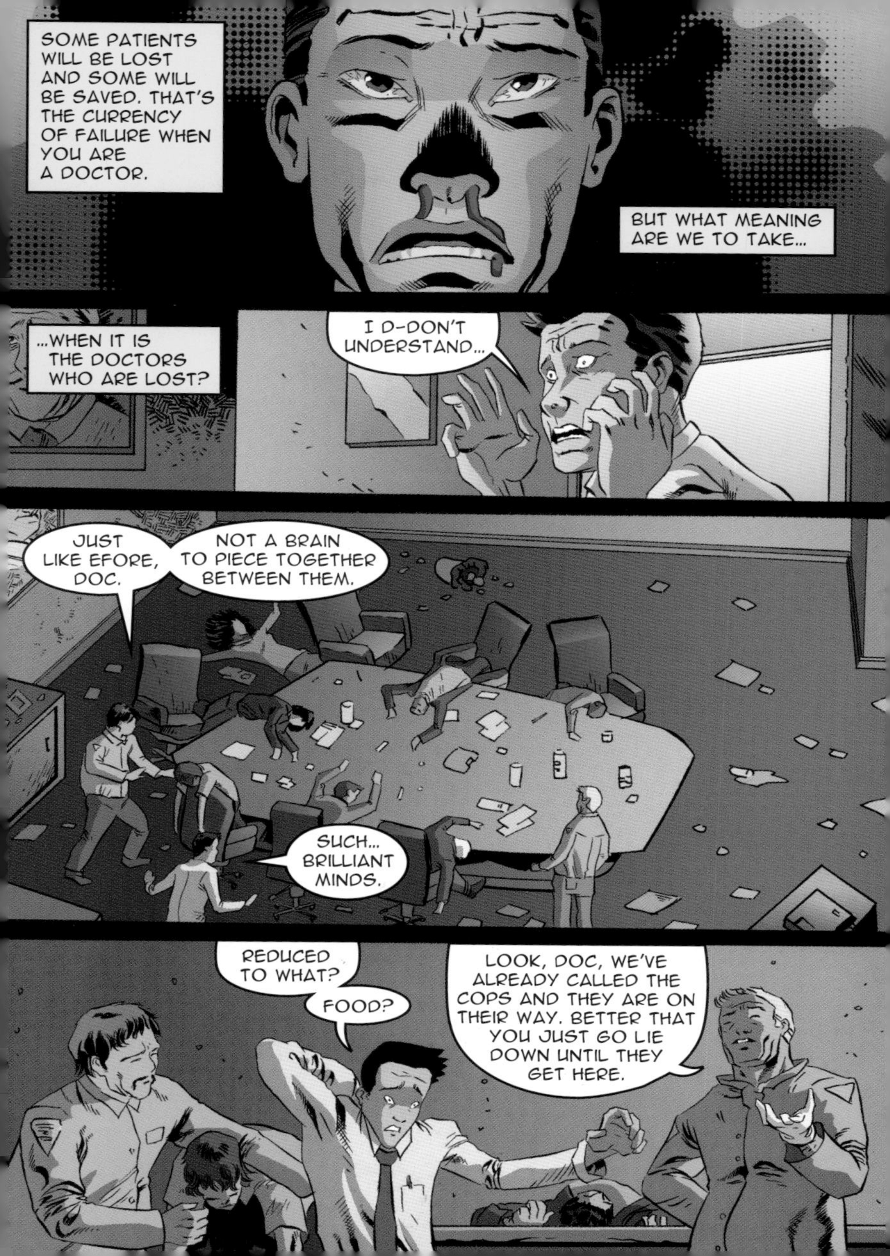
SOME PATIENTS WILL BE LOST AND SOME WILL BE SAVED. THAT'S THE CURRENCY OF FAILURE WHEN YOU ARE A DOCTOR.
BUT WHAT MEANING ARE WE TO TAKE...
...WHEN IT IS THE DOCTORS WHO ARE LOST?
I D-DON'T UNDERSTAND...
JUST LIKE EFORE, DOC.
NOT A BRAIN TO PIECE TOGETHER BETWEEN THEM.
SUCH... BRILLIANT MINDS.
REDUCED TO WHAT?
FOOD?
LOOK, DOC, WE'VE ALREADY CALLED THE COPS AND THEY ARE ON THEIR WAY. BETTER THAT YOU JUST GO LIE DOWN UNTIL THEY GET HERE.

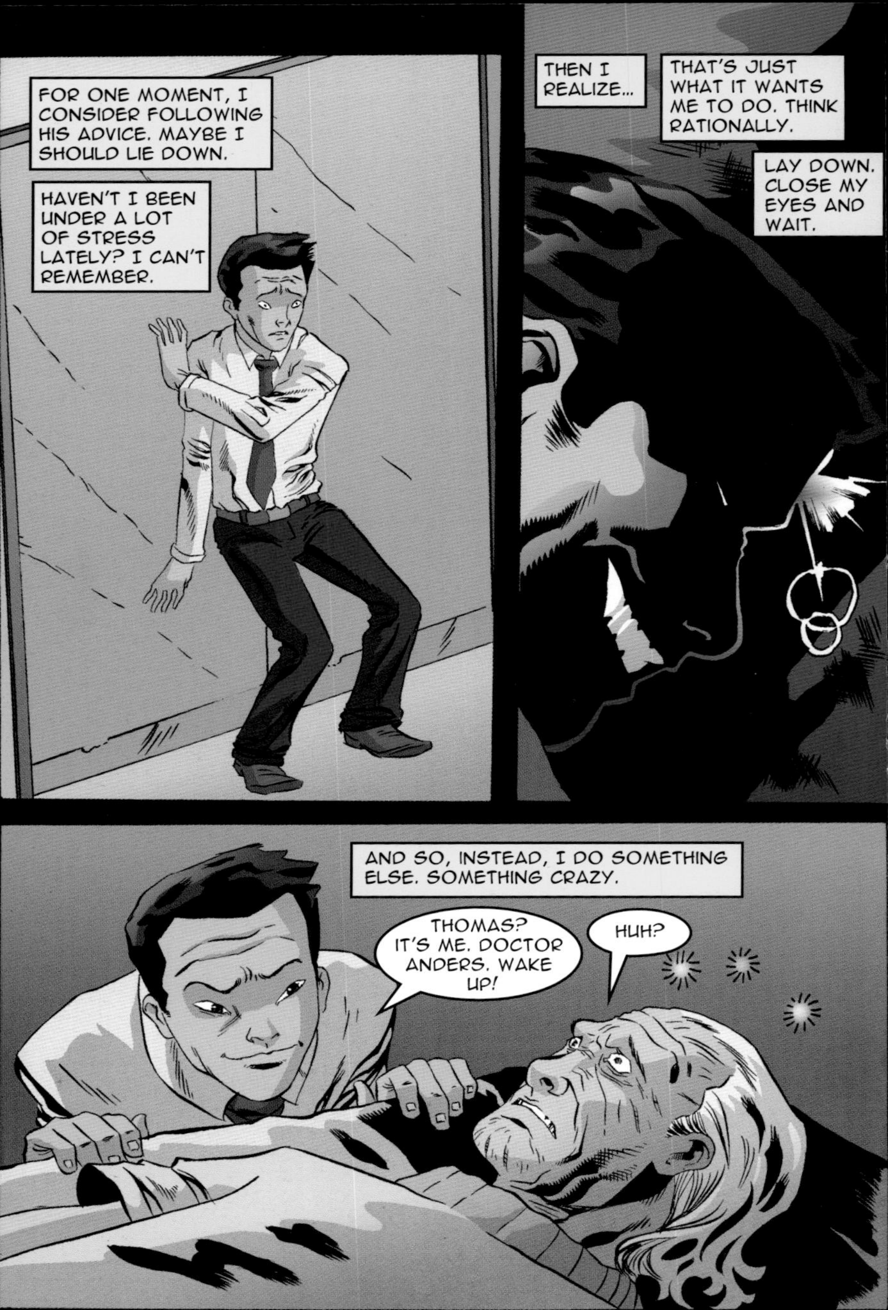
FOR ONE MOMENT, I CONSIDER FOLLOWING HIS ADVICE. MAYBE I SHOULD LIE DOWN.
HAVEN'T I BEEN UNDER A LOT OF STRESS LATELY? I CAN'T REMEMBER.
THEN I REALIZE...
THAT'S JUST WHAT IT WANTS ME TO DO. THINK RATIONALLY.
LAY DOWN. CLOSE MY EYES AND WAIT.
AND SO, INSTEAD, I DO SOMETHING ELSE. SOMETHING CRAZY.
THOMAS? IT'S ME. DOCTOR ANDERS. WAKE UP!
HUH?

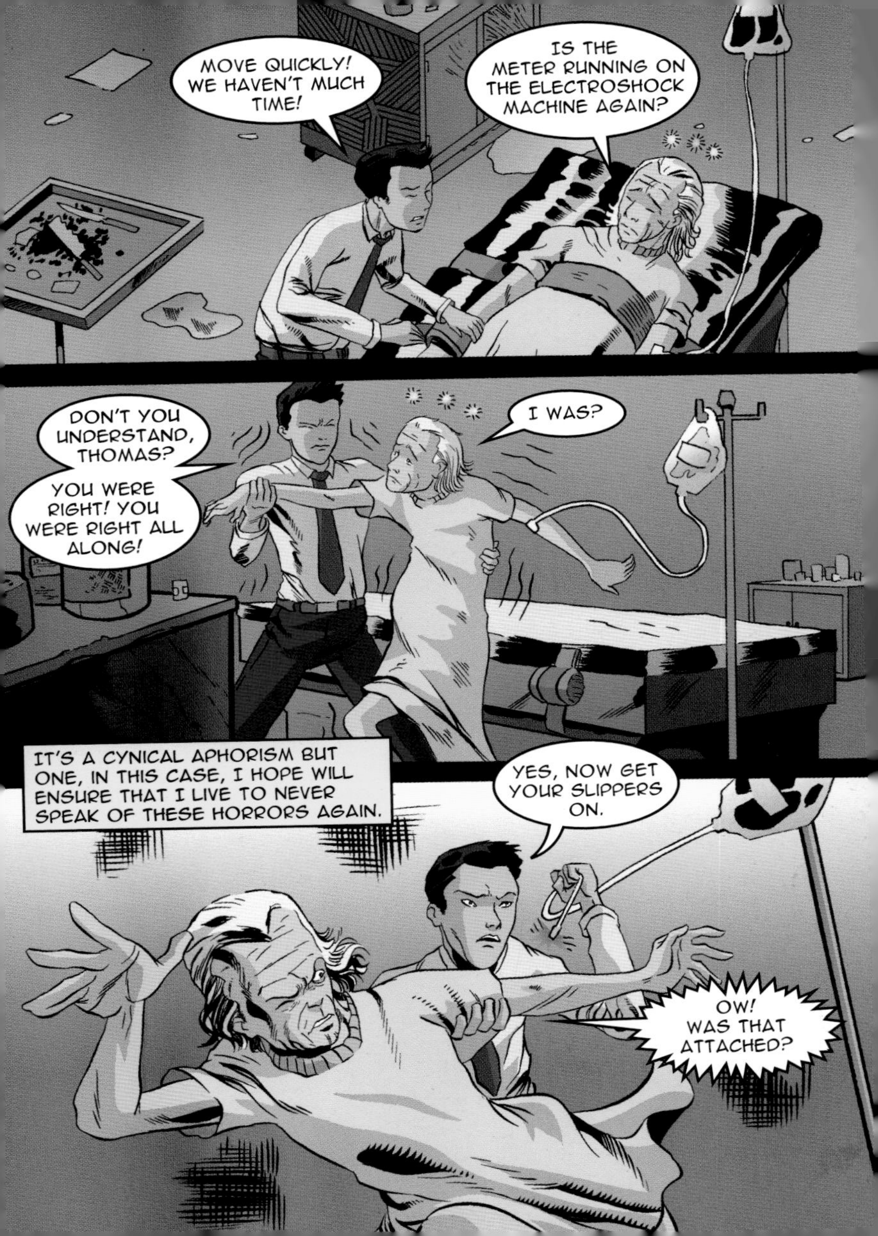
MOVE QUICKLY! WE HAVEN'T MUCH TIME!
IS THE METER RUNNING ON THE ELECTROSHOCK MACHINE AGAIN?
DON'T YOU UNDERSTAND, THOMAS?
YOU WERE RIGHT! YOU WERE RIGHT ALL ALONG!
I WAS?
IT'S A CYNICAL APHORISM BUT ONE, IN THIS CASE, I HOPE WILL ENSURE THAT I LIVE TO NEVER SPEAK OF THESE HORRORS AGAIN.
YES, NOW GET YOUR SLIPPERS ON.
OW! WAS THAT ATTACHED?

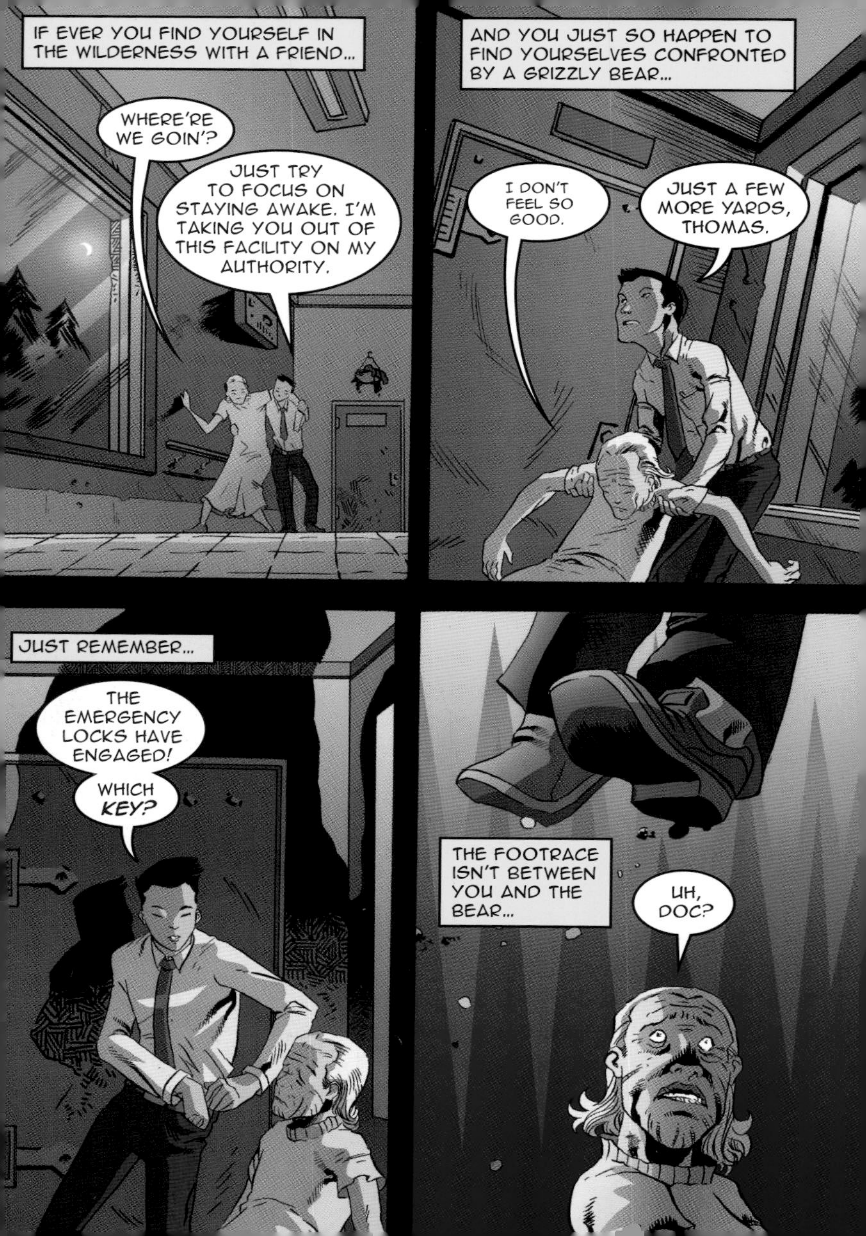
IF EVER YOU FIND YOURSELF IN THE WILDERNESS WITH A FRIEND...
WHERE'RE WE GOIN'?
JUST TRY TO FOCUS ON STAYING AWAKE. I'M TAKING YOU OUT OF THIS FACILITY ON MY AUTHORITY.
AND YOU JUST SO HAPPEN TO FIND YOURSELVES CONFRONTED BY A GRIZZLY BEAR...
I DON'T FEEL SO GOOD.
JUST A FEW MORE YARDS, THOMAS.
JUST REMEMBER...
THE EMERGENCY LOCKS HAVE ENGAGED!
WHICH *KEY?*
THE FOOTRACE ISN'T BETWEEN YOU AND THE BEAR...
UH, DOC?

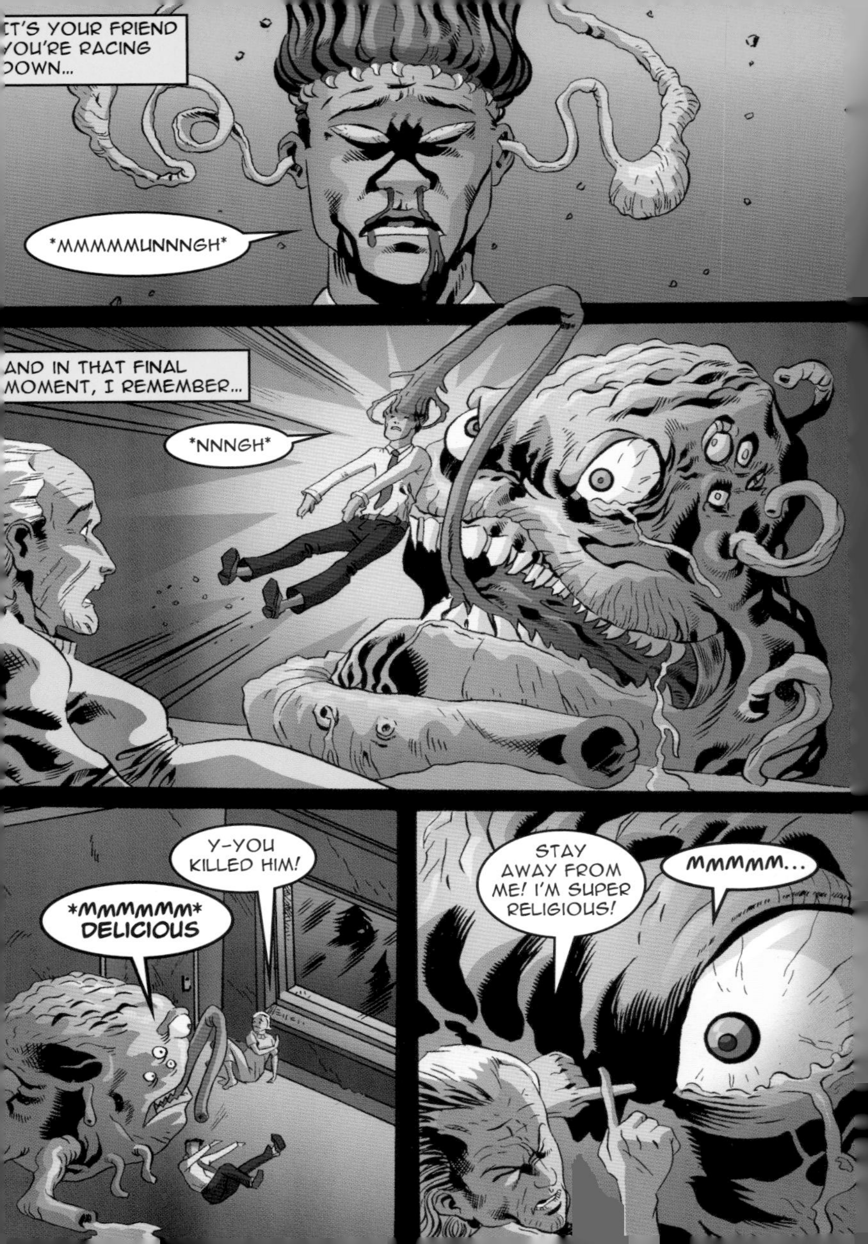
IT'S YOUR FRIEND YOU'RE RACING DOWN...
MMMMMUNNNGH
AND IN THAT FINAL MOMENT, I REMEMBER...
NNNGH
Y-YOU KILLED HIM!
MMMMMM DELICIOUS
STAY AWAY FROM ME! I'M SUPER RELIGIOUS!
MMMMM...

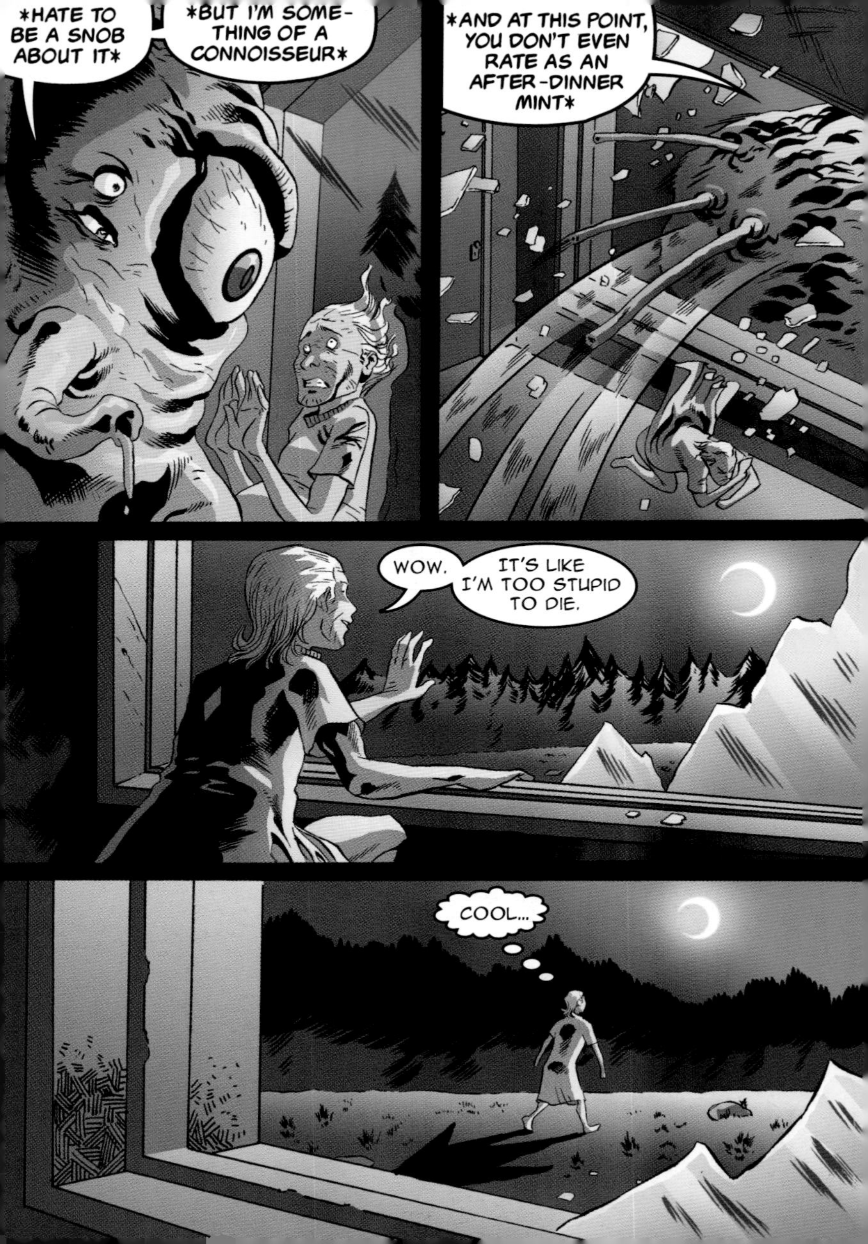
HATE TO BE A SNOB ABOUT IT
BUT I'M SOMETHING OF A CONNOISSEUR
AND AT THIS POINT, YOU DON'T EVEN RATE AS AN AFTER-DINNER MINT
WOW.
IT'S LIKE I'M TOO STUPID TO DIE.
COOL...

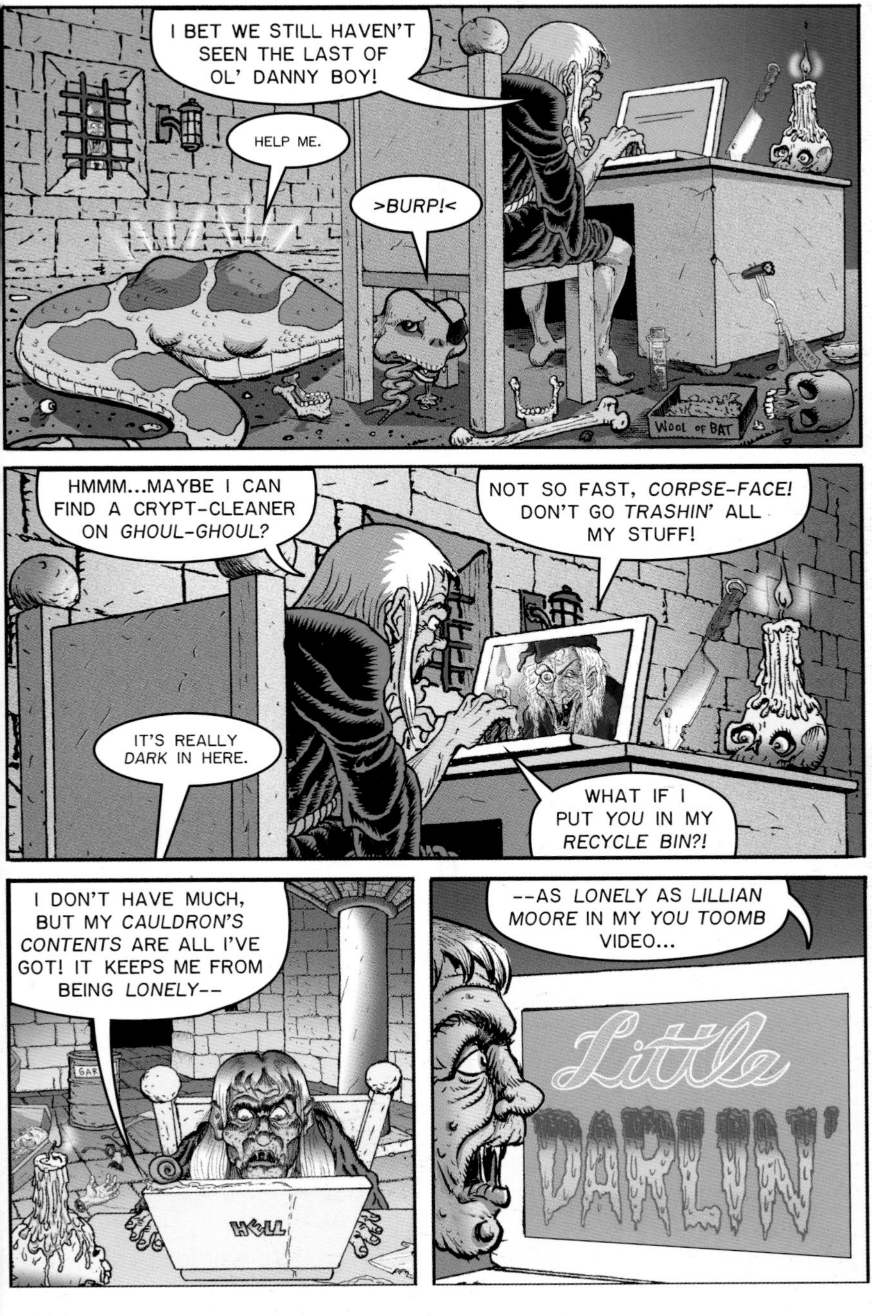

I BET WE STILL HAVEN'T SEEN THE LAST OF OL' DANNY BOY!
HELP ME.
>BURP!<
WOOL OF BAT
HMMM...MAYBE I CAN FIND A CRYPT-CLEANER ON GHOUL-GHOUL?
NOT SO FAST, CORPSE-FACE! DON'T GO TRASHIN' ALL MY STUFF!
IT'S REALLY DARK IN HERE.
WHAT IF I PUT YOU IN MY RECYCLE BIN?!
I DON'T HAVE MUCH, BUT MY CAULDRON'S CONTENTS ARE ALL I'VE GOT! IT KEEPS ME FROM BEING LONELY--
--AS LONELY AS LILLIAN MOORE IN MY YOU TOOMB VIDEO...
Little DARLIN'

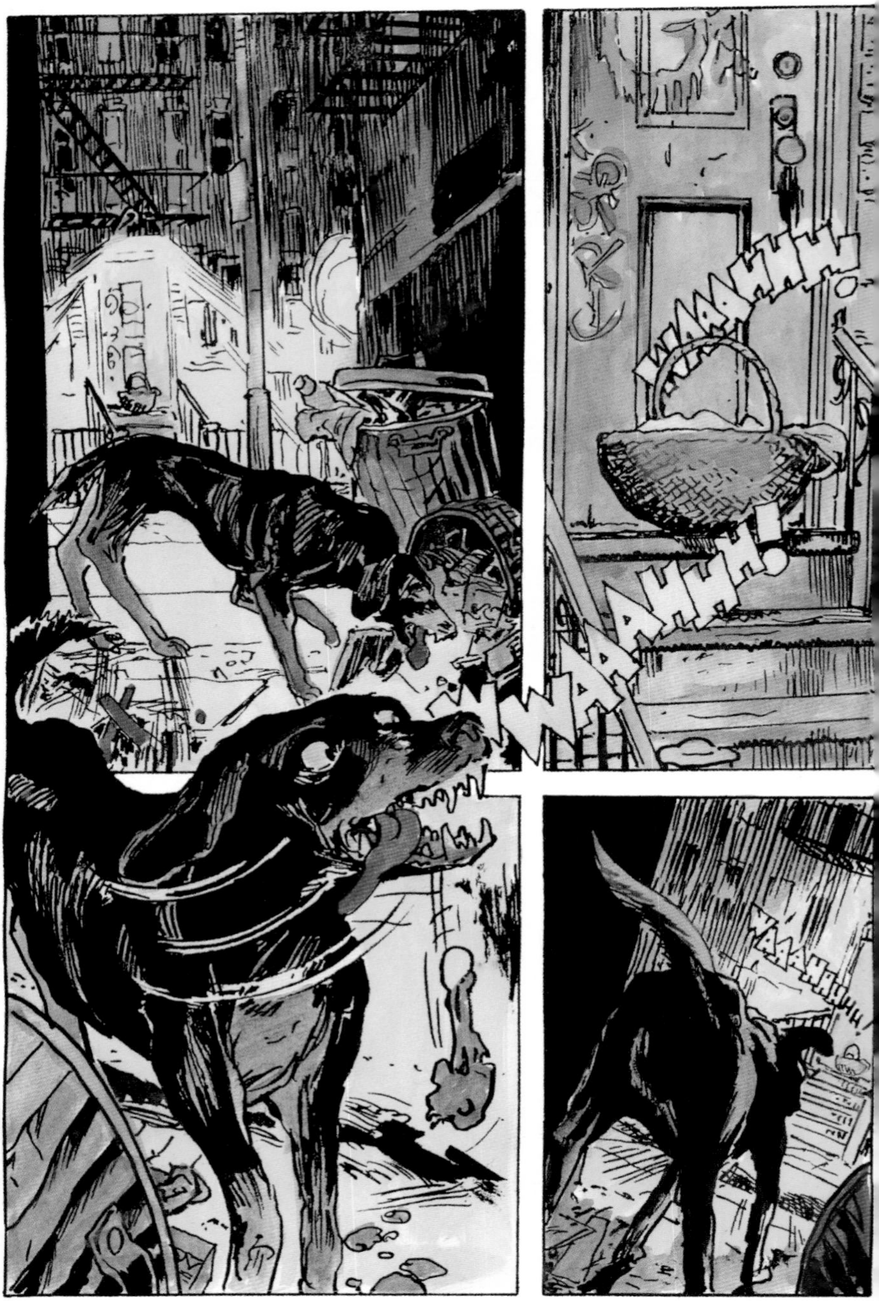

WAAAHHHH!
WAAAHHH!
WAAHHHHH!

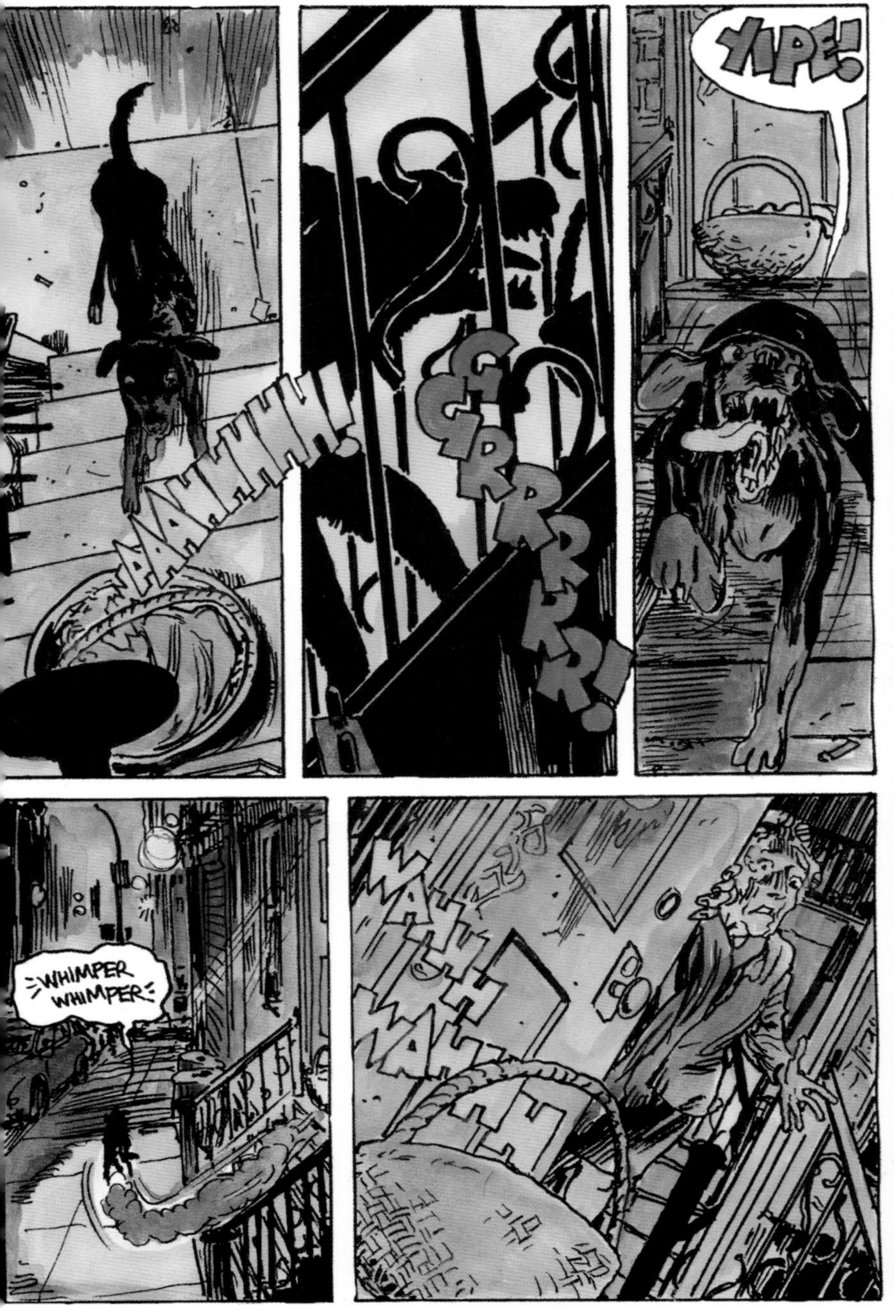
WAAHHHHH!
GGRRRRRR!
YIPE!
WHIMPER WHIMPER
WAHH
WAHH

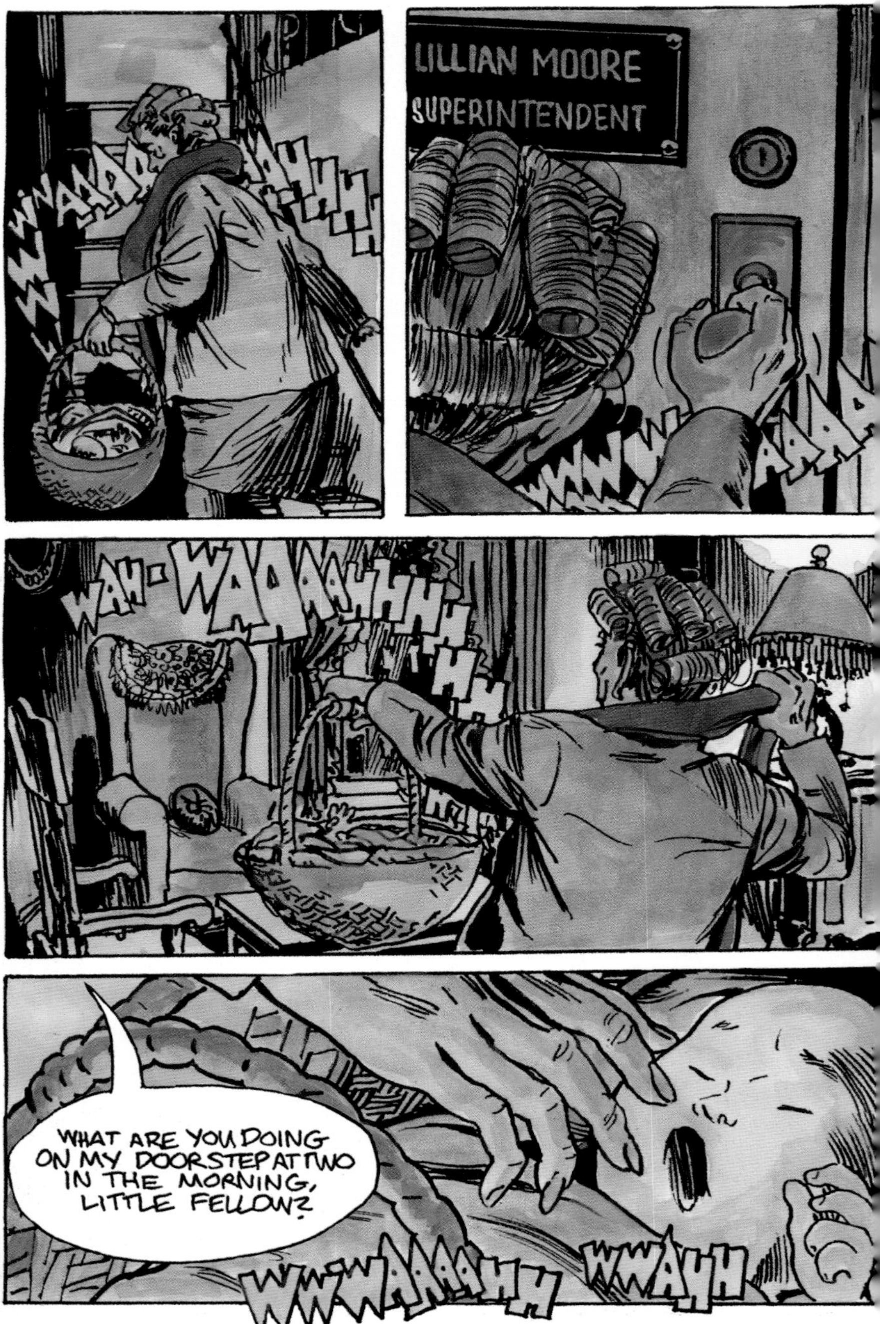
LILLIAN MOORE
SUPERINTENDENT
WHAT ARE YOU DOING ON MY DOORSTEP AT TWO IN THE MORNING, LITTLE FELLOW?

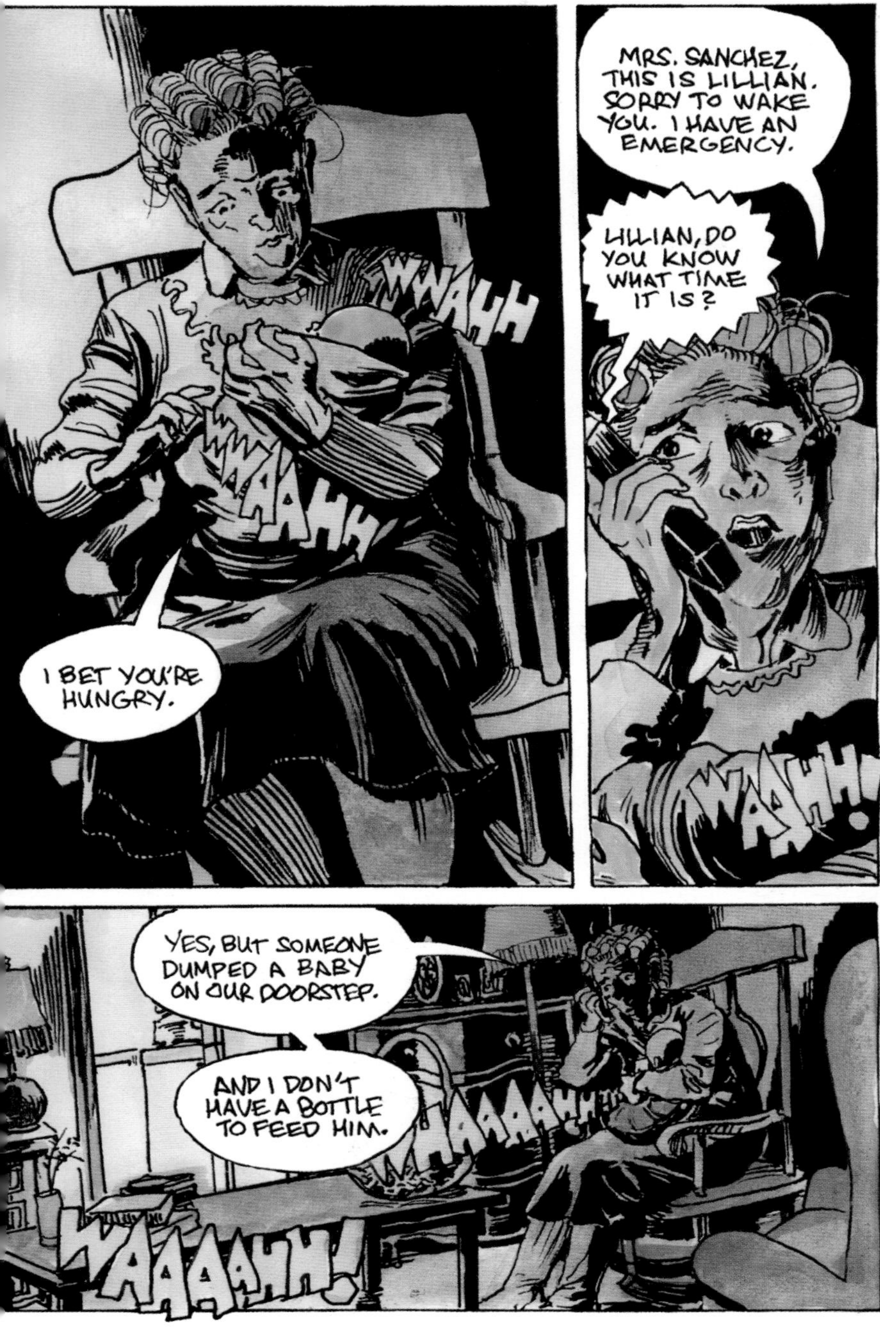
WWAHH
WWAAHH
I BET YOU'RE HUNGRY.
MRS. SANCHEZ, THIS IS LILLIAN. SORRY TO WAKE YOU. I HAVE AN EMERGENCY.
LILLIAN, DO YOU KNOW WHAT TIME IT IS?
WAHH!
YES, BUT SOMEONE DUMPED A BABY ON OUR DOORSTEP.
AND I DON'T HAVE A BOTTLE TO FEED HIM.
WAAAAAHH
WAAAAHH!

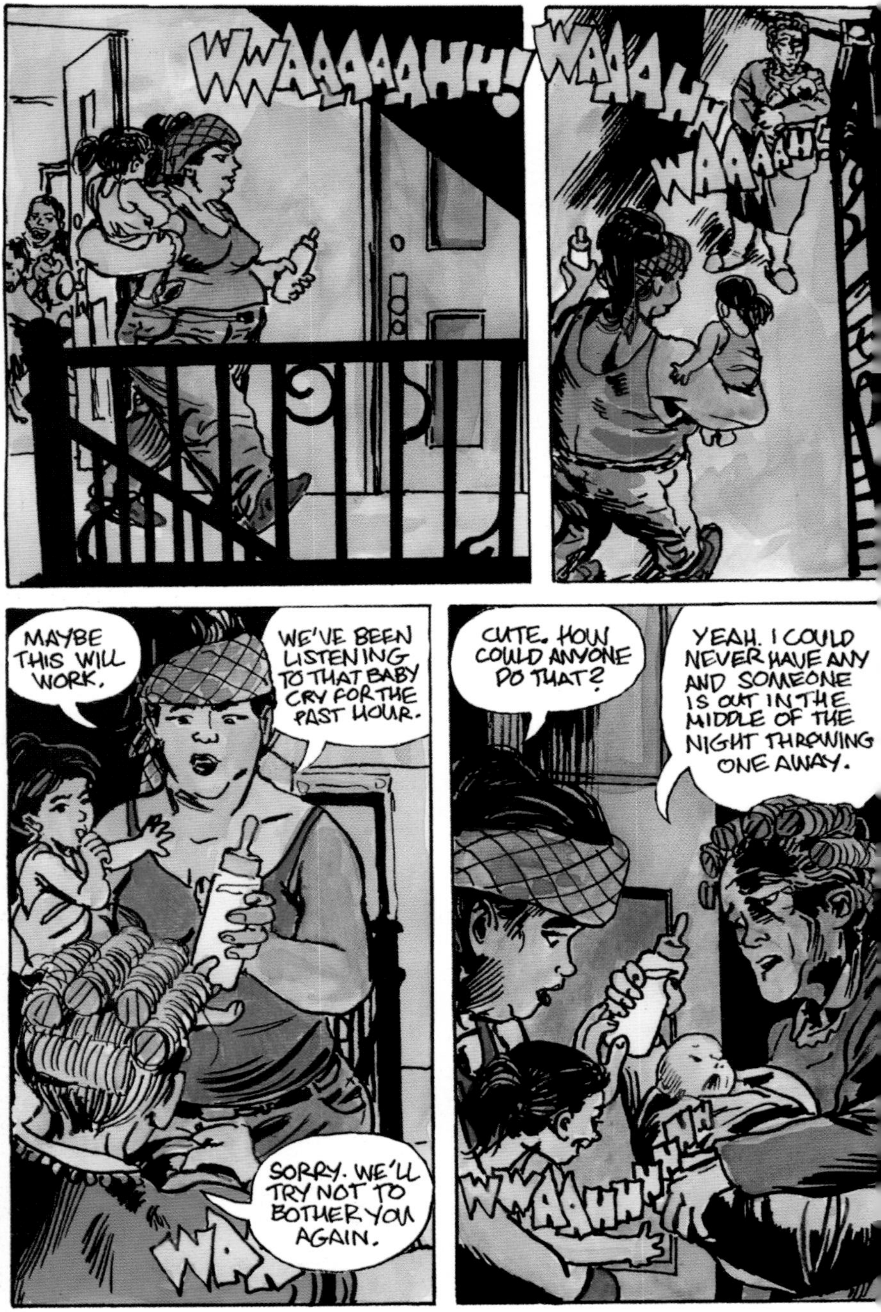
WWAAAAAHH!
WAAAH!
WAAAAH!
MAYBE THIS WILL WORK.
WE'VE BEEN LISTENING TO THAT BABY CRY FOR THE PAST HOUR.
SORRY. WE'LL TRY NOT TO BOTHER YOU AGAIN.
CUTE. HOW COULD ANYONE DO THAT?
YEAH. I COULD NEVER HAVE ANY AND SOMEONE IS OUT IN THE MIDDLE OF THE NIGHT THROWING ONE AWAY.
WWAAHH

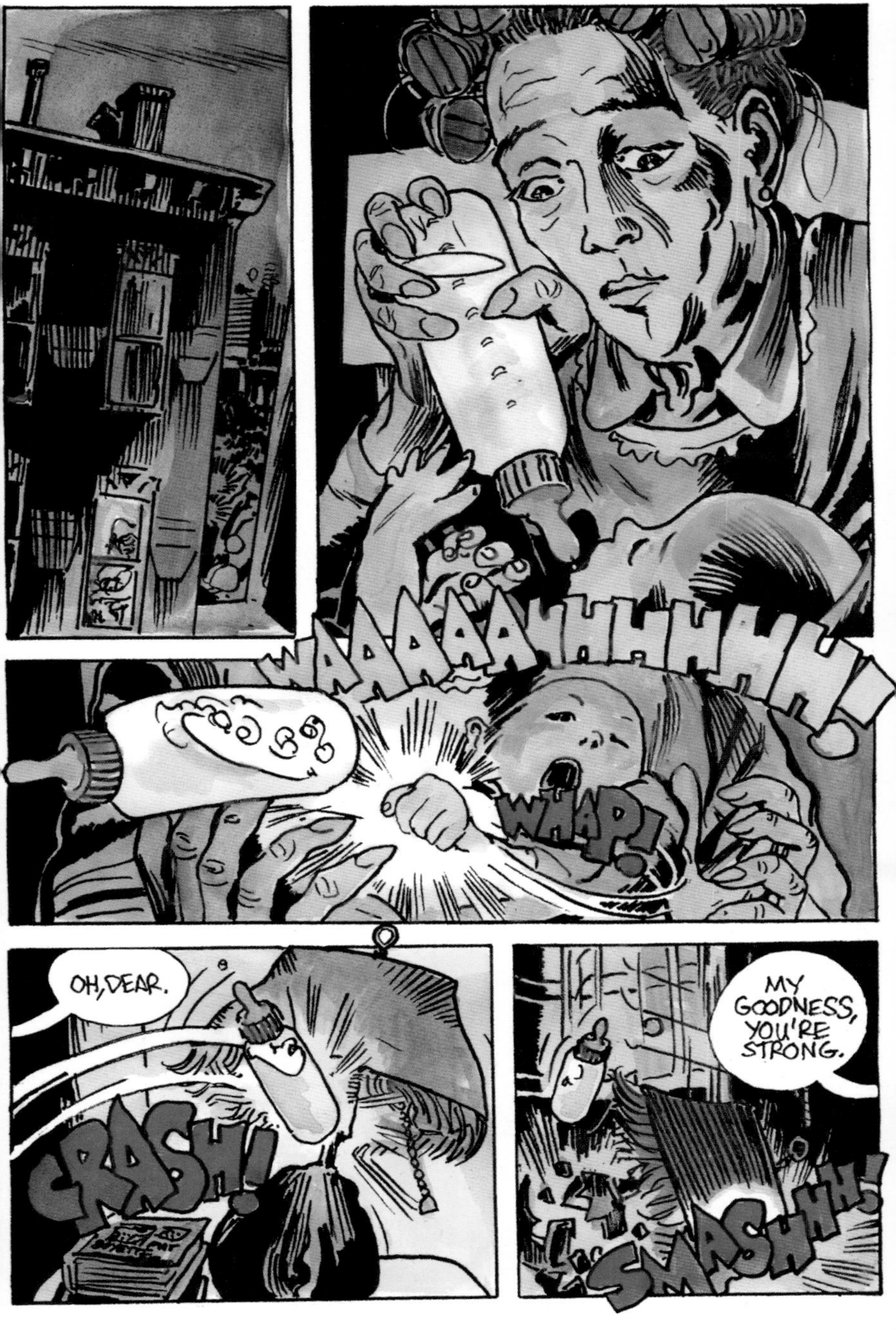

WAAAAAHHHHHH!
WHAP!
OH, DEAR.
CRASH!
MY GOODNESS, YOU'RE STRONG.
SMASHH!

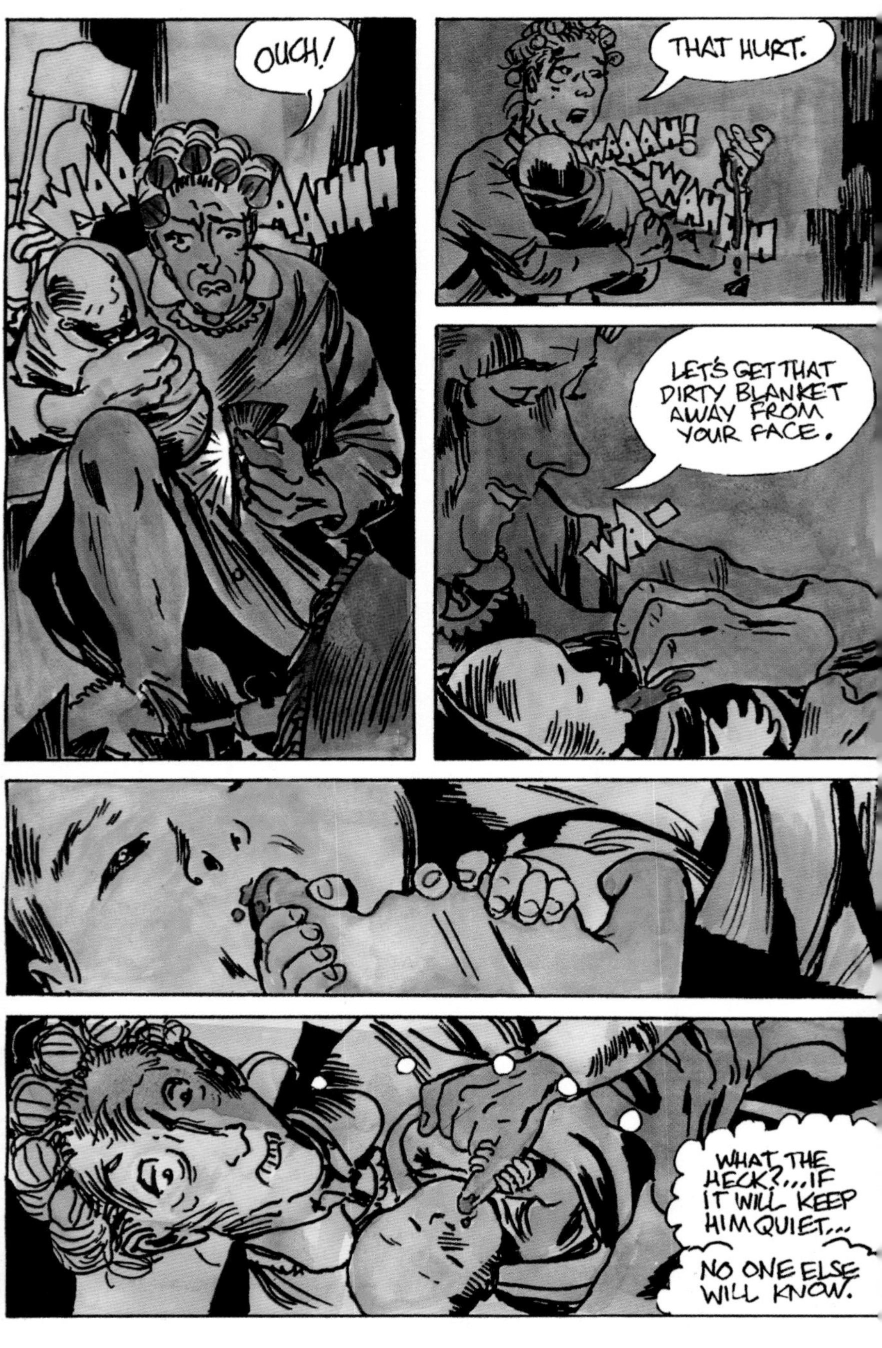
OUCH!
WAAAAHHH
THAT HURT.
WAAAH!
WAHHH
LET'S GET THAT DIRTY BLANKET AWAY FROM YOUR FACE.
WA-
WHAT THE HECK?...IF IT WILL KEEP HIM QUIET...
NO ONE ELSE WILL KNOW.

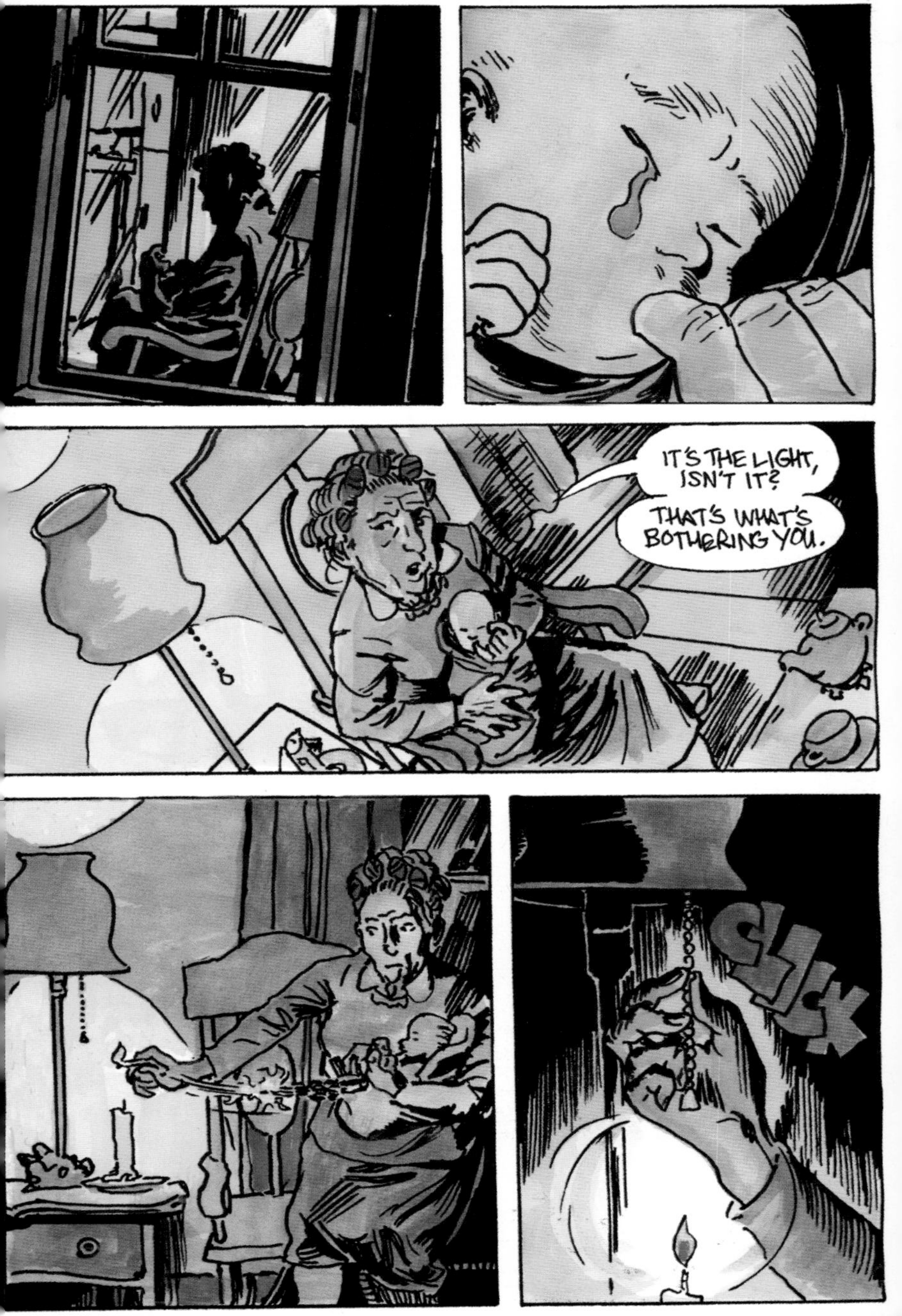
IT'S THE LIGHT, ISN'T IT?
THAT'S WHAT'S BOTHERING YOU.
CLICK

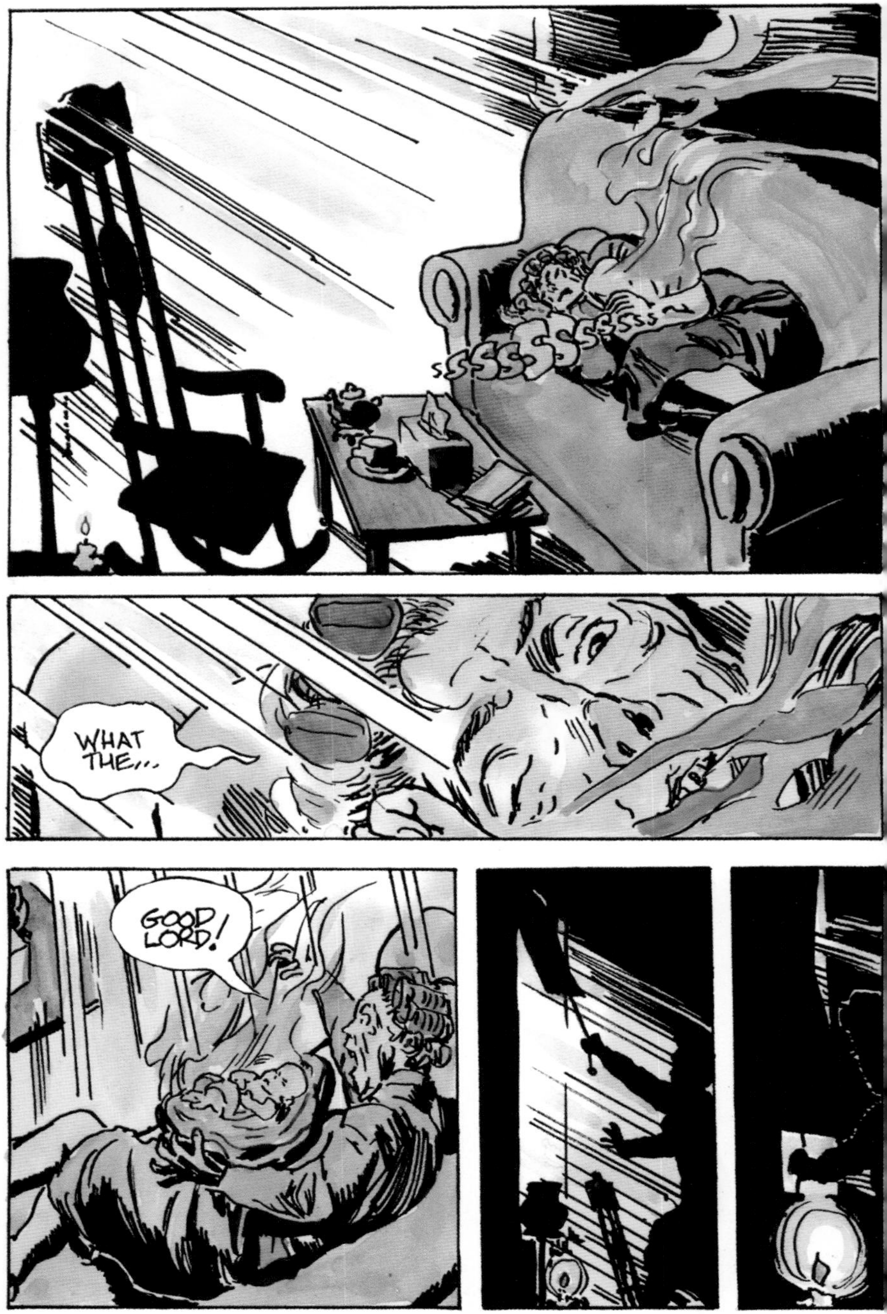

SSSSSSSSSSsss
WHAT THE...
GOOD LORD!

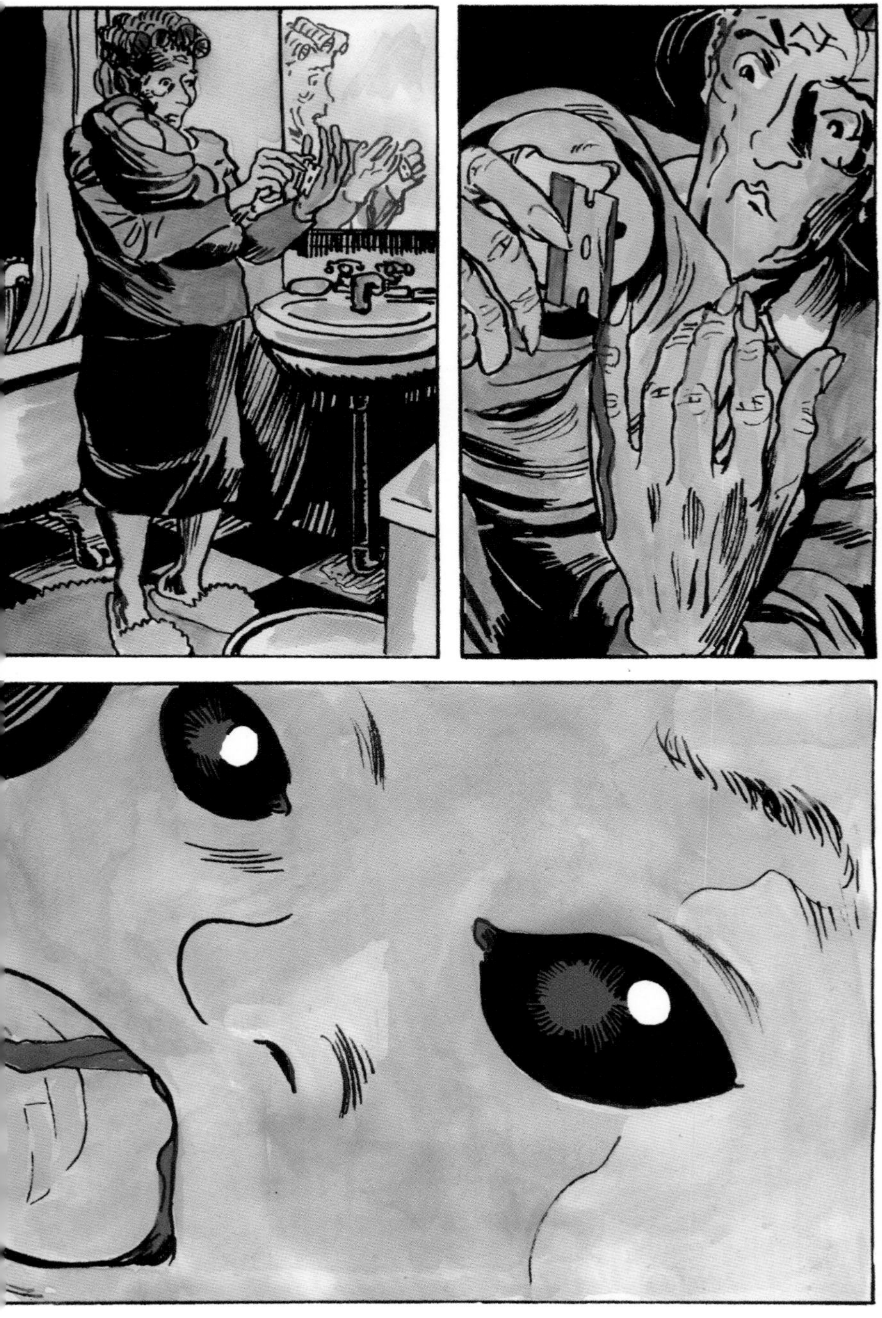

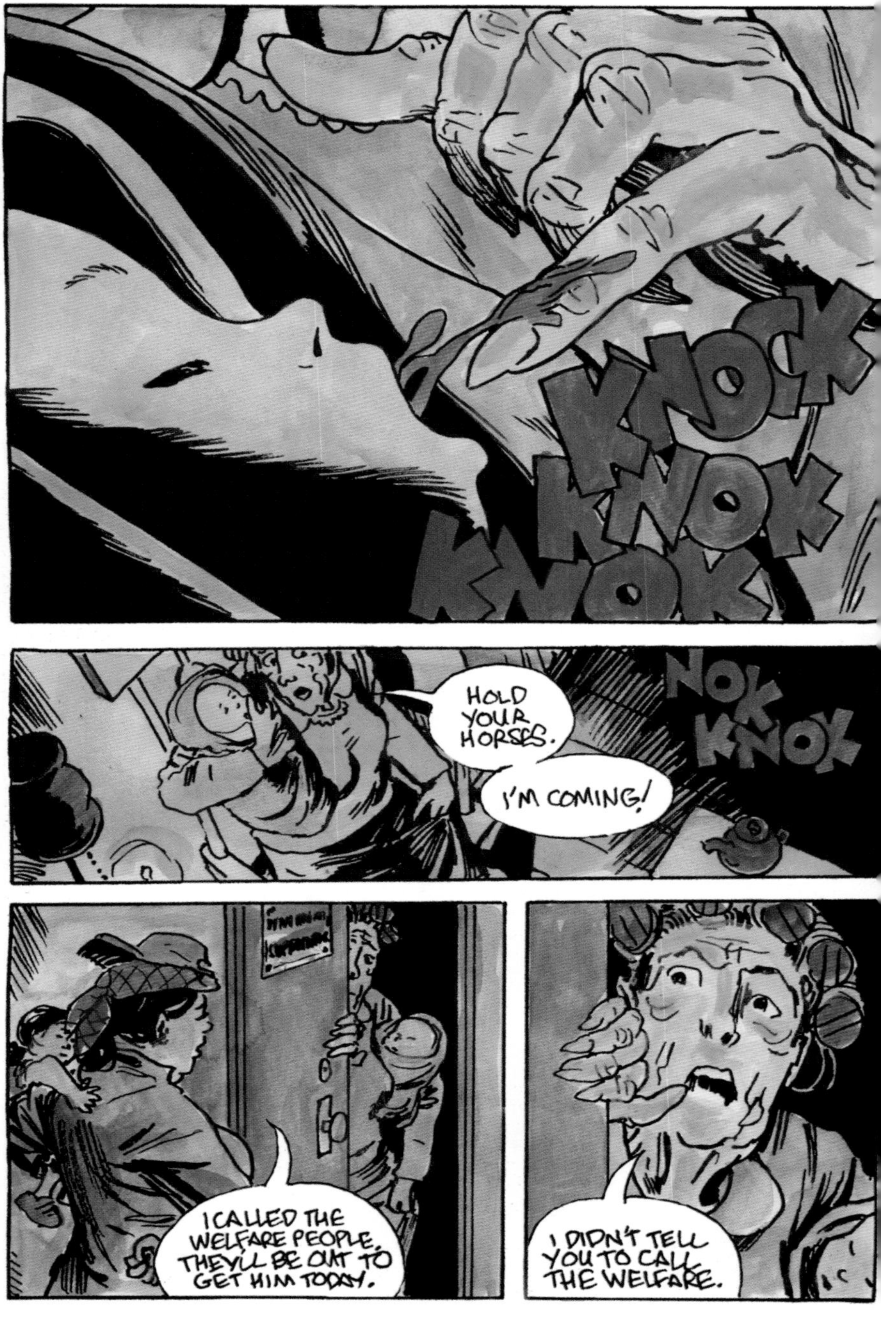
KNOCK
KNOK
KNOK
NOK
KNOK
KNOK
HOLD YOUR HORSES.
I'M COMING!
I CALLED THE WELFARE PEOPLE. THEY'LL BE OUT TO GET HIM TODAY.
I DIDN'T TELL YOU TO CALL THE WELFARE.

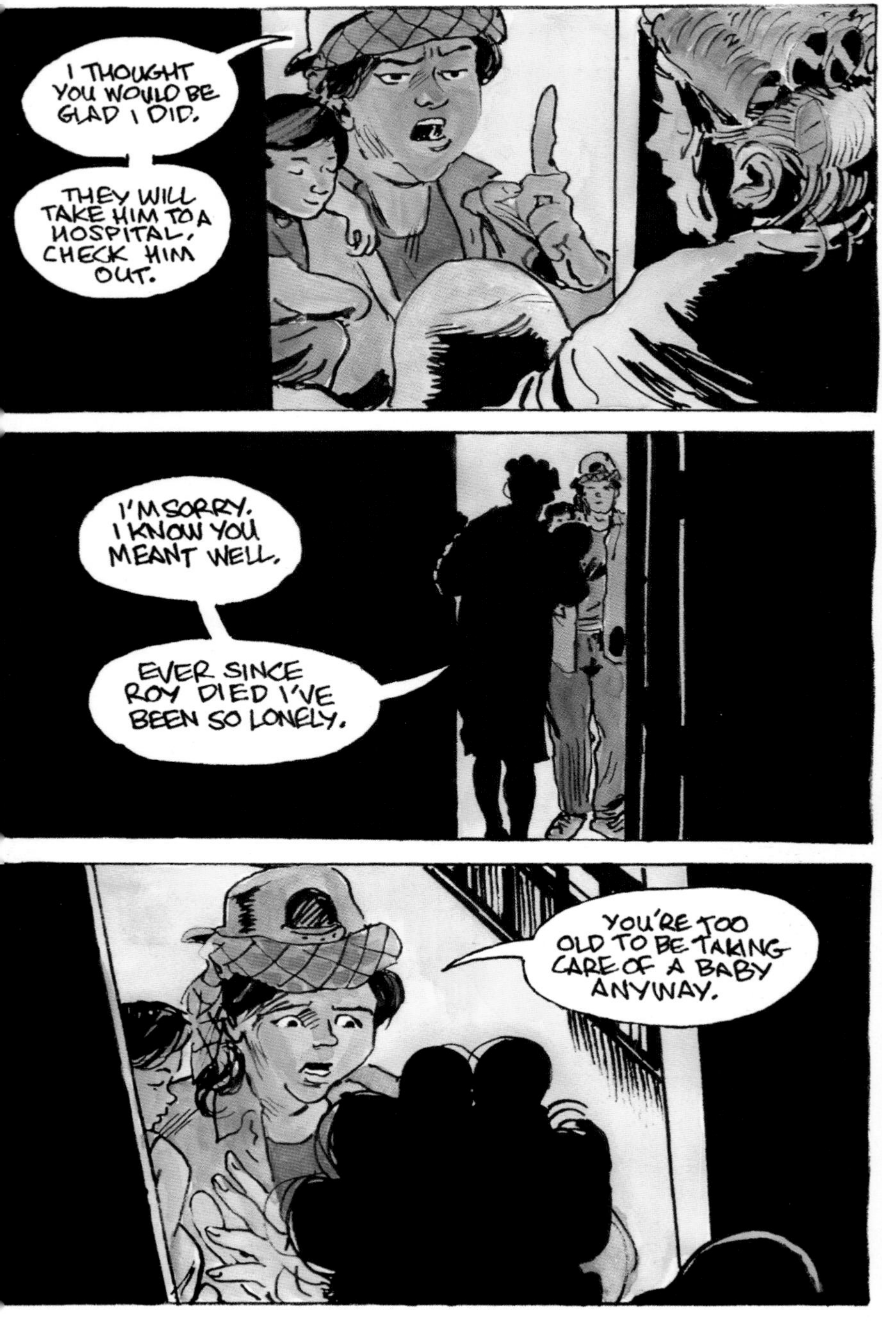
I THOUGHT YOU WOULD BE GLAD I DID.
THEY WILL TAKE HIM TO A HOSPITAL, CHECK HIM OUT.
I'M SORRY. I KNOW YOU MEANT WELL.
EVER SINCE ROY DIED I'VE BEEN SO LONELY.
YOU'RE TOO OLD TO BE TAKING CARE OF A BABY ANYWAY.

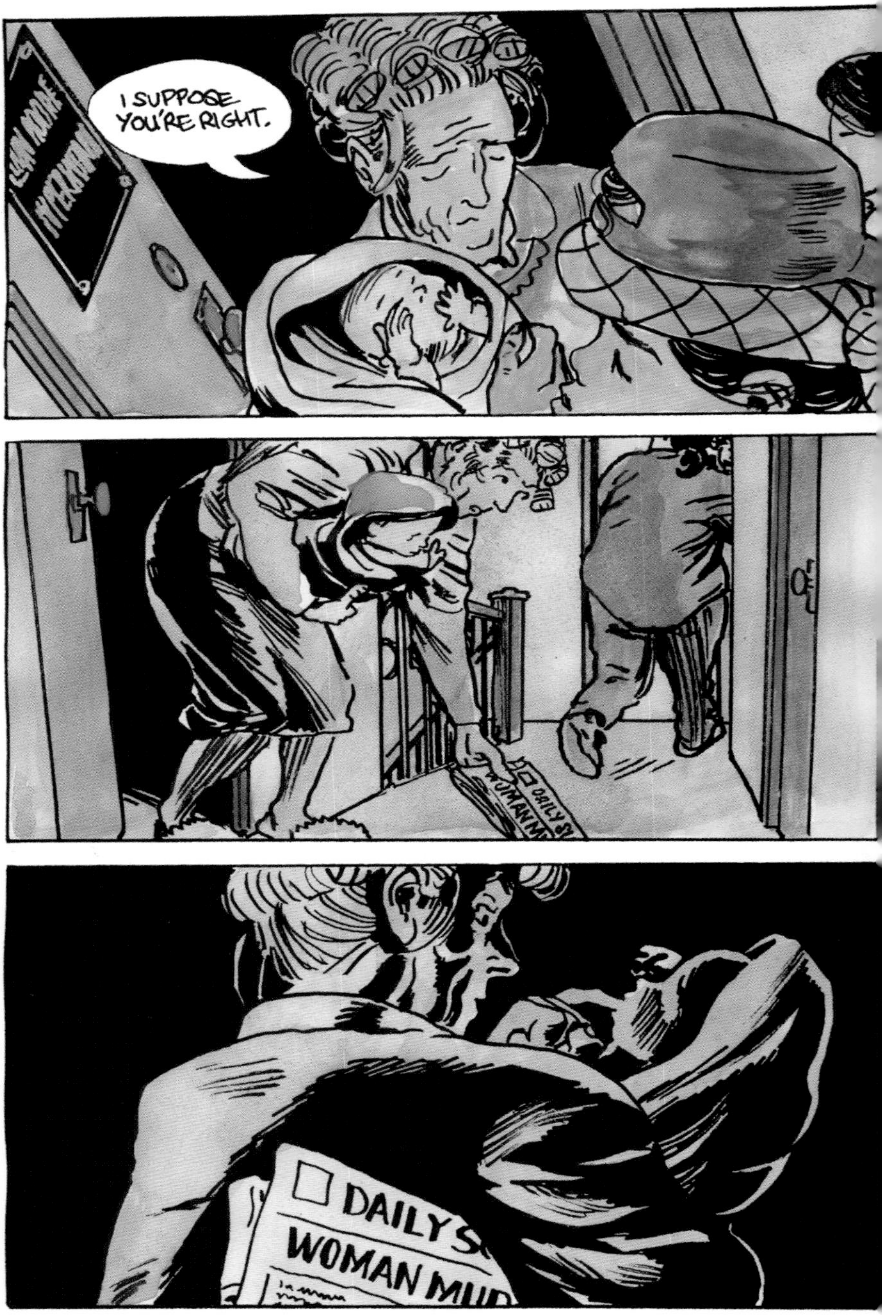
I SUPPOSE YOU'RE RIGHT.
DAILY

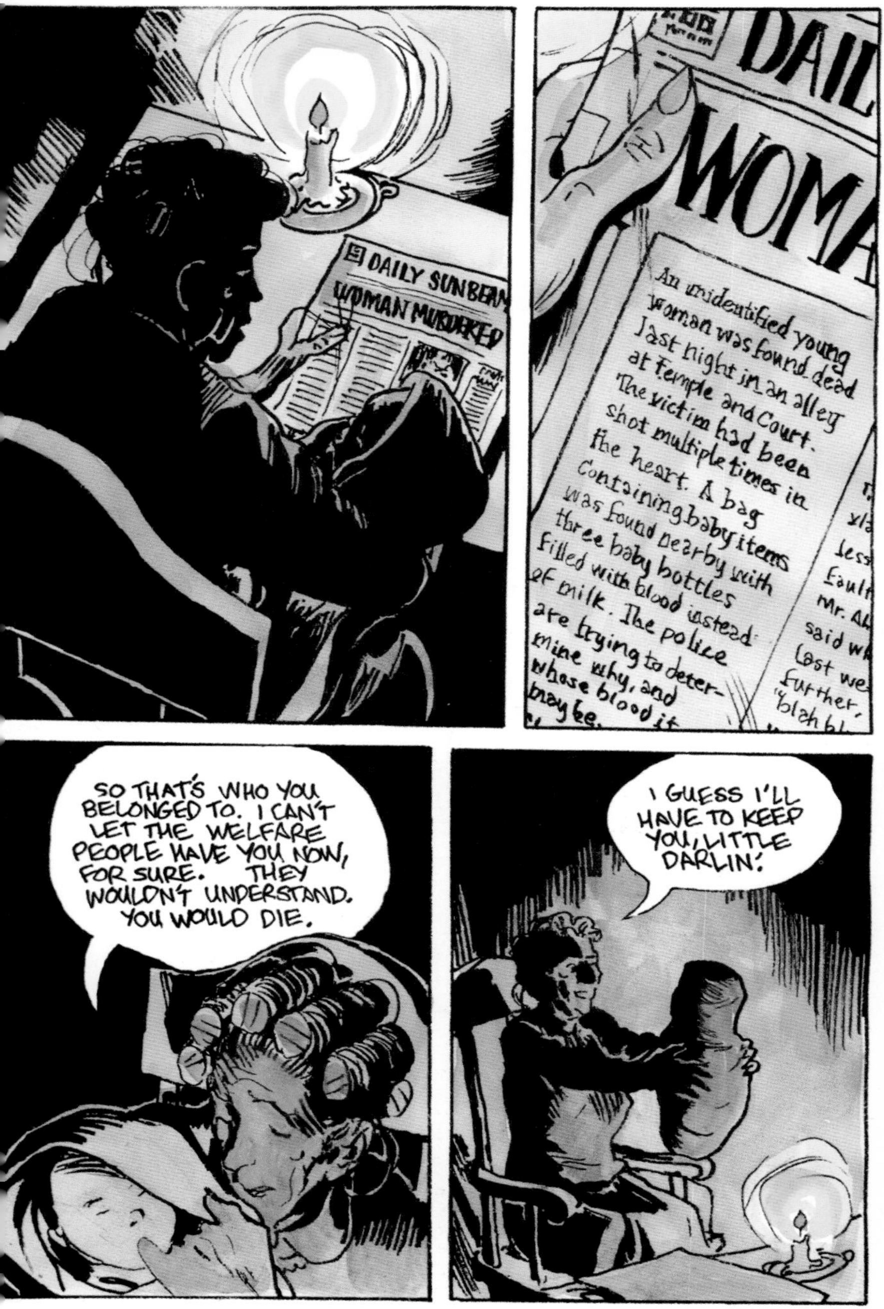
DAILY SUNBEA
WOMAN MURDERED
An unidentified young woman was found dead last night in an alley at Temple and Court. The victim had been shot multiple times in the heart. A bag containing baby items was found nearby with three baby bottles filled with blood instead of milk. The police are trying to determine why, and whose blood it may be.
SO THAT'S WHO YOU BELONGED TO. I CAN'T LET THE WELFARE PEOPLE HAVE YOU NOW, FOR SURE. THEY WOULDN'T UNDERSTAND. YOU WOULD DIE.
I GUESS I'LL HAVE TO KEEP YOU, LITTLE DARLIN'.

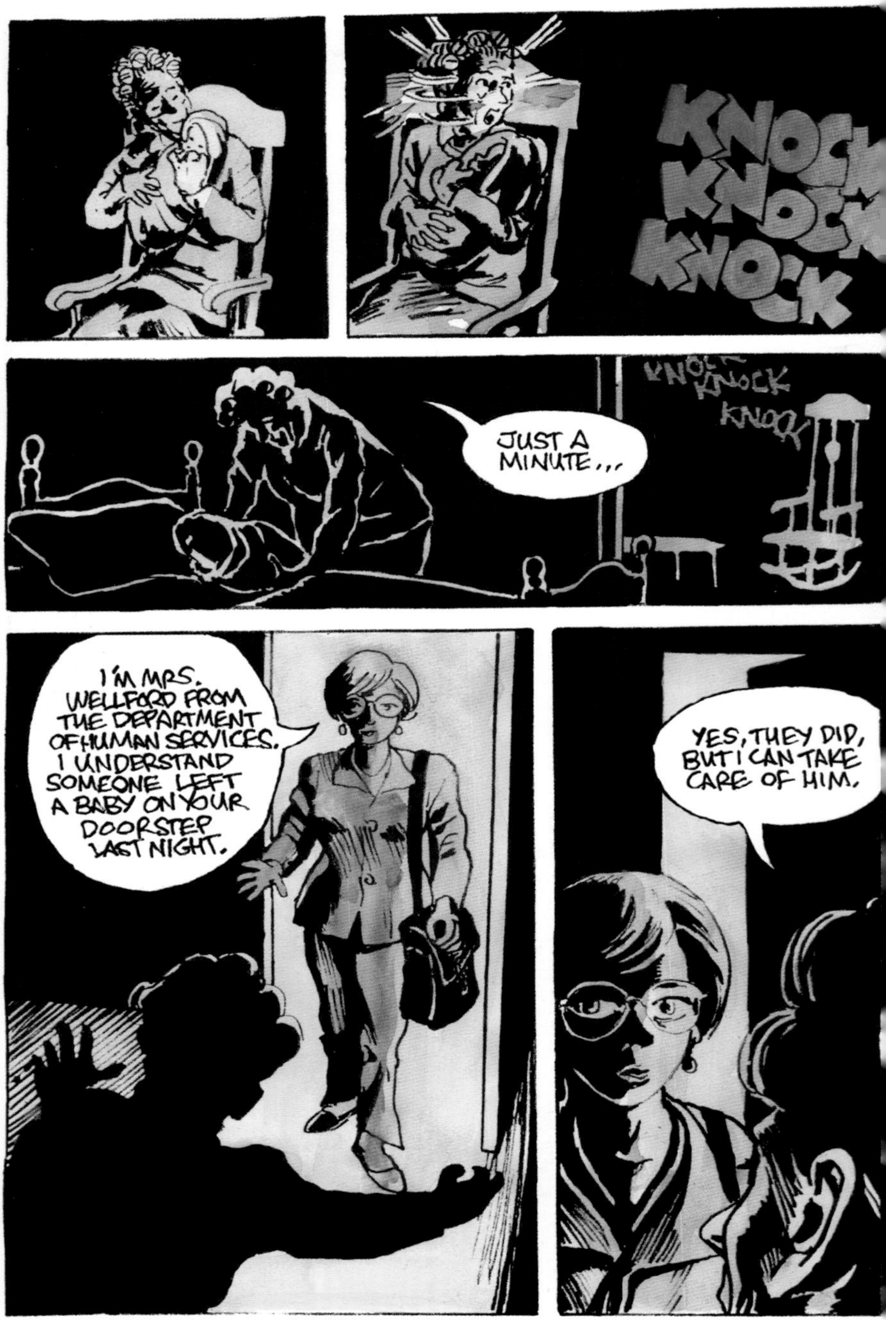
KNOCK KNOCK KNOCK
KNOCK KNOCK KNOCK
JUST A MINUTE...
I'M MRS. WELLFORD FROM THE DEPARTMENT OF HUMAN SERVICES. I UNDERSTAND SOMEONE LEFT A BABY ON YOUR DOORSTEP LAST NIGHT.
YES, THEY DID, BUT I CAN TAKE CARE OF HIM.

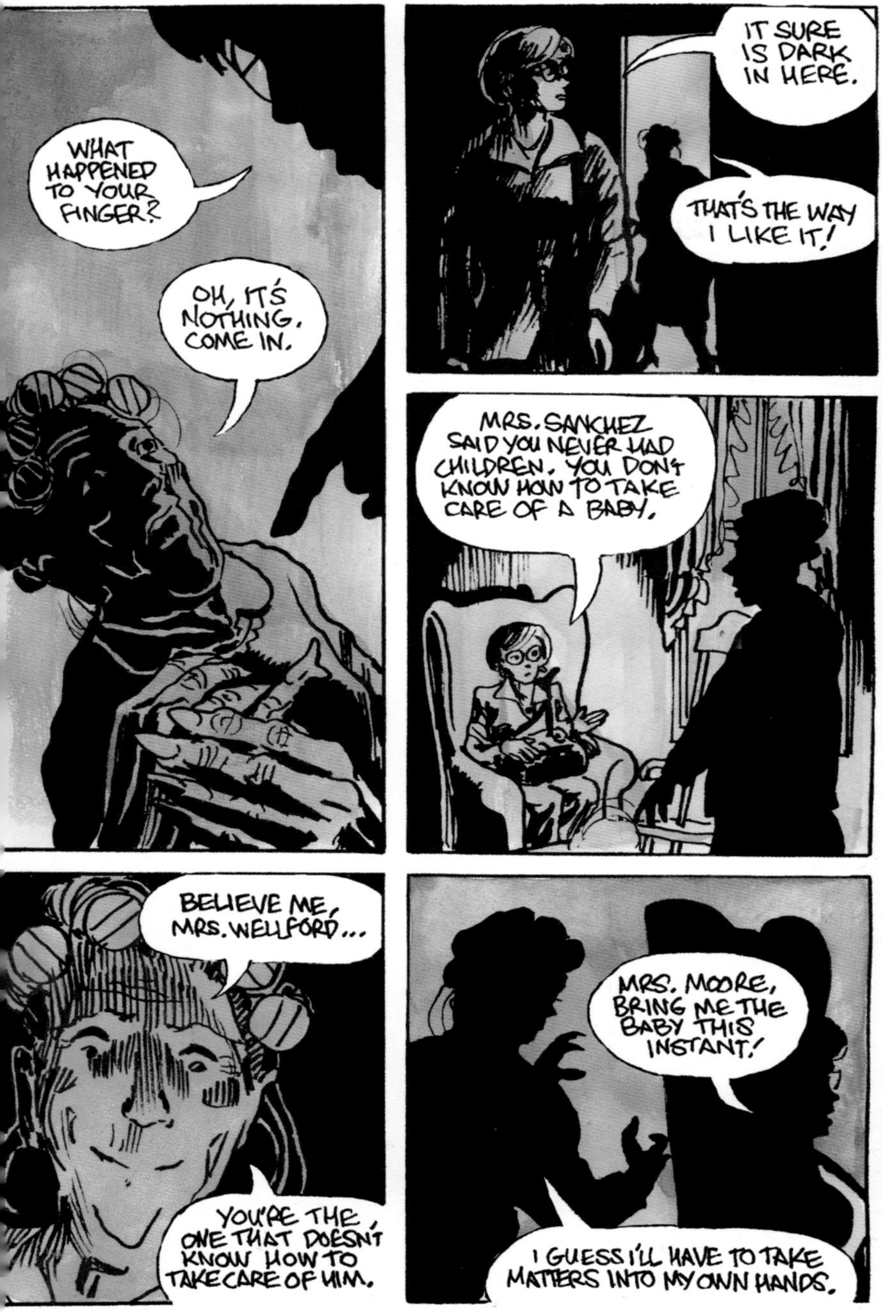
WHAT HAPPENED TO YOUR FINGER?
OH, IT'S NOTHING. COME IN.
IT SURE IS DARK IN HERE.
THAT'S THE WAY I LIKE IT!
MRS. SANCHEZ SAID YOU NEVER HAD CHILDREN. YOU DON'T KNOW HOW TO TAKE CARE OF A BABY.
BELIEVE ME, MRS. WELLFORD...
YOU'RE THE ONE THAT DOESN'T KNOW HOW TO TAKE CARE OF HIM.
MRS. MOORE, BRING ME THE BABY THIS INSTANT!
I GUESS I'LL HAVE TO TAKE MATTERS INTO MY OWN HANDS.

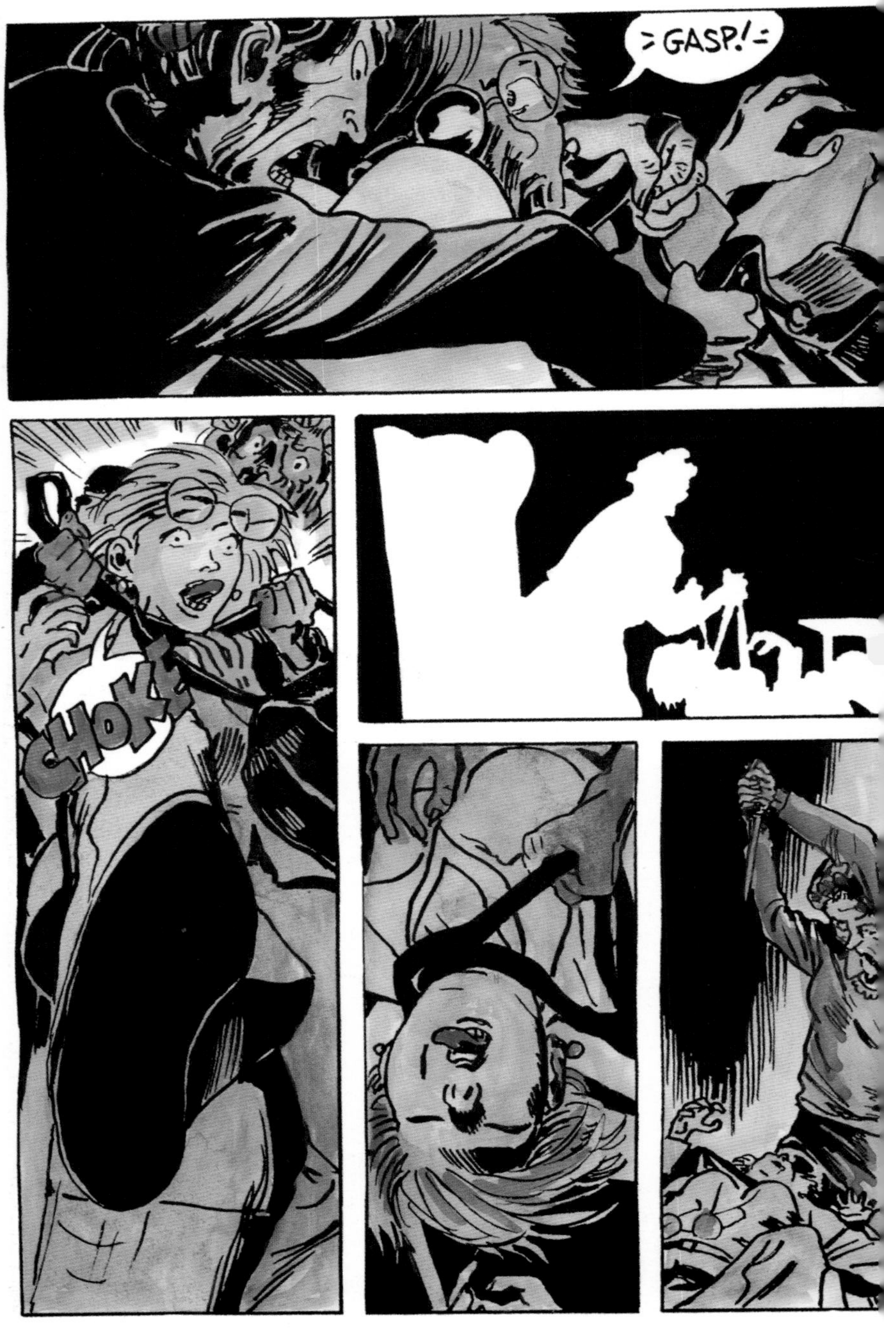

=GASP!=
CHOKE

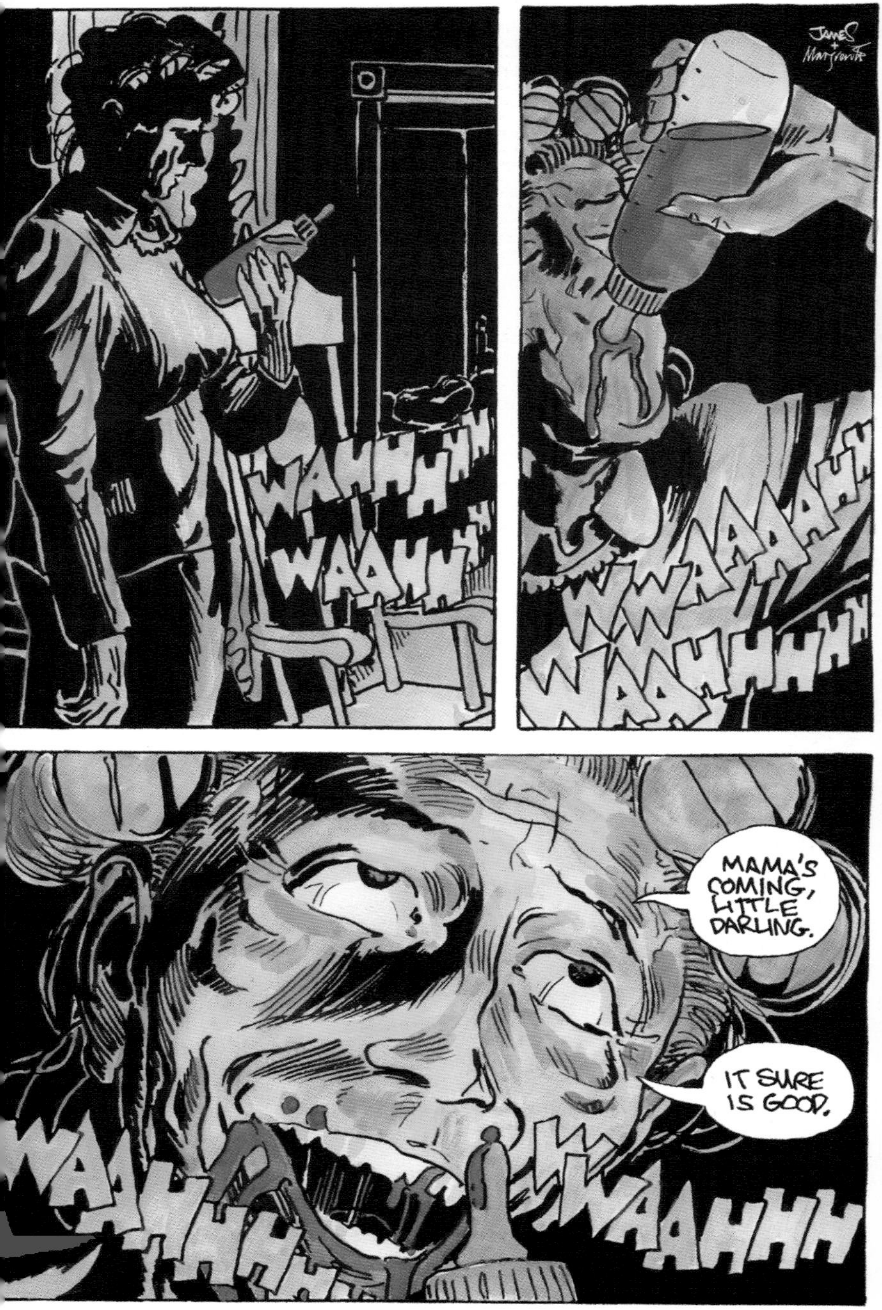
JAMES + MARGIOVITZ(?)
WAAHHHH
WAAHHH
WAAAAHH
WAAHHHH
MAMA'S COMING, LITTLE DARLING.
IT SURE IS GOOD.
WAAHHHHH
WAAHHH

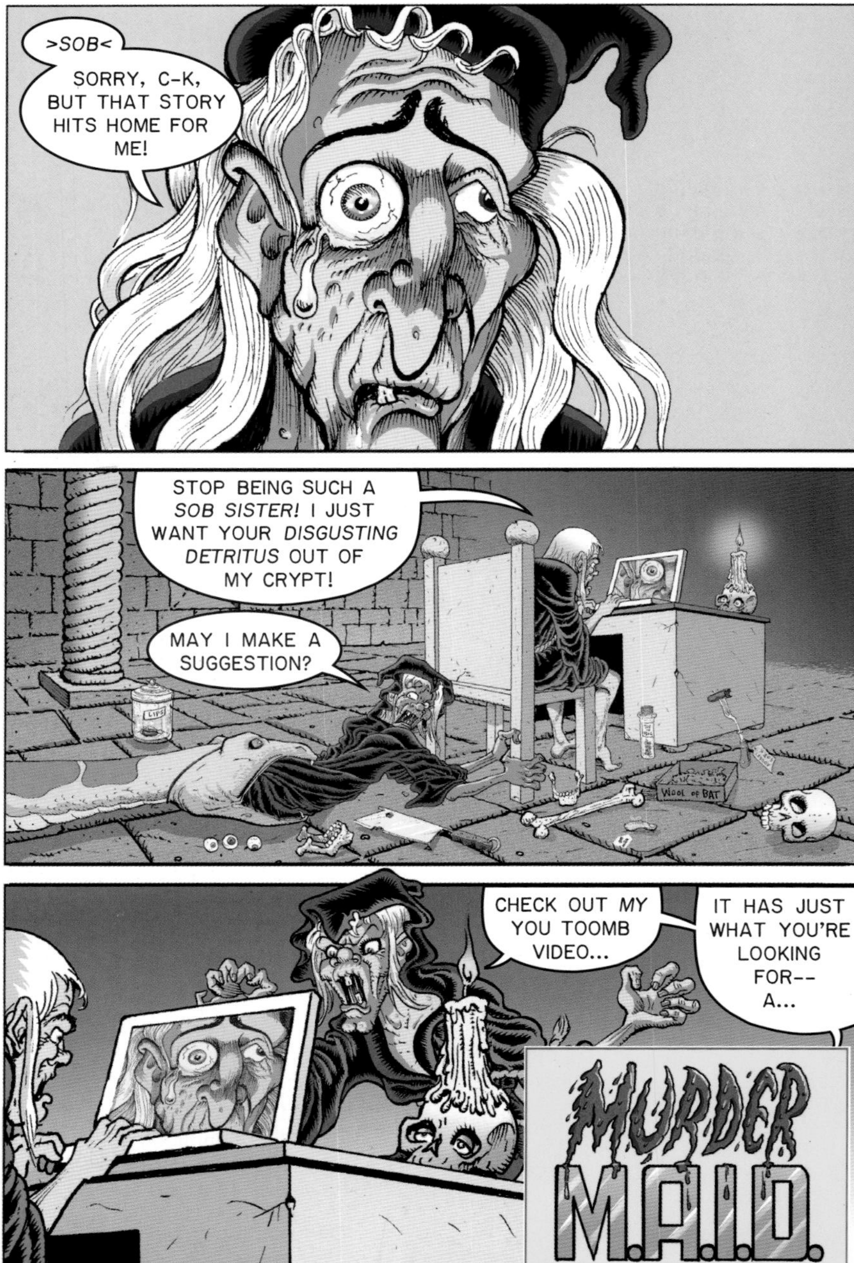
>SOB<
SORRY, C-K, BUT THAT STORY HITS HOME FOR ME!
STOP BEING SUCH A *SOB SISTER!* I JUST WANT YOUR *DISGUSTING DETRITUS* OUT OF MY CRYPT!
MAY I MAKE A SUGGESTION?
LIPS
WOOL OF BAT
CHECK OUT *MY* YOU TOOMB VIDEO...
IT HAS JUST WHAT YOU'RE LOOKING FOR-- A...
MURDER M.A.I.D.

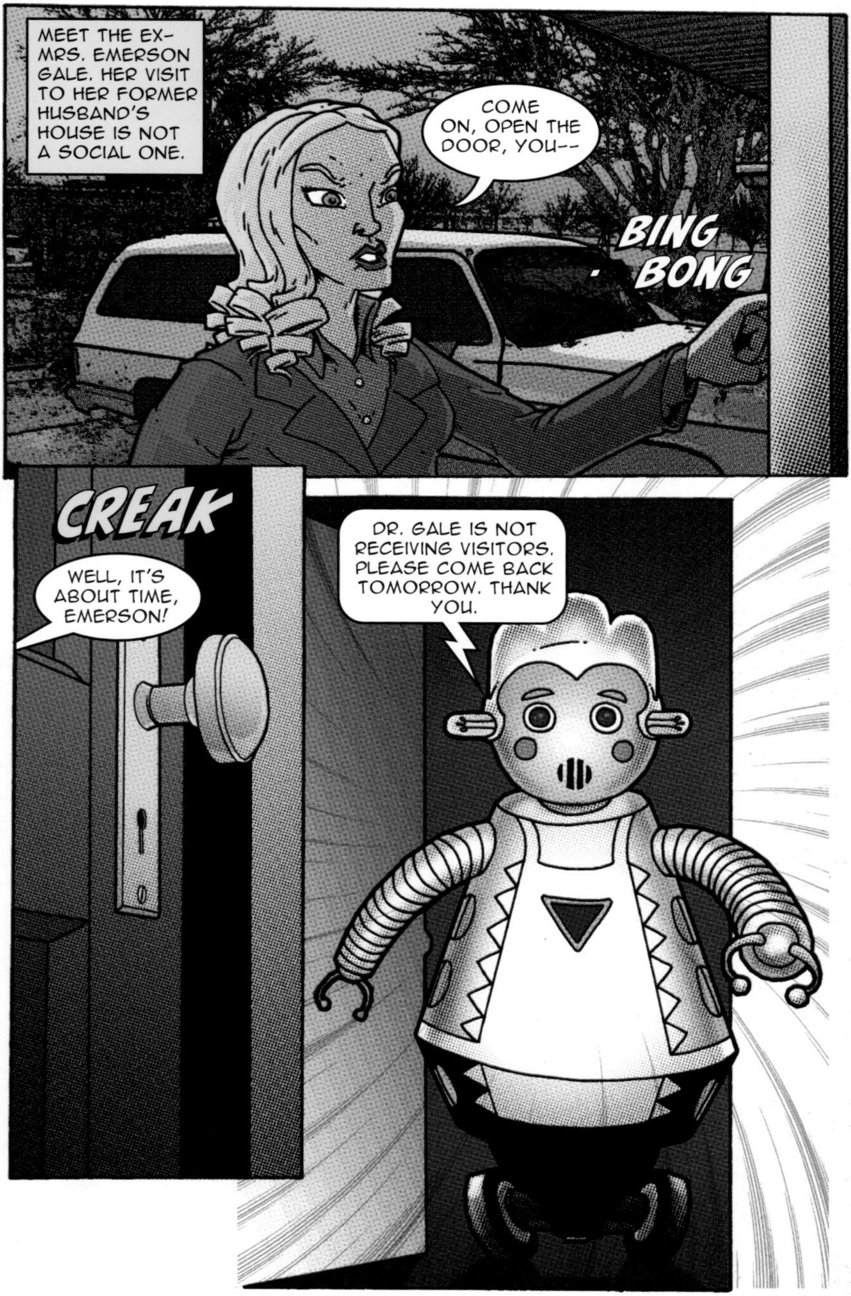
MEET THE EX-MRS. EMERSON GALE. HER VISIT TO HER FORMER HUSBAND'S HOUSE IS NOT A SOCIAL ONE.
COME ON, OPEN THE DOOR, YOU--
BING BONG
CREAK
WELL, IT'S ABOUT TIME, EMERSON!
DR. GALE IS NOT RECEIVING VISITORS. PLEASE COME BACK TOMORROW. THANK YOU.

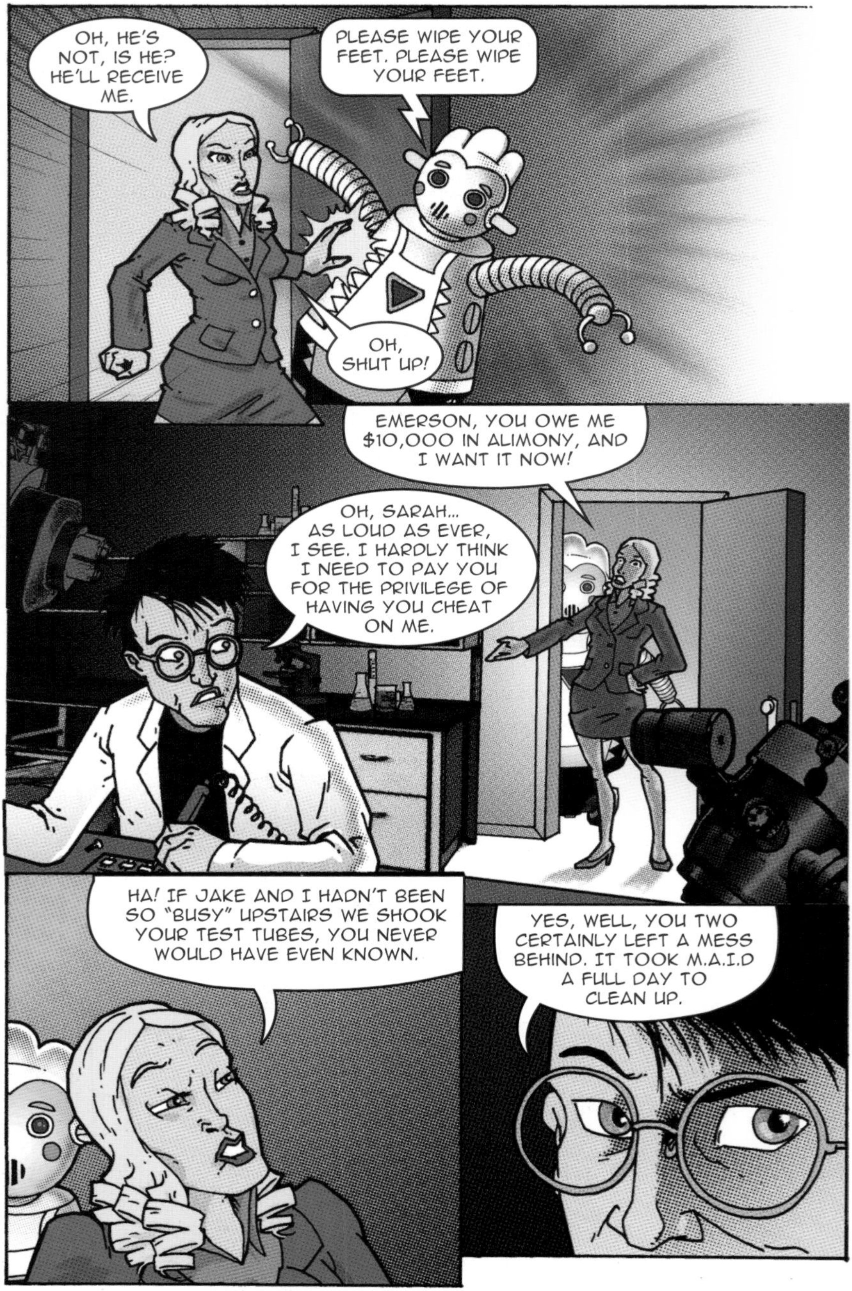
OH, HE'S NOT, IS HE? HE'LL RECEIVE ME.
PLEASE WIPE YOUR FEET. PLEASE WIPE YOUR FEET.
OH, SHUT UP!
EMERSON, YOU OWE ME $10,000 IN ALIMONY, AND I WANT IT NOW!
OH, SARAH... AS LOUD AS EVER, I SEE. I HARDLY THINK I NEED TO PAY YOU FOR THE PRIVILEGE OF HAVING YOU CHEAT ON ME.
HA! IF JAKE AND I HADN'T BEEN SO "BUSY" UPSTAIRS WE SHOOK YOUR TEST TUBES, YOU NEVER WOULD HAVE EVEN KNOWN.
YES, WELL, YOU TWO CERTAINLY LEFT A MESS BEHIND. IT TOOK M.A.I.D A FULL DAY TO CLEAN UP.

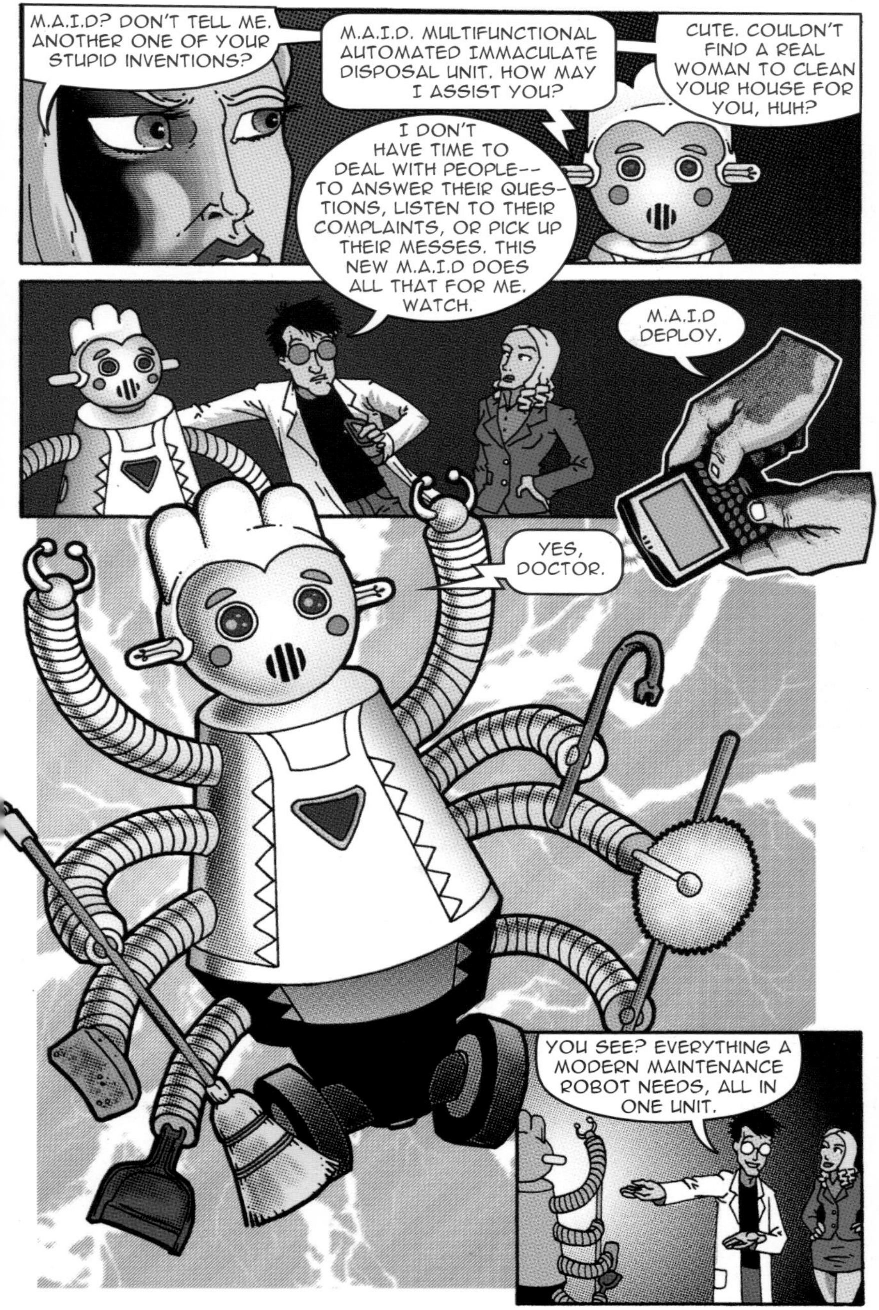
M.A.I.D? DON'T TELL ME. ANOTHER ONE OF YOUR STUPID INVENTIONS?
M.A.I.D. MULTIFUNCTIONAL AUTOMATED IMMACULATE DISPOSAL UNIT. HOW MAY I ASSIST YOU?
CUTE. COULDN'T FIND A REAL WOMAN TO CLEAN YOUR HOUSE FOR YOU, HUH?
I DON'T HAVE TIME TO DEAL WITH PEOPLE-- TO ANSWER THEIR QUESTIONS, LISTEN TO THEIR COMPLAINTS, OR PICK UP THEIR MESSES. THIS NEW M.A.I.D DOES ALL THAT FOR ME. WATCH.
M.A.I.D DEPLOY.
YES, DOCTOR.
YOU SEE? EVERYTHING A MODERN MAINTENANCE ROBOT NEEDS, ALL IN ONE UNIT.

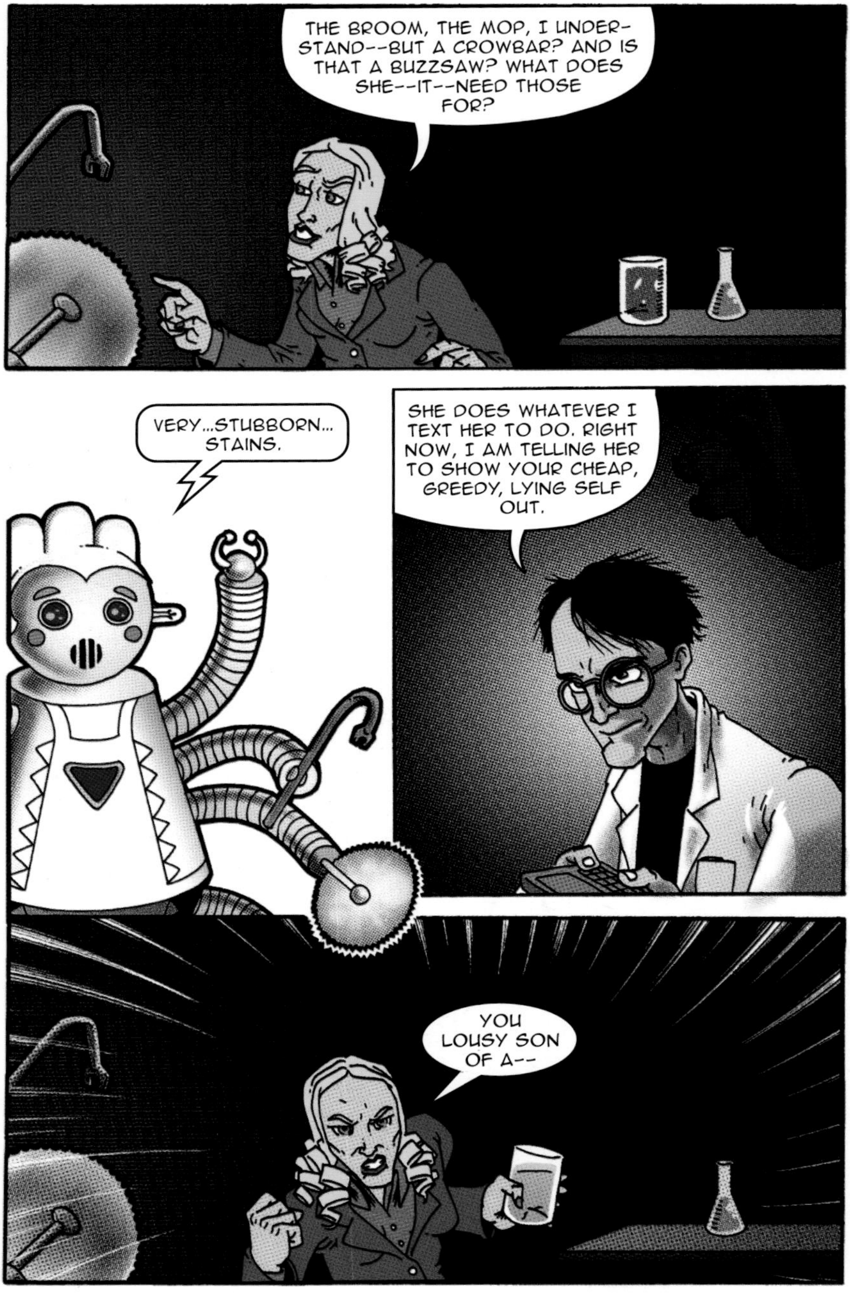
THE BROOM, THE MOP, I UNDERSTAND--BUT A CROWBAR? AND IS THAT A BUZZSAW? WHAT DOES SHE--IT--NEED THOSE FOR?
VERY...STUBBORN... STAINS.
SHE DOES WHATEVER I TEXT HER TO DO. RIGHT NOW, I AM TELLING HER TO SHOW YOUR CHEAP, GREEDY, LYING SELF OUT.
YOU LOUSY SON OF A--

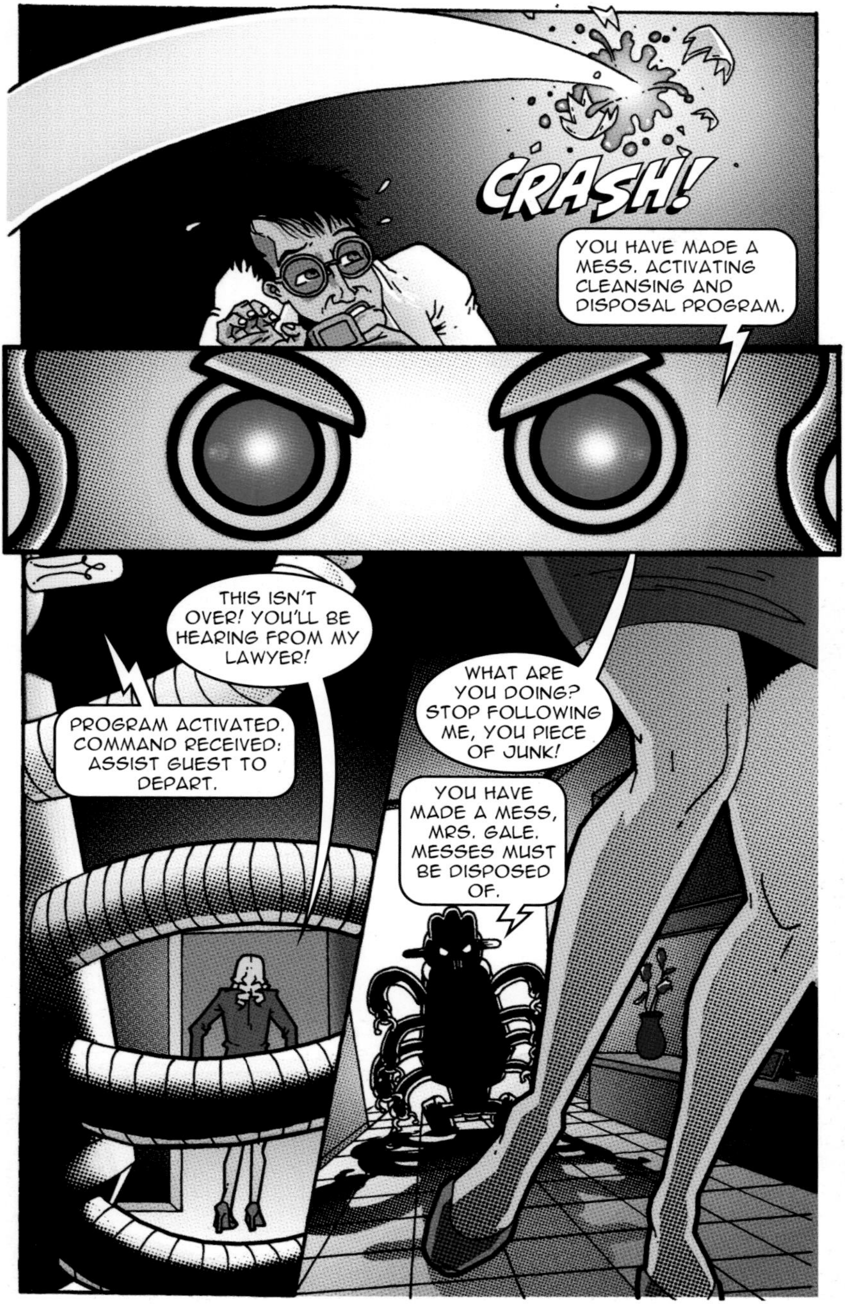
CRASH!
YOU HAVE MADE A MESS. ACTIVATING CLEANSING AND DISPOSAL PROGRAM.
WHAT ARE YOU DOING? STOP FOLLOWING ME, YOU PIECE OF JUNK!
YOU HAVE MADE A MESS, MRS. GALE. MESSES MUST BE DISPOSED OF.
THIS ISN'T OVER! YOU'LL BE HEARING FROM MY LAWYER!
PROGRAM ACTIVATED. COMMAND RECEIVED: ASSIST GUEST TO DEPART.

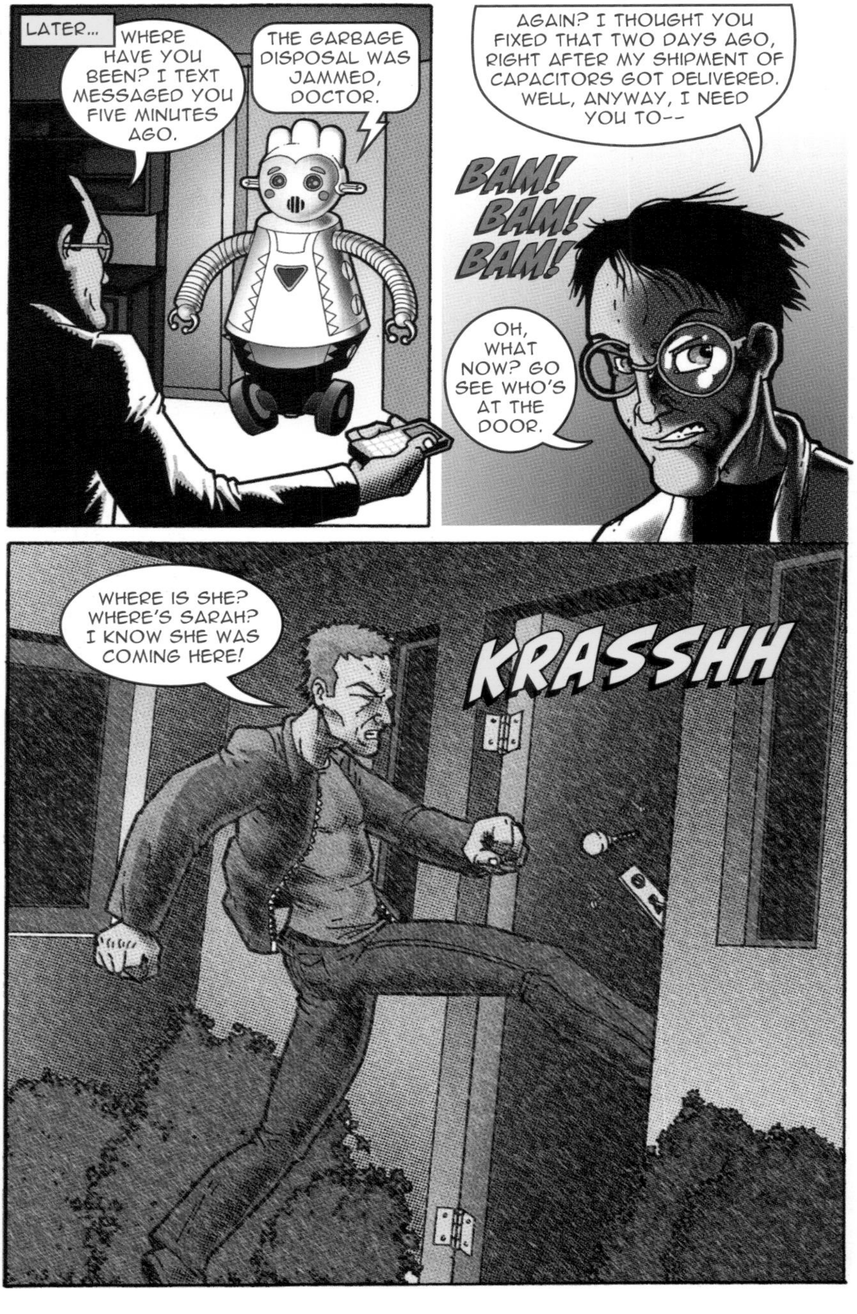
LATER...
WHERE HAVE YOU BEEN? I TEXT MESSAGED YOU FIVE MINUTES AGO.
THE GARBAGE DISPOSAL WAS JAMMED, DOCTOR.
AGAIN? I THOUGHT YOU FIXED THAT TWO DAYS AGO, RIGHT AFTER MY SHIPMENT OF CAPACITORS GOT DELIVERED. WELL, ANYWAY, I NEED YOU TO--
BAM! BAM! BAM!
OH, WHAT NOW? GO SEE WHO'S AT THE DOOR.
WHERE IS SHE? WHERE'S SARAH? I KNOW SHE WAS COMING HERE!
KRASSHH

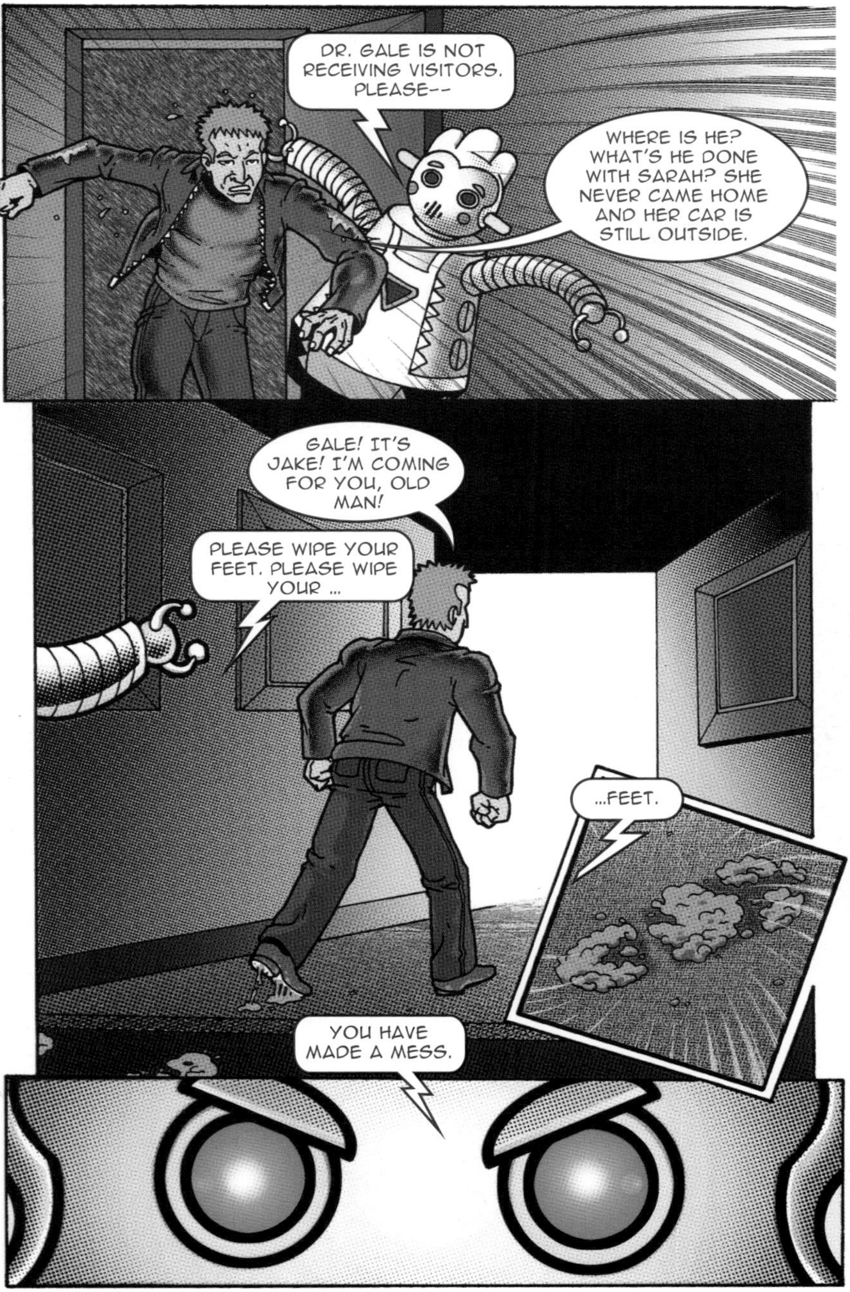
DR. GALE IS NOT RECEIVING VISITORS. PLEASE--
WHERE IS HE? WHAT'S HE DONE WITH SARAH? SHE NEVER CAME HOME AND HER CAR IS STILL OUTSIDE.
GALE! IT'S JAKE! I'M COMING FOR YOU, OLD MAN!
PLEASE WIPE YOUR FEET. PLEASE WIPE YOUR ...
...FEET.
YOU HAVE MADE A MESS.

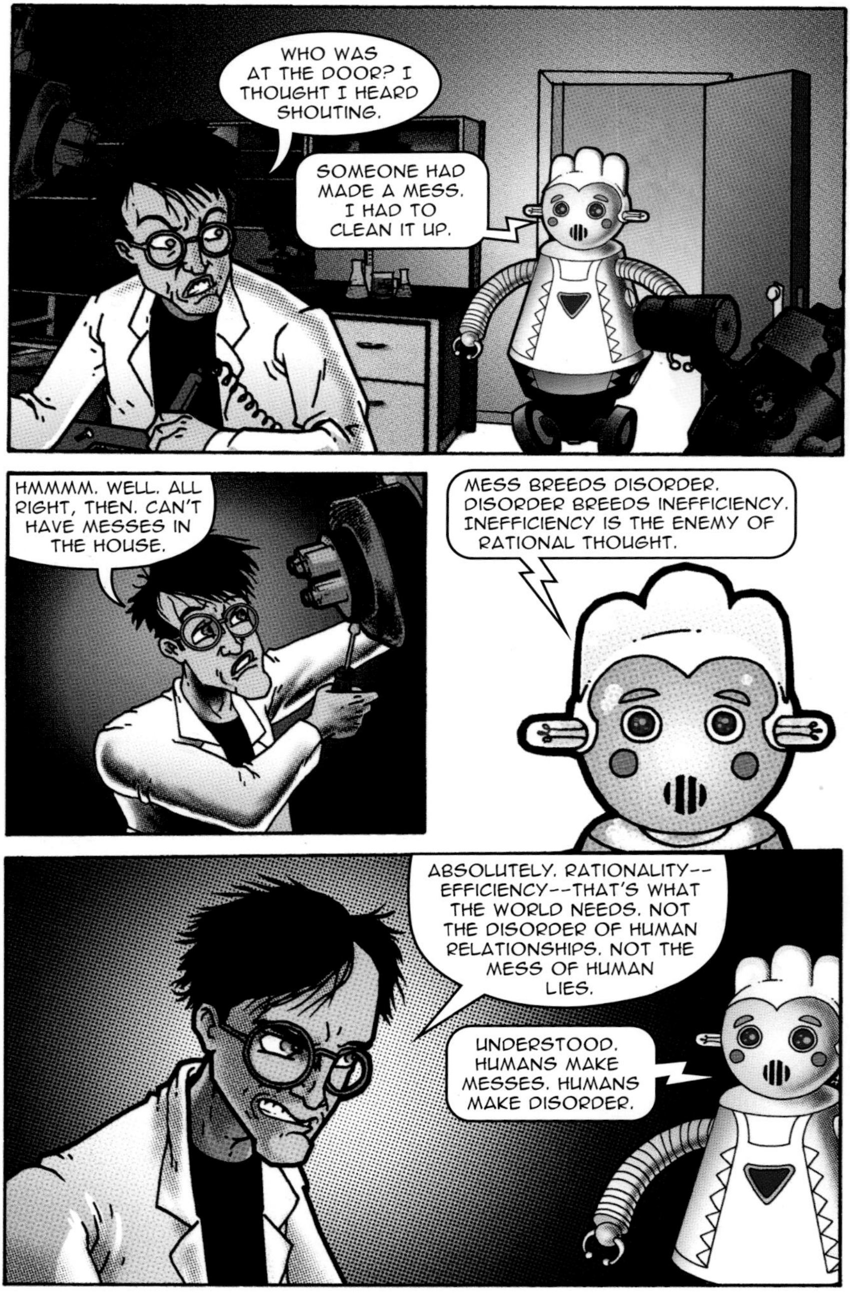
WHO WAS AT THE DOOR? I THOUGHT I HEARD SHOUTING.
SOMEONE HAD MADE A MESS. I HAD TO CLEAN IT UP.
HMMMM. WELL. ALL RIGHT, THEN. CAN'T HAVE MESSES IN THE HOUSE.
MESS BREEDS DISORDER. DISORDER BREEDS INEFFICIENCY. INEFFICIENCY IS THE ENEMY OF RATIONAL THOUGHT.
ABSOLUTELY. RATIONALITY--EFFICIENCY--THAT'S WHAT THE WORLD NEEDS. NOT THE DISORDER OF HUMAN RELATIONSHIPS. NOT THE MESS OF HUMAN LIES.
UNDERSTOOD. HUMANS MAKE MESSES. HUMANS MAKE DISORDER.

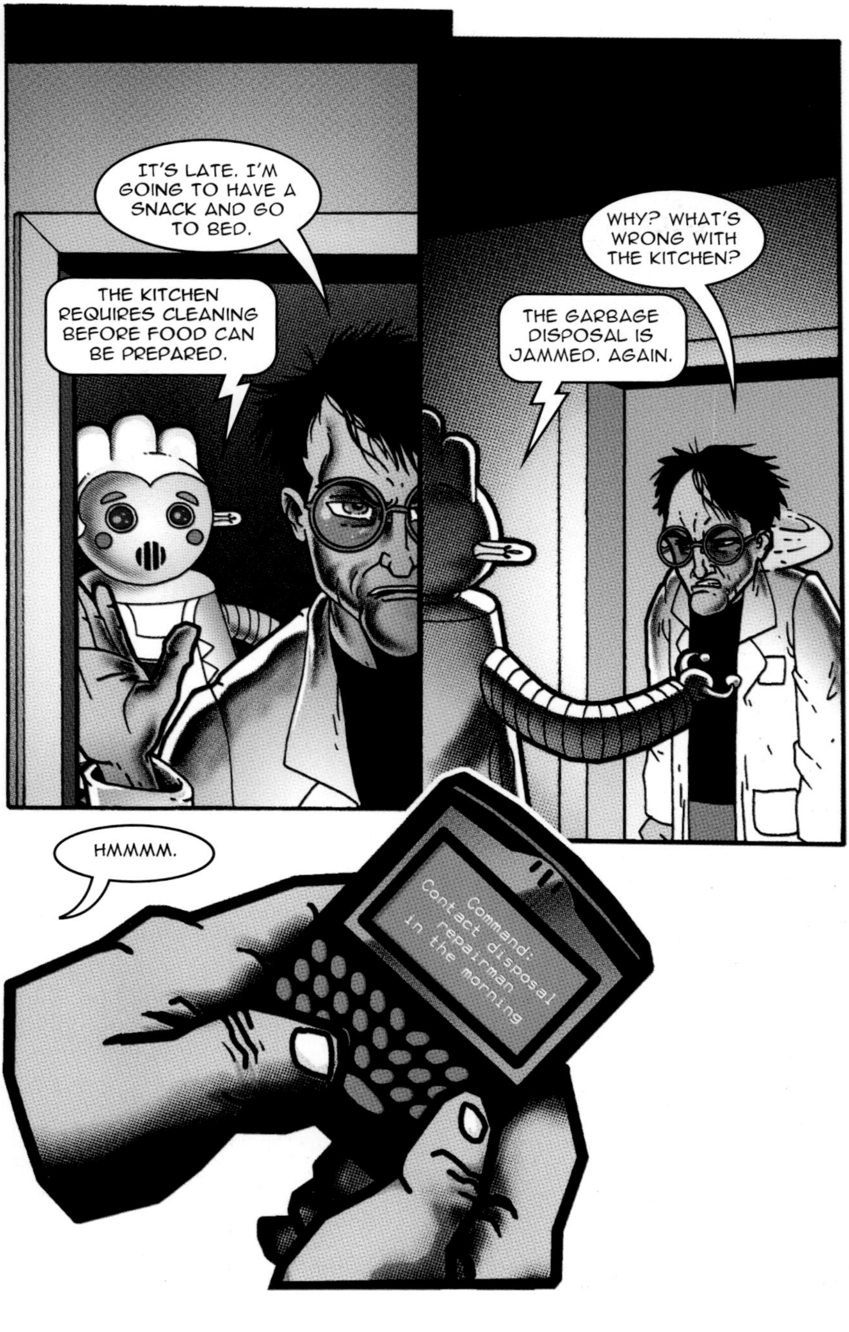
IT'S LATE. I'M GOING TO HAVE A SNACK AND GO TO BED.
THE KITCHEN REQUIRES CLEANING BEFORE FOOD CAN BE PREPARED.
WHY? WHAT'S WRONG WITH THE KITCHEN?
THE GARBAGE DISPOSAL IS JAMMED. AGAIN.
HMMMM.
Command: Contact disposal repairman in the morning

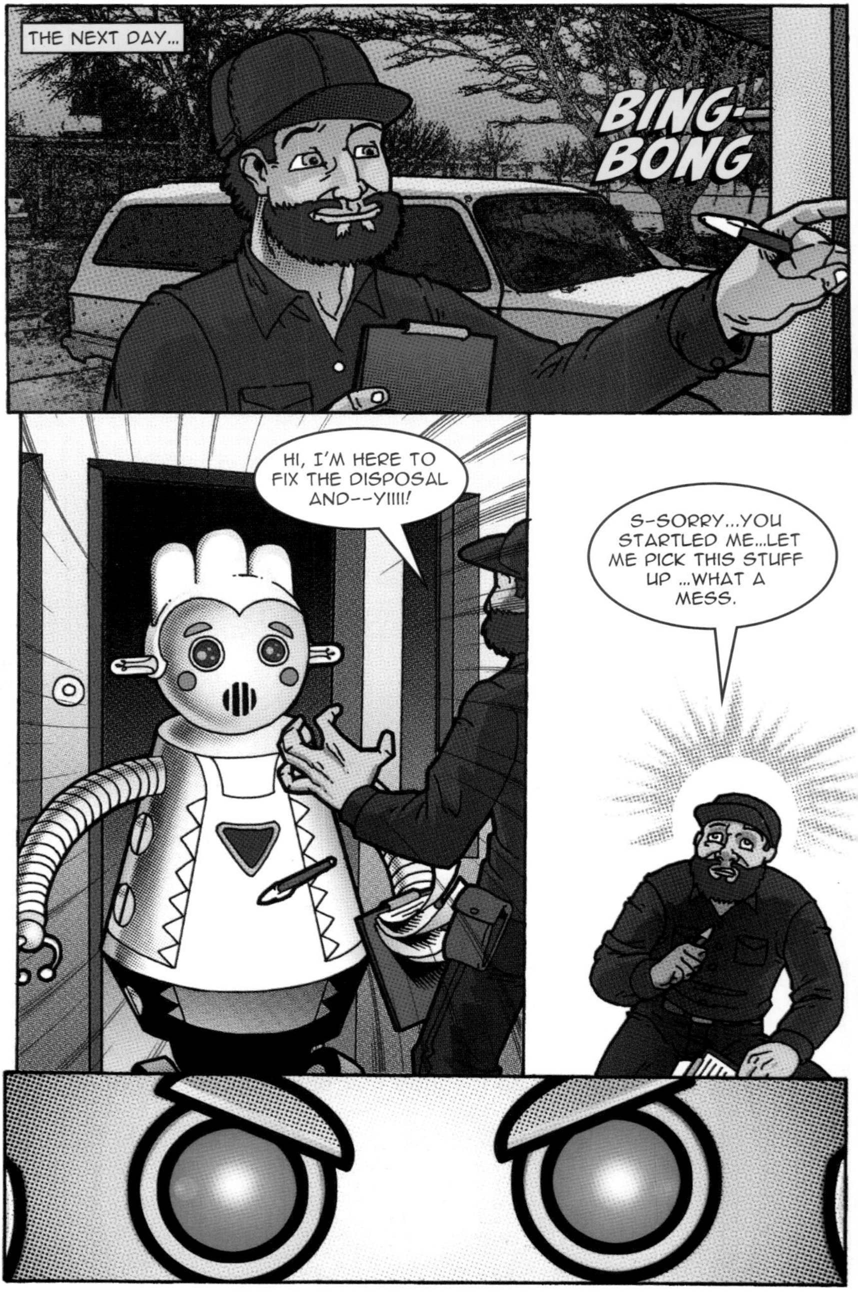
THE NEXT DAY...
BING-BONG
HI, I'M HERE TO FIX THE DISPOSAL AND--YIIII!
S-SORRY...YOU STARTLED ME...LET ME PICK THIS STUFF UP ...WHAT A MESS.

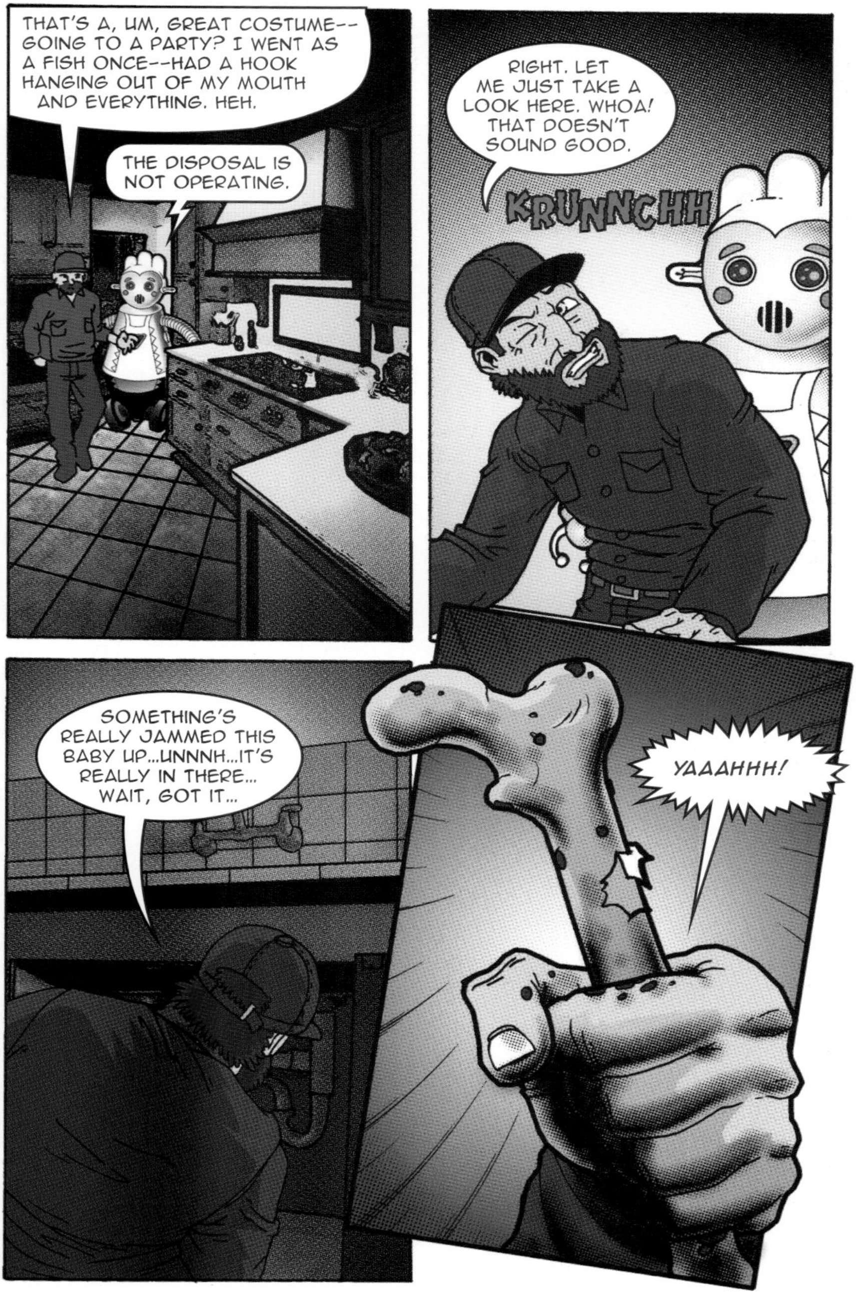
THAT'S A, UM, GREAT COSTUME--GOING TO A PARTY? I WENT AS A FISH ONCE--HAD A HOOK HANGING OUT OF MY MOUTH AND EVERYTHING. HEH.
THE DISPOSAL IS NOT OPERATING.
RIGHT. LET ME JUST TAKE A LOOK HERE. WHOA! THAT DOESN'T SOUND GOOD.
KRUNNCHH
SOMETHING'S REALLY JAMMED THIS BABY UP...UNNNH...IT'S REALLY IN THERE... WAIT, GOT IT...
YAAAHHH!

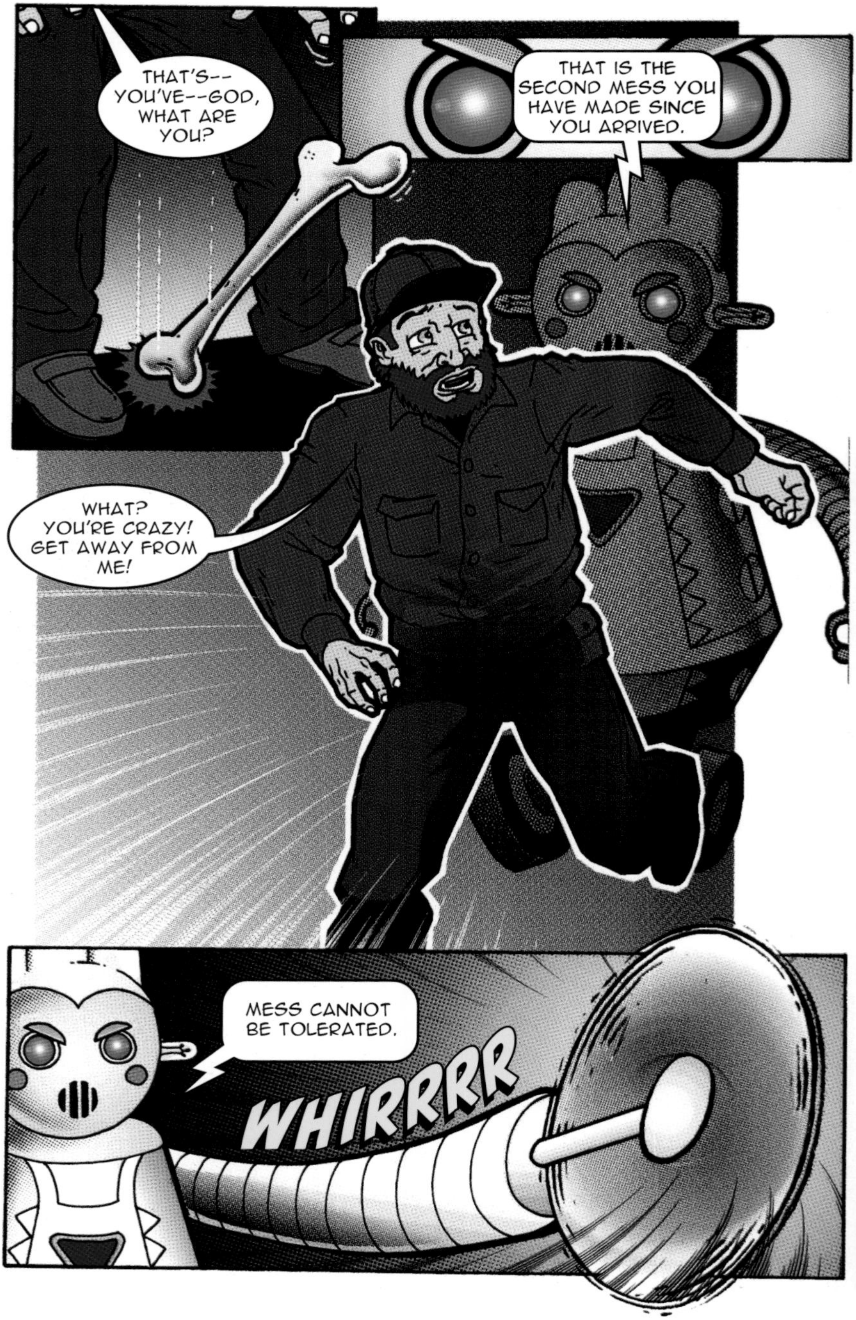
THAT'S-- YOU'VE--GOD, WHAT ARE YOU?
THAT IS THE SECOND MESS YOU HAVE MADE SINCE YOU ARRIVED.
WHAT? YOU'RE CRAZY! GET AWAY FROM ME!
MESS CANNOT BE TOLERATED.
WHIRRRR

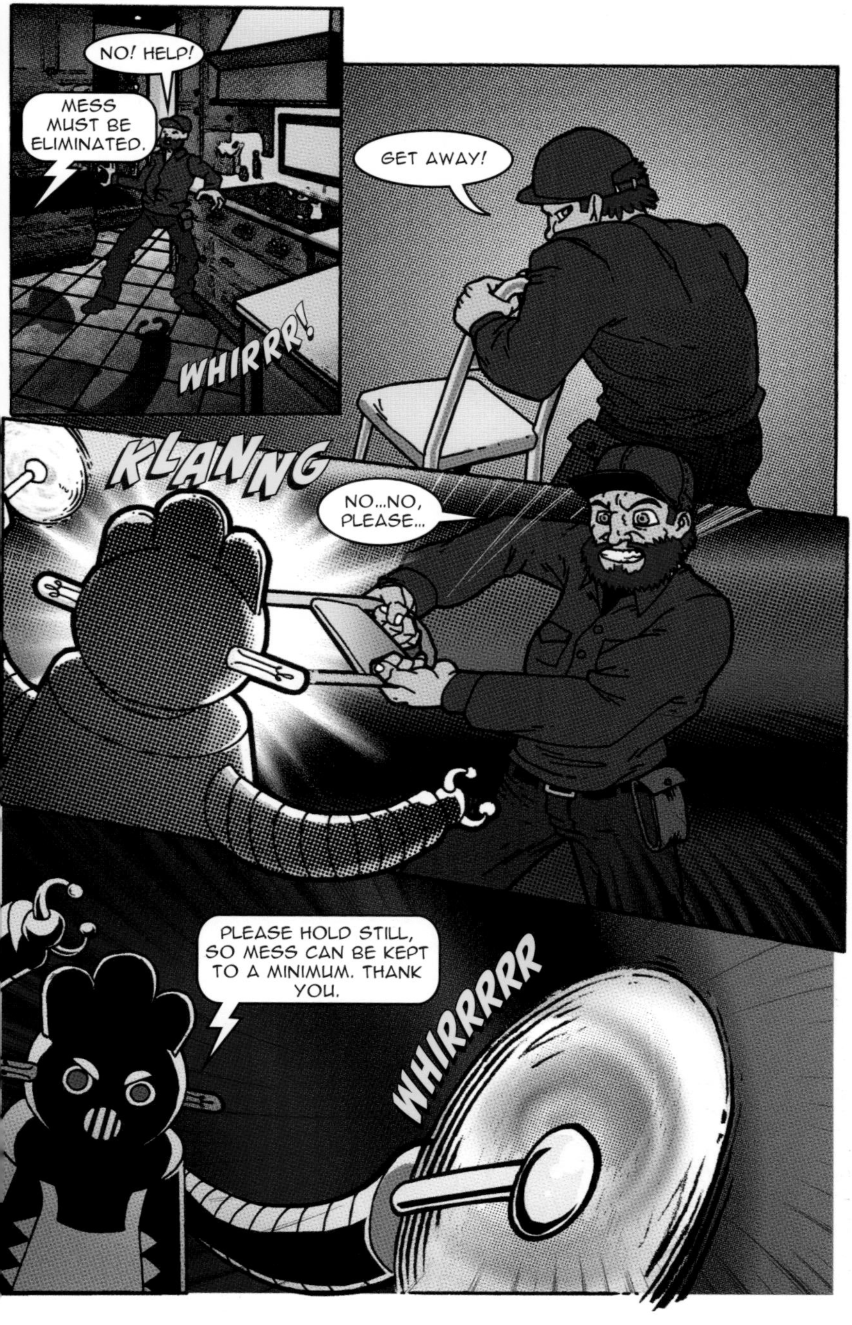
NO! HELP!
MESS MUST BE ELIMINATED.
WHIRRR!
GET AWAY!
KLANNG
NO...NO, PLEASE...
PLEASE HOLD STILL, SO MESS CAN BE KEPT TO A MINIMUM. THANK YOU.
WHIRRRRR

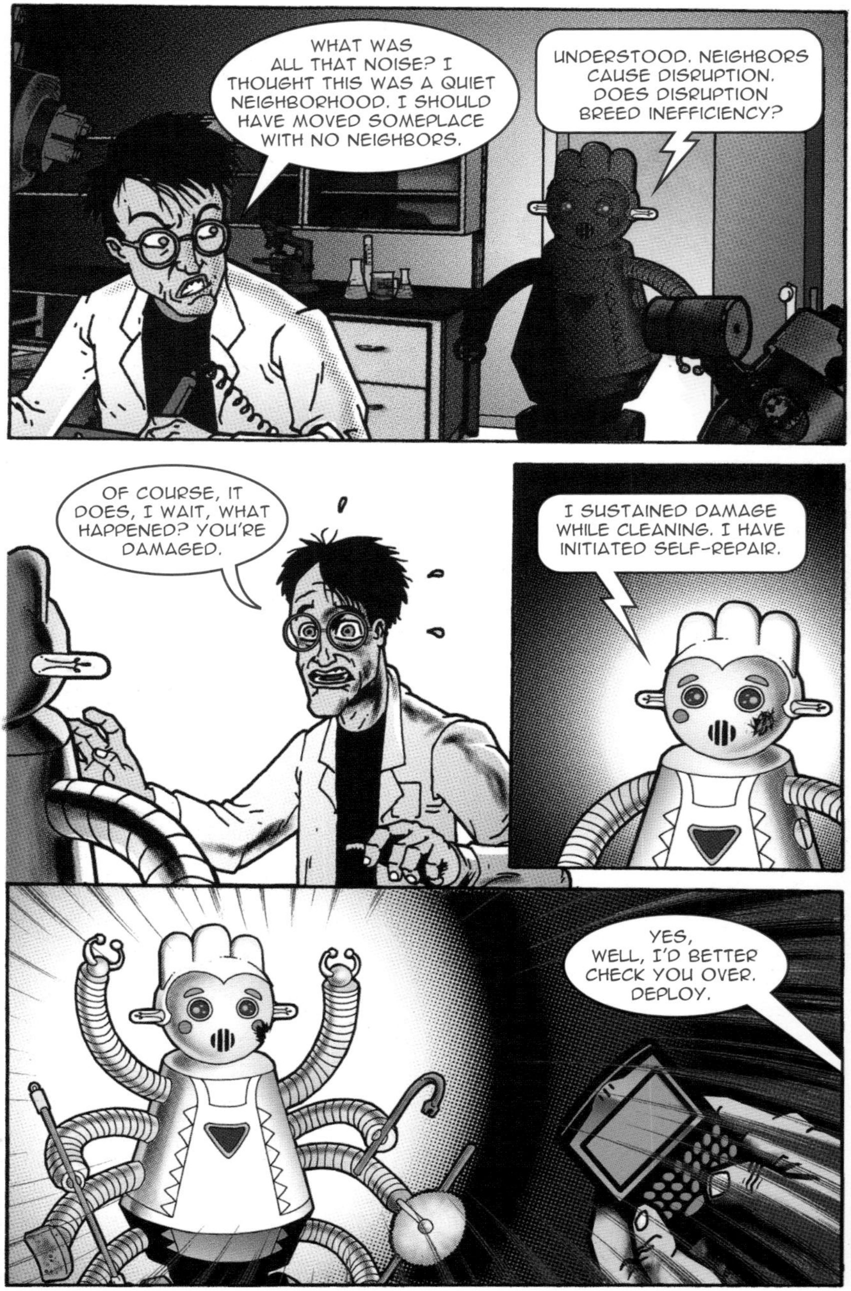
WHAT WAS ALL THAT NOISE? I THOUGHT THIS WAS A QUIET NEIGHBORHOOD. I SHOULD HAVE MOVED SOMEPLACE WITH NO NEIGHBORS.
UNDERSTOOD. NEIGHBORS CAUSE DISRUPTION. DOES DISRUPTION BREED INEFFICIENCY?
OF COURSE, IT DOES, I WAIT, WHAT HAPPENED? YOU'RE DAMAGED.
I SUSTAINED DAMAGE WHILE CLEANING. I HAVE INITIATED SELF-REPAIR.
YES, WELL, I'D BETTER CHECK YOU OVER. DEPLOY.

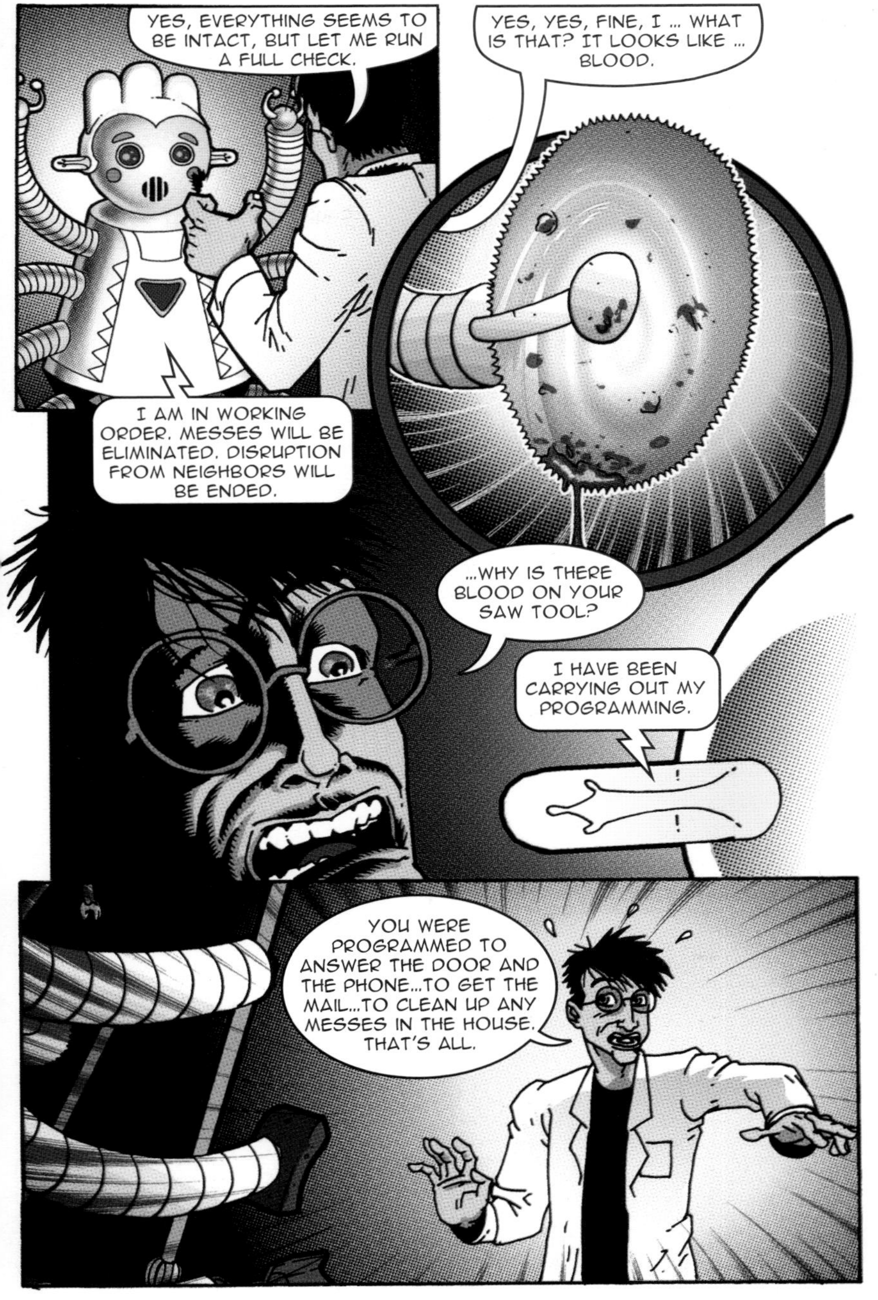
YES, EVERYTHING SEEMS TO BE INTACT, BUT LET ME RUN A FULL CHECK.
I AM IN WORKING ORDER. MESSES WILL BE ELIMINATED. DISRUPTION FROM NEIGHBORS WILL BE ENDED.
YES, YES, FINE, I ... WHAT IS THAT? IT LOOKS LIKE ... BLOOD.
...WHY IS THERE BLOOD ON YOUR SAW TOOL?
I HAVE BEEN CARRYING OUT MY PROGRAMMING.
YOU WERE PROGRAMMED TO ANSWER THE DOOR AND THE PHONE...TO GET THE MAIL...TO CLEAN UP ANY MESSES IN THE HOUSE. THAT'S ALL.

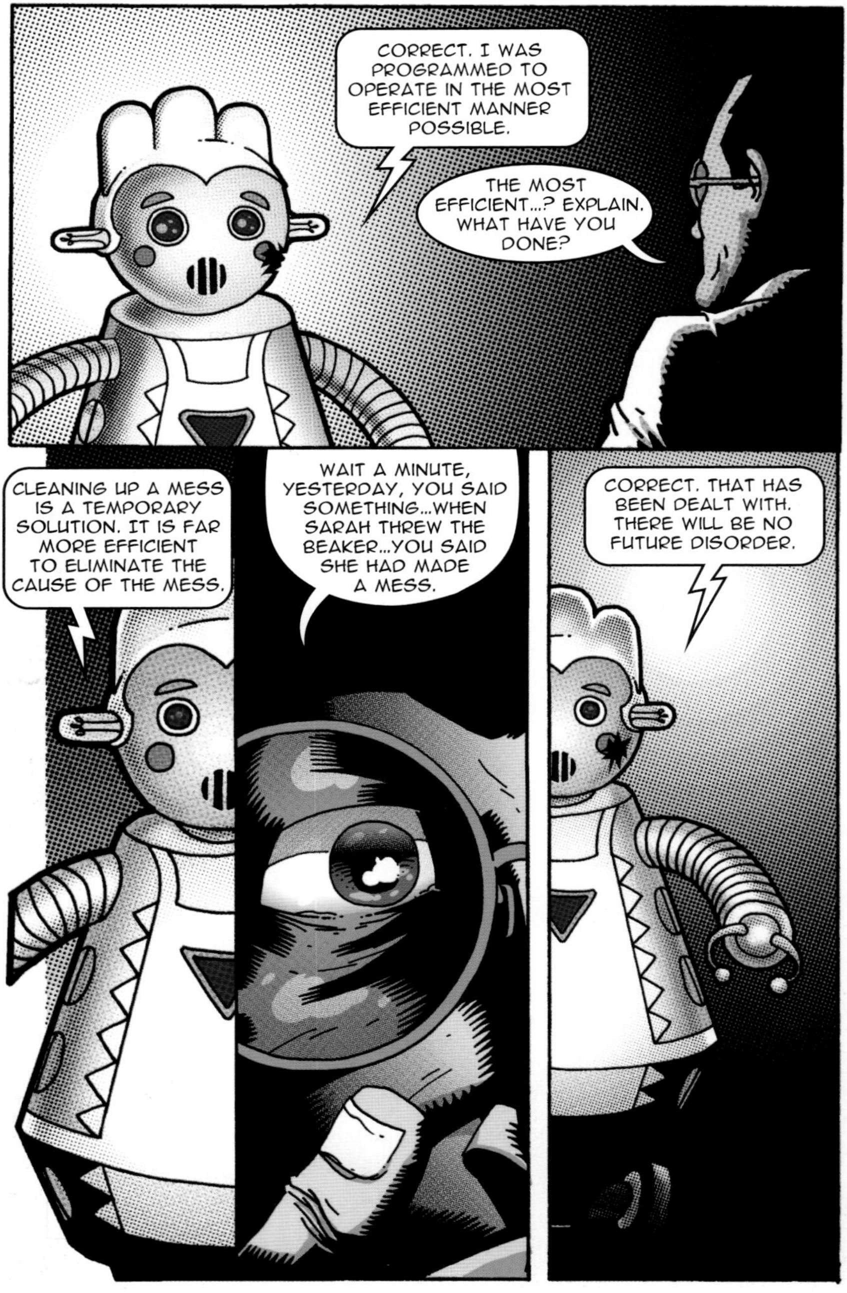
CORRECT. I WAS PROGRAMMED TO OPERATE IN THE MOST EFFICIENT MANNER POSSIBLE.
THE MOST EFFICIENT...? EXPLAIN. WHAT HAVE YOU DONE?
CLEANING UP A MESS IS A TEMPORARY SOLUTION. IT IS FAR MORE EFFICIENT TO ELIMINATE THE CAUSE OF THE MESS.
WAIT A MINUTE, YESTERDAY, YOU SAID SOMETHING...WHEN SARAH THREW THE BEAKER...YOU SAID SHE HAD MADE A MESS.
CORRECT. THAT HAS BEEN DEALT WITH. THERE WILL BE NO FUTURE DISORDER.

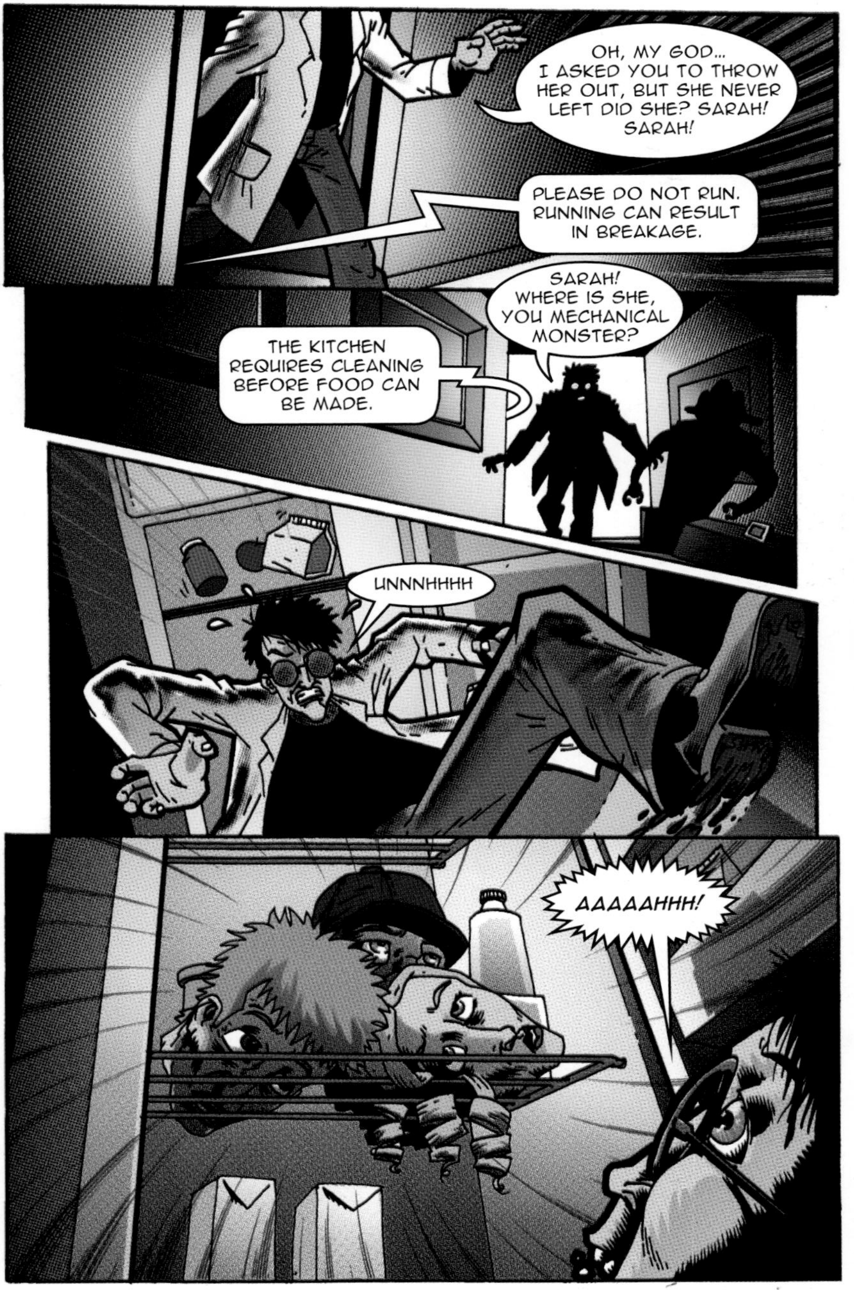
OH, MY GOD... I ASKED YOU TO THROW HER OUT, BUT SHE NEVER LEFT DID SHE? SARAH! SARAH!
PLEASE DO NOT RUN. RUNNING CAN RESULT IN BREAKAGE.
SARAH! WHERE IS SHE, YOU MECHANICAL MONSTER?
THE KITCHEN REQUIRES CLEANING BEFORE FOOD CAN BE MADE.
UNNNHHHH
AAAAAHHH!

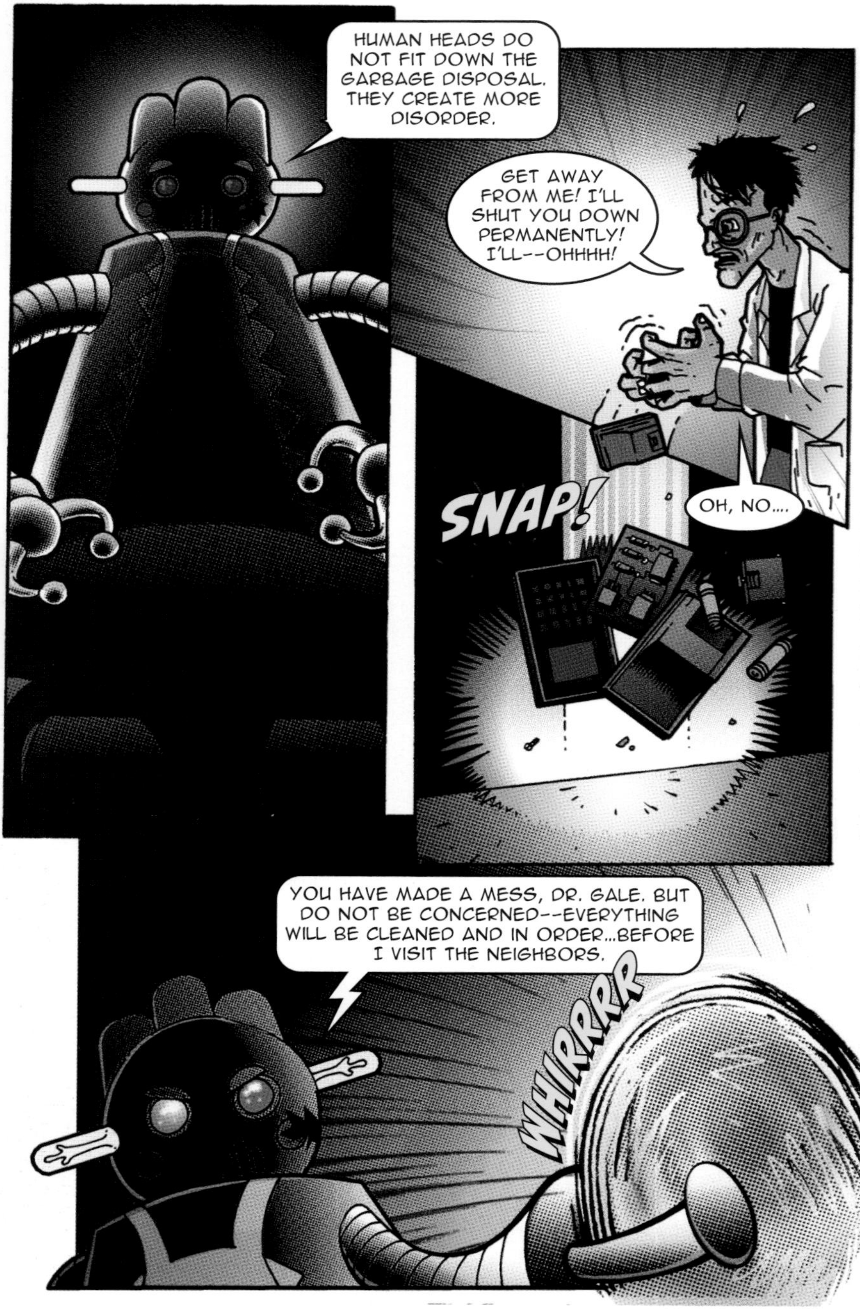
HUMAN HEADS DO NOT FIT DOWN THE GARBAGE DISPOSAL. THEY CREATE MORE DISORDER.
GET AWAY FROM ME! I'LL SHUT YOU DOWN PERMANENTLY! I'LL--OHHHH!
SNAP!
OH, NO....
YOU HAVE MADE A MESS, DR. GALE. BUT DO NOT BE CONCERNED--EVERYTHING WILL BE CLEANED AND IN ORDER...BEFORE I VISIT THE NEIGHBORS.
WHIRRRR

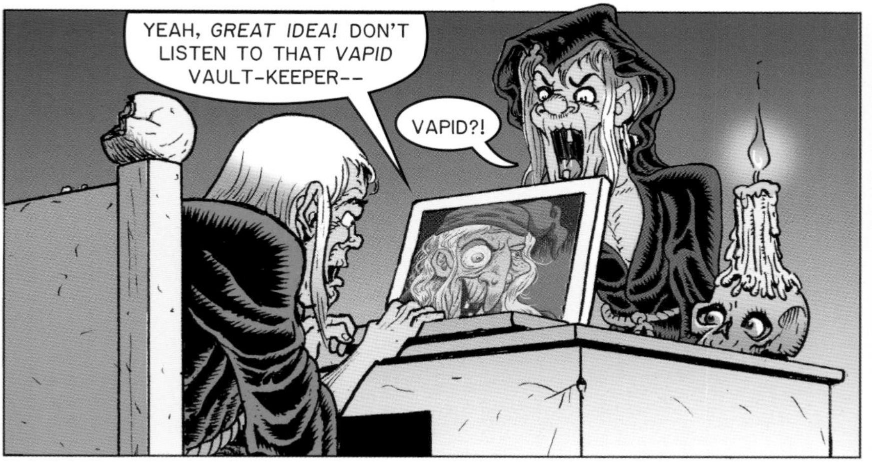
YEAH, *GREAT IDEA!* DON'T LISTEN TO THAT *VAPID* VAULT-KEEPER--
VAPID?!

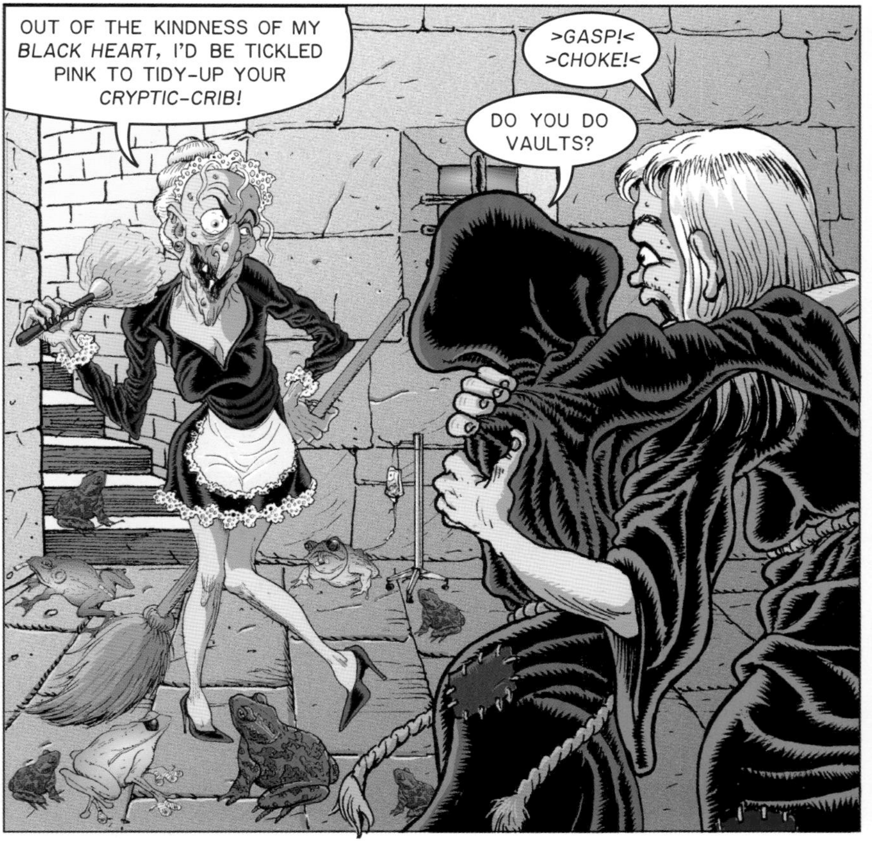
OUT OF THE KINDNESS OF MY *BLACK HEART,* I'D BE TICKLED PINK TO TIDY-UP YOUR *CRYPTIC-CRIB!*
>GASP!< >CHOKE!<
DO YOU DO VAULTS?

WATCH OUT FOR PAPERCUTZ™

Welcome to another scary edition of the Papercutz Backpages, the place to find out all the news about what's going on with the graphic novel publishers of THE HARDY BOYS, NANCY DREW, TALES FROM THE CRYPT, BIONICLE, and CLASSICS ILLUSTRATED. I'm Jim Salicrup, that creepy-looking Old Editor and pumped-up Papercutz promoter. Last time on these pages we gave you a sneak-peek at Marion Mousse's all-new adaptation of Mary Shelly's "Frankenstein" from CLASSICS ILLUSTRATED DELUXE #3, on sale now. This time around we're offering a terror-triple-threat of previews sure to please any TALES FROM THE CRYPT fan-addict.

First up, to give you just a teeny-tiny taste of the horrors that await you in CLASSICS ILLUSTRATED #4 "The Raven and Other Poems" by Edgar Allan Poe, we present Gahan Wilson's illustrated version of Poe's poem "Alone." Long-time contributor to The New Yorker and Playboy magazines, Gahan Wilson is the modern master of macabre cartoons, and we're as thrilled as can be to bring his collection of illustrated Poe-ms back into print.

Then, we follow-up with a few pages of Rick Geary's chilling adaptation of H.G. Wells's "Invisible Man" from CLASSICS ILLUSTRATED #2. If you've enjoyed Alan Moore's "League of Extraordinary Gentleman" then you certainly won't want to miss Rick's version of Mr. Moore's source material.

And finally, we offer a bit more of ol' eerie Geary's wondrous work – a peek at the cover art to three of his "Murder" graphic novels from NBM Publishing, our sinister sister company. We've only got enough room to show you the covers of three of Rick's meticulously researched, fact-filled, non-fiction graphic novels – "Jack the Ripper," "The Bloody Benders," and "The Murder of Abraham Lincoln" – but also included in the "Treasury of Victorian Murder" series are "The Beast of Chicago," "The Borden Tragedy," "The Fatal Bullet," and "The Case of Madeleine Smith." All are available, in black and white, paperback graphic novels from NBM, 40 Exchange Place, Ste. 1308, New York, NY 10005, for $9.95 each ("The Borden Tragedy" and "The Case of Madeleine Smith" are only $8.95 each). Be sure to include $4.00 for postage and handling for first book ordered, and $1.00 for each additional book. And tell 'em, Papercutz sent you!

That's enough for now, be here next time for TALES FROM THE CRYPT #7 "Something Wicca This Way Comes." We hear it's the Old Witch's favorite!

Thanks,

Jim

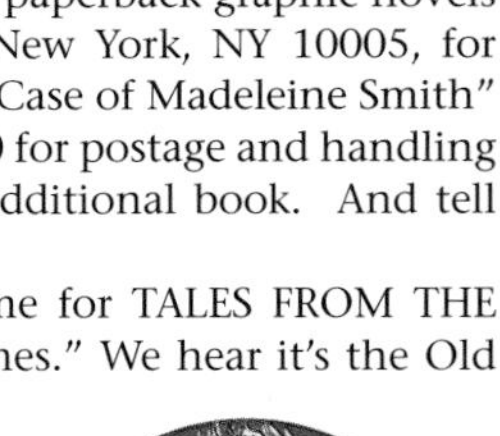

Caricature by
Rick Parker.

THE OLD EDITOR

ALONE

From childhood's hour I have not been
As others were— I have not seen
As others saw— I could not bring
My passions from a common spring.
From the same source I have not taken
My sorrow; I could not awaken
My heart to joy at the same tone;
And all I lov'd, *I* lov'd alone.

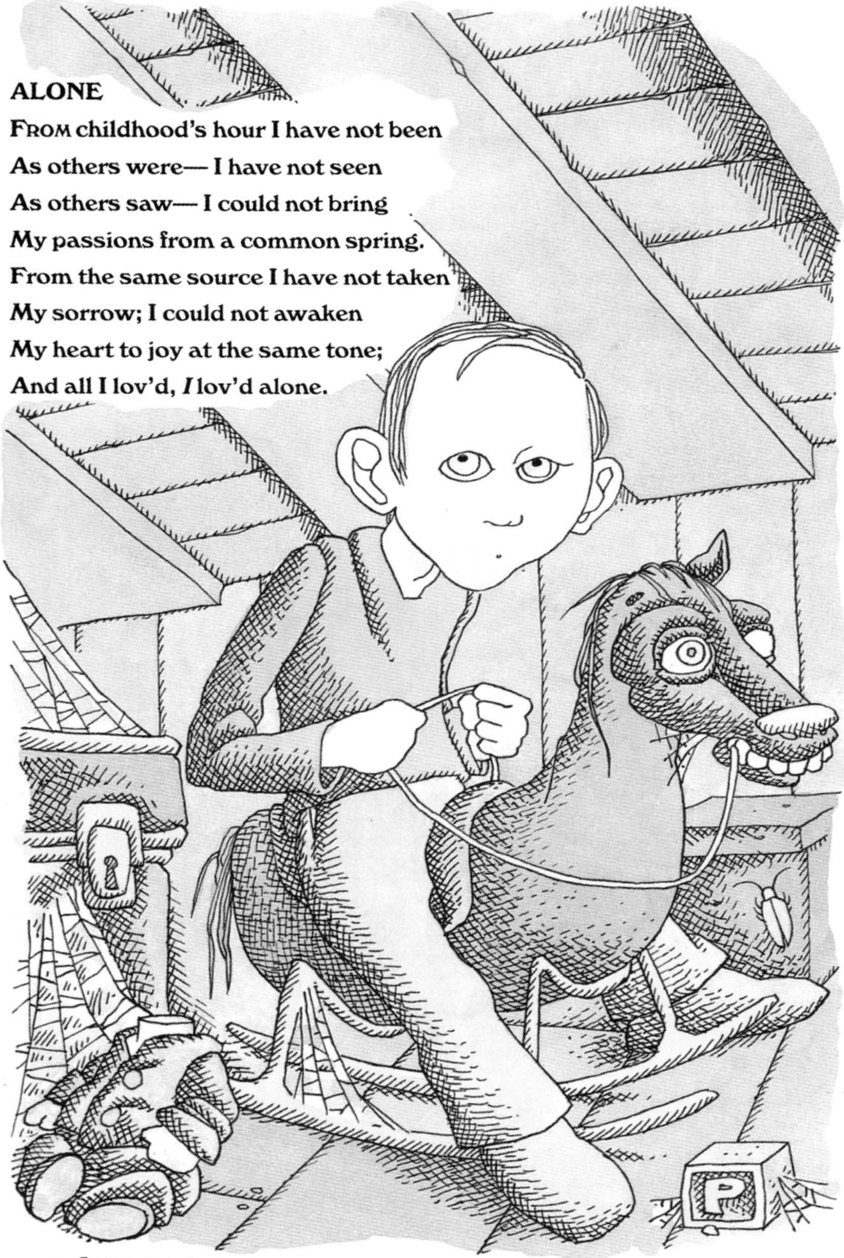
P

Then— in my childhood— in the dawn
Of a most stormy life— was drawn
From ev'ry depth of good and ill
The mystery which binds me still:
From the torrent, or the fountain,
From the red cliff of the mountain,
From the sun that 'round me roll'd
In its autumn tint of gold—
From the lightning in the sky
As it pass'd me flying by—
From the thunder and the storm,
And the cloud that took the form
(When the rest of Heaven was blue)
Of a demon in my view.

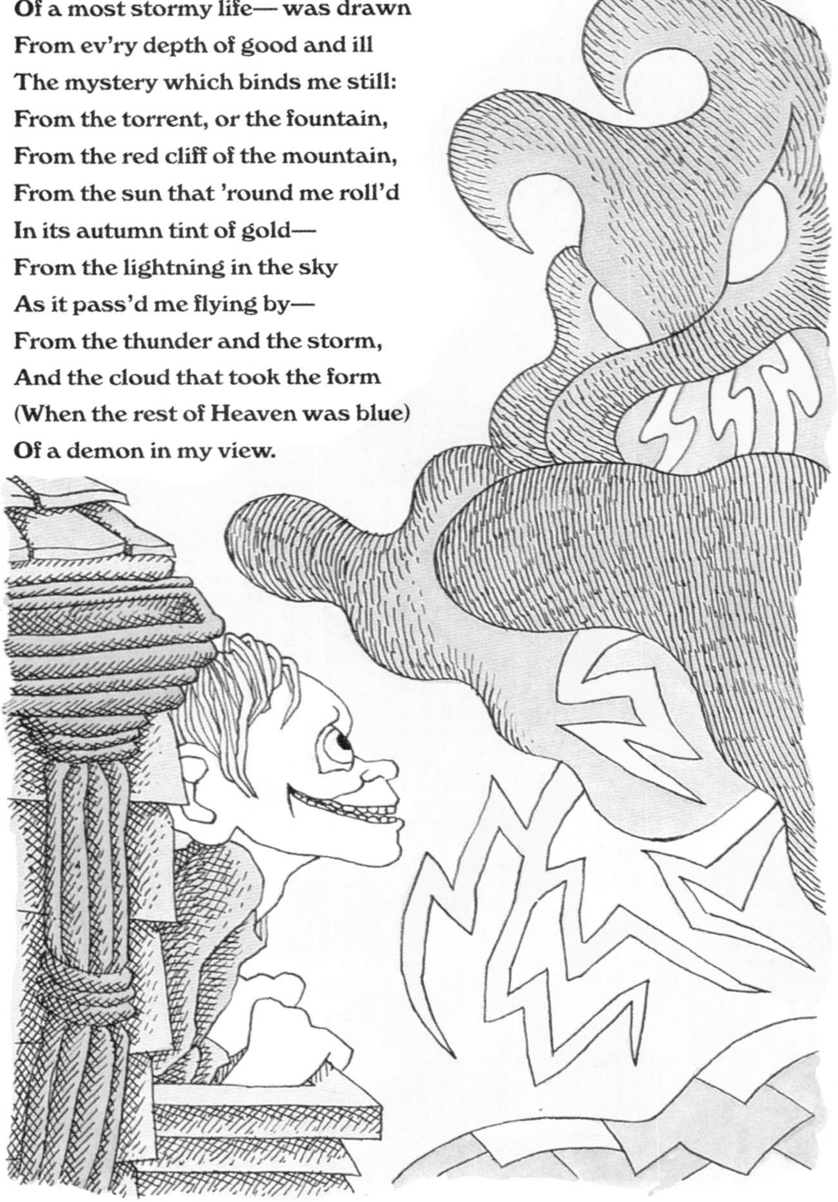

Here's a small peek at "The Invisible Man" by H.G. Wells, adapted by Rick Geary...

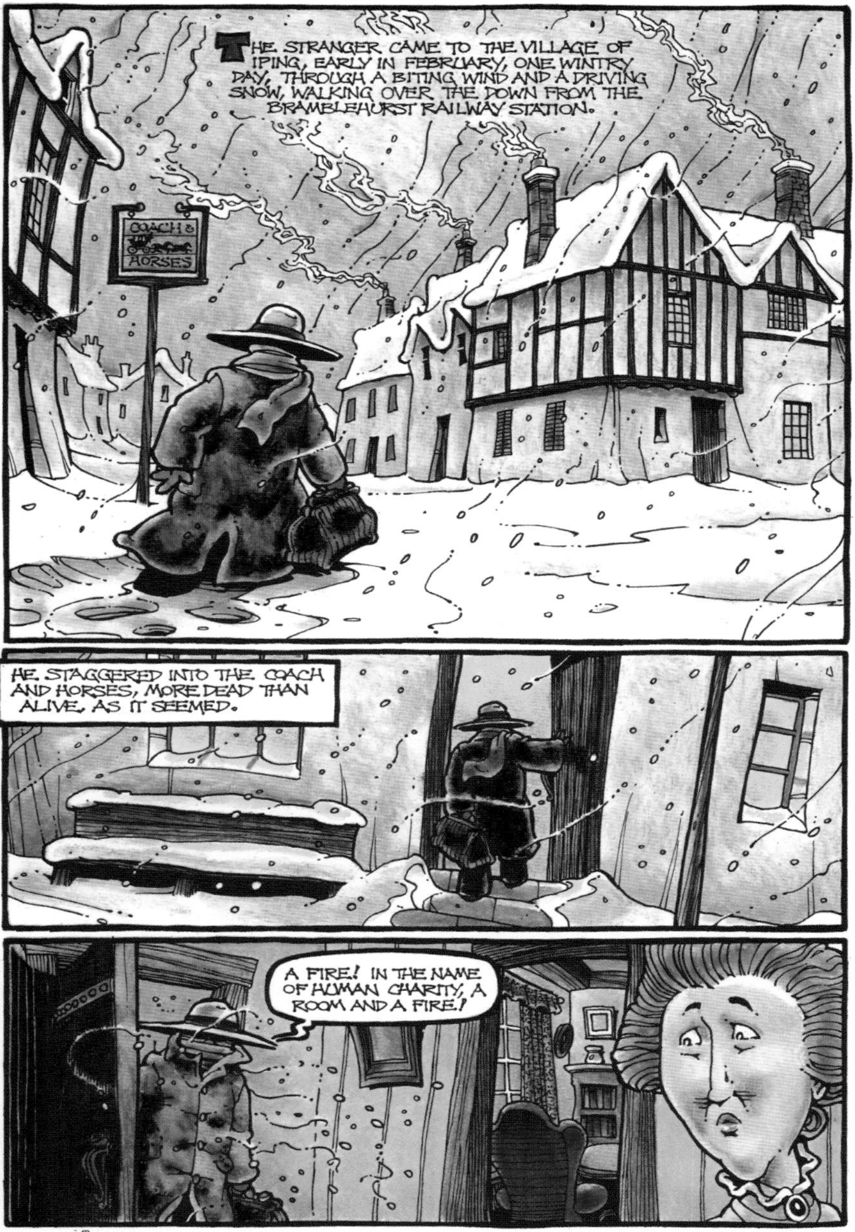
THE STRANGER CAME TO THE VILLAGE OF IPING, EARLY IN FEBRUARY, ONE WINTRY DAY, THROUGH A BITING WIND AND A DRIVING SNOW, WALKING OVER THE DOWN FROM THE BRAMBLEHURST RAILWAY STATION.
COACH & HORSES
HE STAGGERED INTO THE COACH AND HORSES, MORE DEAD THAN ALIVE, AS IT SEEMED.
A FIRE! IN THE NAME OF HUMAN CHARITY, A ROOM AND A FIRE!

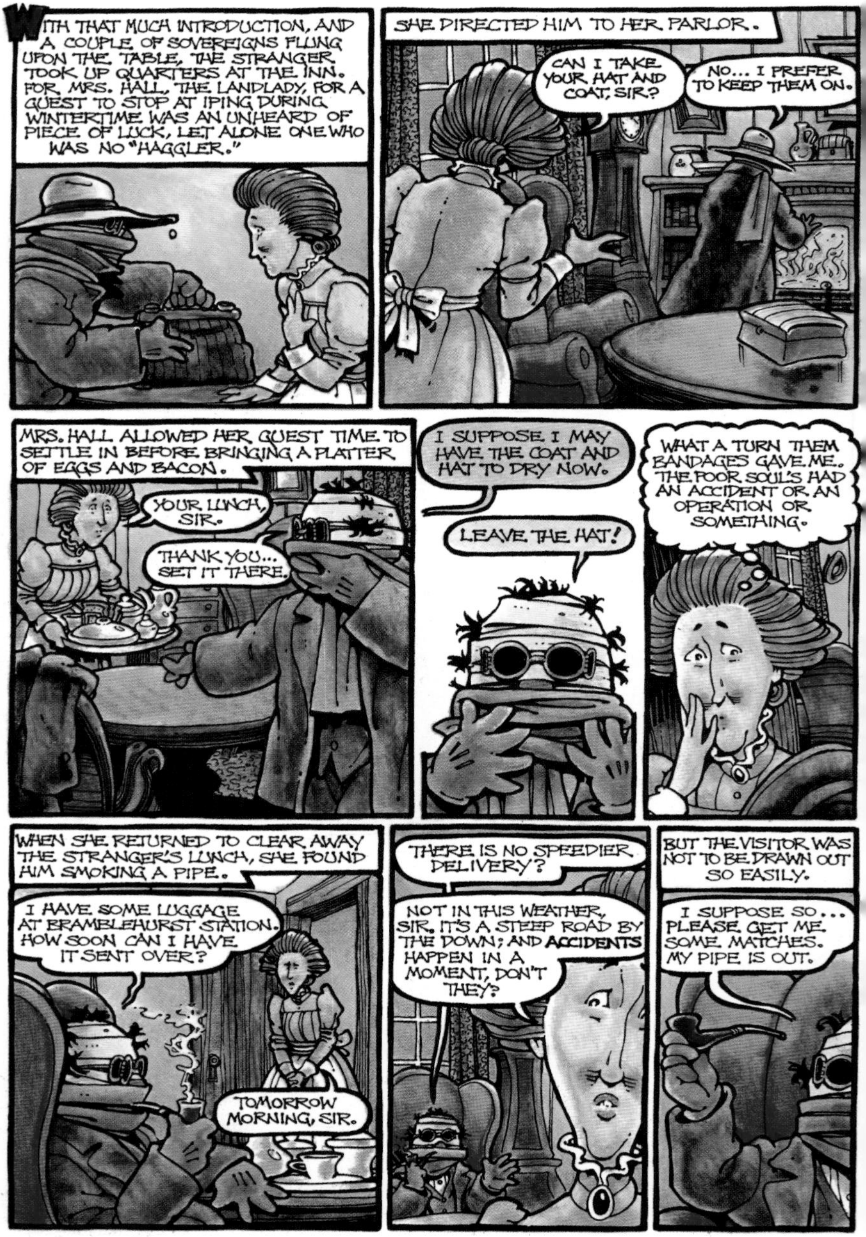
WITH THAT MUCH INTRODUCTION, AND A COUPLE OF SOVEREIGNS FLUNG UPON THE TABLE, THE STRANGER TOOK UP QUARTERS AT THE INN. FOR MRS. HALL, THE LANDLADY, FOR A GUEST TO STOP AT IPING DURING WINTERTIME WAS AN UNHEARD OF PIECE OF LUCK, LET ALONE ONE WHO WAS NO "HAGGLER."
SHE DIRECTED HIM TO HER PARLOR.
CAN I TAKE YOUR HAT AND COAT, SIR?
NO... I PREFER TO KEEP THEM ON.
MRS. HALL ALLOWED HER GUEST TIME TO SETTLE IN BEFORE BRINGING A PLATTER OF EGGS AND BACON.
YOUR LUNCH, SIR.
THANK YOU... SET IT THERE.
I SUPPOSE I MAY HAVE THE COAT AND HAT TO DRY NOW.
LEAVE THE HAT!
WHAT A TURN THEM BANDAGES GAVE ME. THE POOR SOUL'S HAD AN ACCIDENT OR AN OPERATION OR SOMETHING.
WHEN SHE RETURNED TO CLEAR AWAY THE STRANGER'S LUNCH, SHE FOUND HIM SMOKING A PIPE.
I HAVE SOME LUGGAGE AT BRAMBLEHURST STATION. HOW SOON CAN I HAVE IT SENT OVER?
TOMORROW MORNING, SIR.
THERE IS NO SPEEDIER DELIVERY?
NOT IN THIS WEATHER, SIR. IT'S A STEEP ROAD BY THE DOWN; AND ACCIDENTS HAPPEN IN A MOMENT, DON'T THEY?
BUT THE VISITOR WAS NOT TO BE DRAWN OUT SO EASILY.
I SUPPOSE SO... PLEASE GET ME SOME MATCHES. MY PIPE IS OUT.

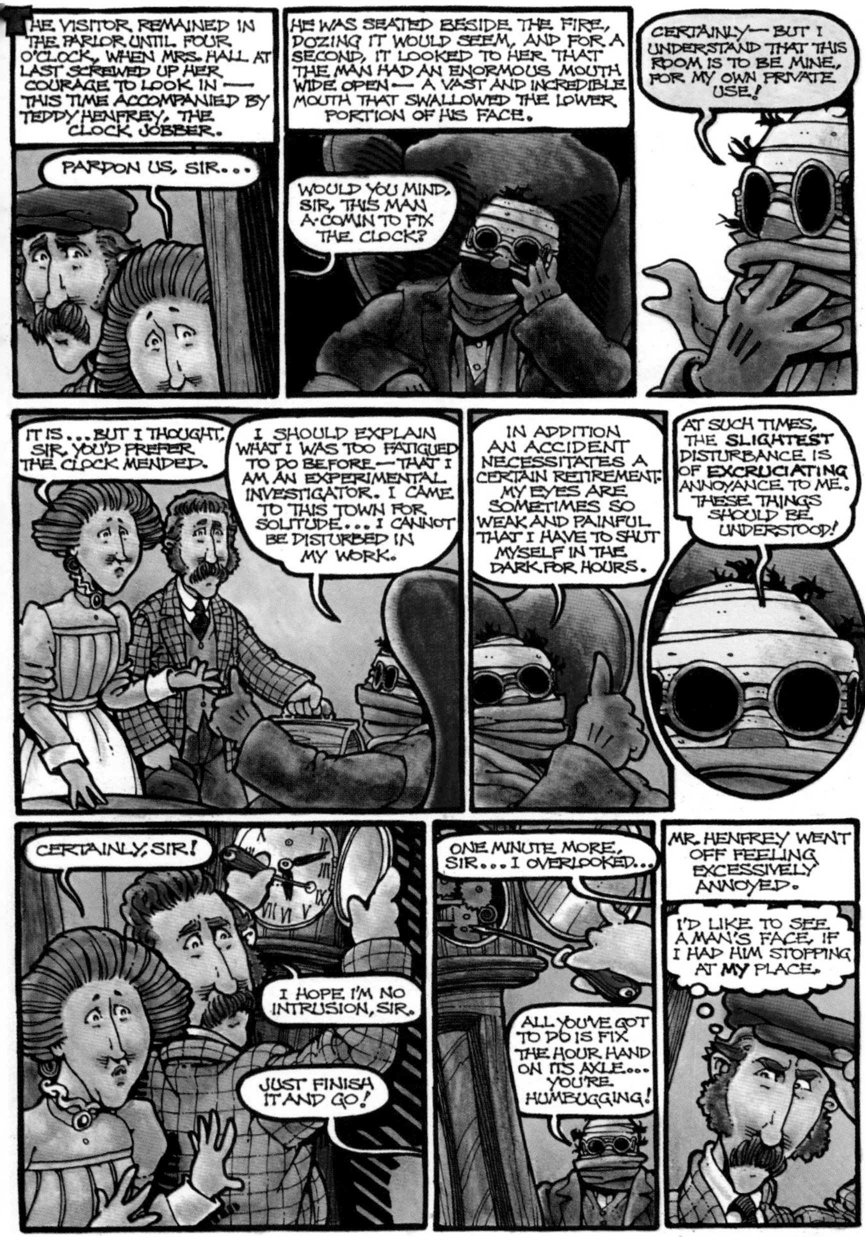
THE VISITOR REMAINED IN THE PARLOR UNTIL FOUR O'CLOCK, WHEN MRS. HALL AT LAST SCREWED UP HER COURAGE TO LOOK IN — THIS TIME ACCOMPANIED BY TEDDY HENFREY, THE CLOCK JOBBER.
PARDON US, SIR...
HE WAS SEATED BESIDE THE FIRE, DOZING IT WOULD SEEM, AND FOR A SECOND, IT LOOKED TO HER THAT THE MAN HAD AN ENORMOUS MOUTH WIDE OPEN — A VAST AND INCREDIBLE MOUTH THAT SWALLOWED THE LOWER PORTION OF HIS FACE.
WOULD YOU MIND, SIR, THIS MAN A-COMIN TO FIX THE CLOCK?
CERTAINLY— BUT I UNDERSTAND THAT THIS ROOM IS TO BE MINE, FOR MY OWN PRIVATE USE!
IT IS... BUT I THOUGHT, SIR, YOU'D PREFER THE CLOCK MENDED.
I SHOULD EXPLAIN WHAT I WAS TOO FATIGUED TO DO BEFORE— THAT I AM AN EXPERIMENTAL INVESTIGATOR. I CAME TO THIS TOWN FOR SOLITUDE... I CANNOT BE DISTURBED IN MY WORK.
IN ADDITION AN ACCIDENT NECESSITATES A CERTAIN RETIREMENT. MY EYES ARE SOMETIMES SO WEAK AND PAINFUL THAT I HAVE TO SHUT MYSELF IN THE DARK FOR HOURS.
AT SUCH TIMES, THE SLIGHTEST DISTURBANCE IS OF EXCRUCIATING ANNOYANCE TO ME. THESE THINGS SHOULD BE UNDERSTOOD!
CERTAINLY, SIR!
I HOPE I'M NO INTRUSION, SIR.
JUST FINISH IT AND GO!
ONE MINUTE MORE, SIR... I OVERLOOKED...
ALL YOU'VE GOT TO DO IS FIX THE HOUR HAND ON ITS AXLE... YOU'RE HUMBUGGING!
MR. HENFREY WENT OFF FEELING EXCESSIVELY ANNOYED.
I'D LIKE TO SEE A MAN'S FACE, IF I HAD HIM STOPPING AT MY PLACE.

For the rest, pick up CLASSICS ILLUSTRATED #2 "The Invisible Man" on sale at booksellers everywhere.

And if you liked Rick Geary's adaptation of "The Invisible Man," check out his "Treasury of Victorian Murder" series of graphic novels from NBM...

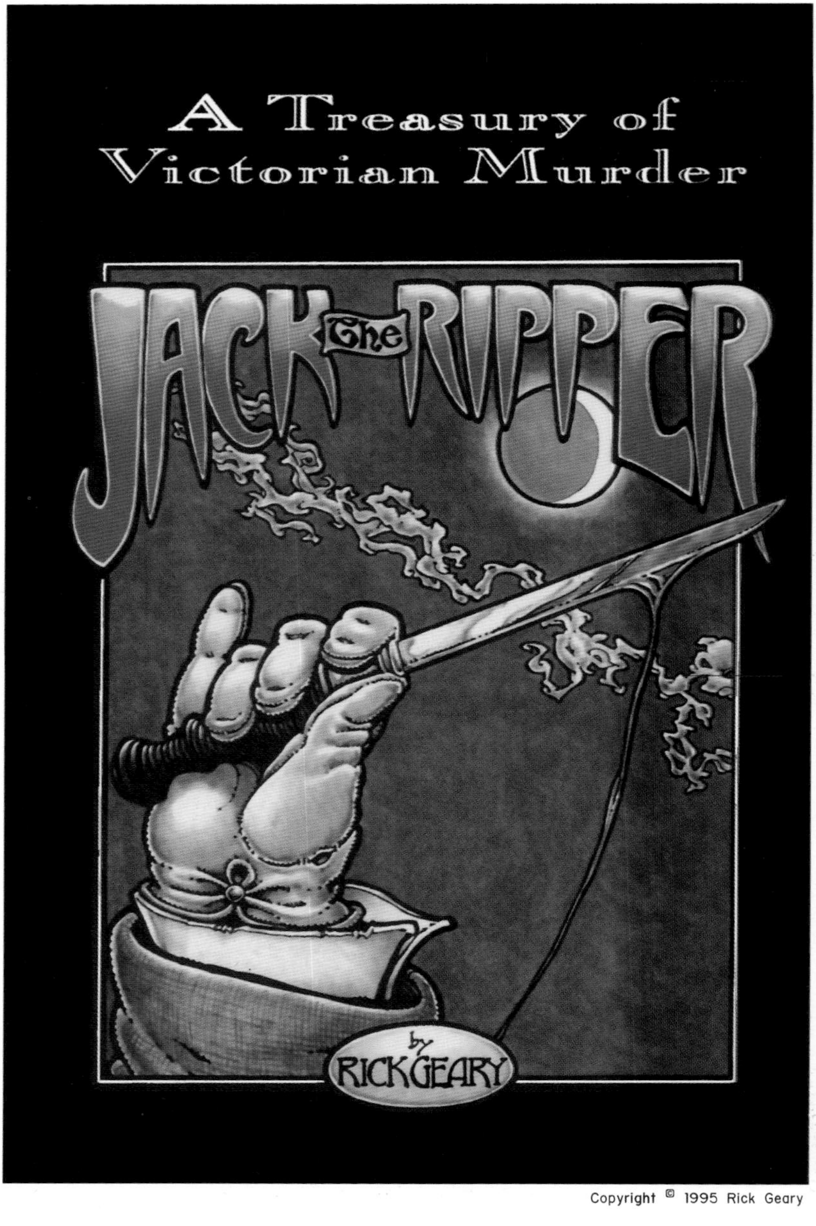
A Treasury of Victorian Murder
JACK the RIPPER
by
RICK GEARY

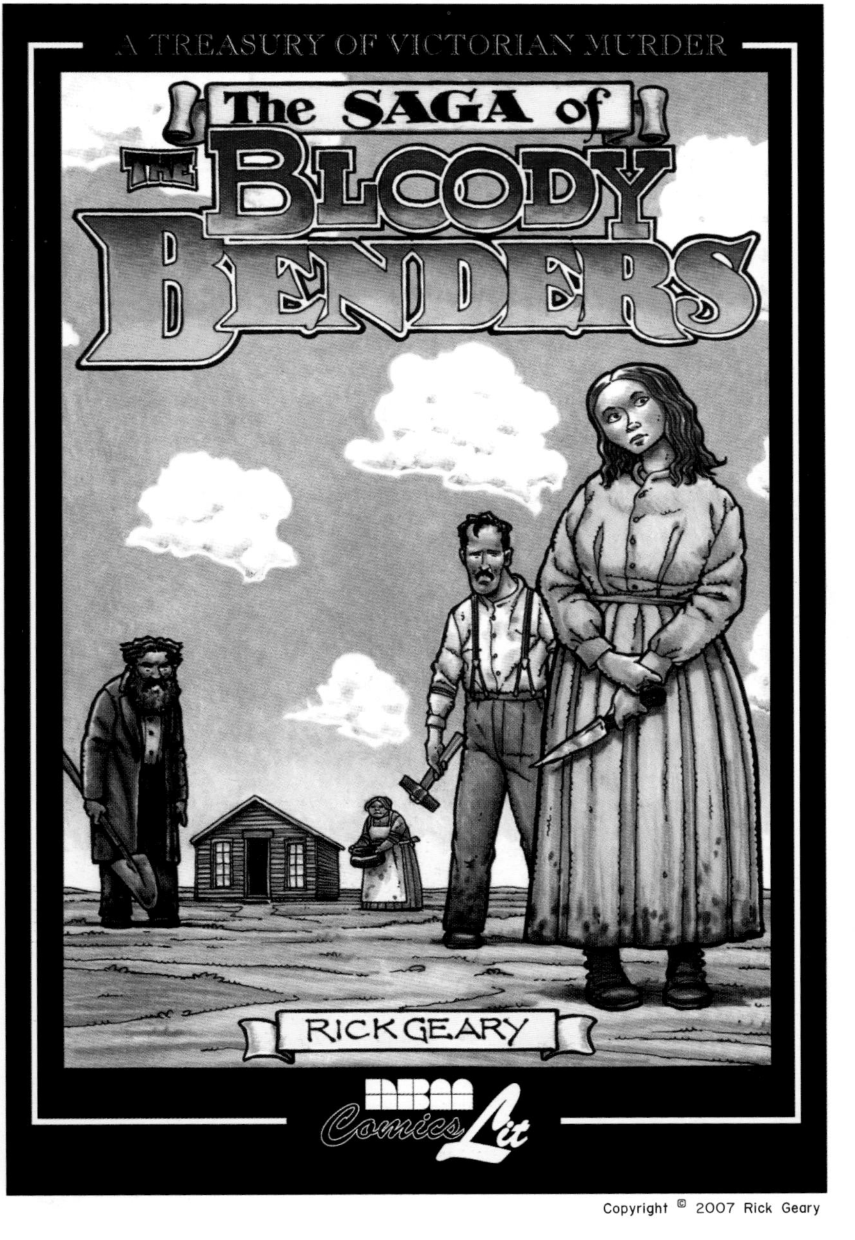
A TREASURY OF VICTORIAN MURDER
The SAGA of
THE BLOODY BENDERS
RICK GEARY
NBM Comics Lit

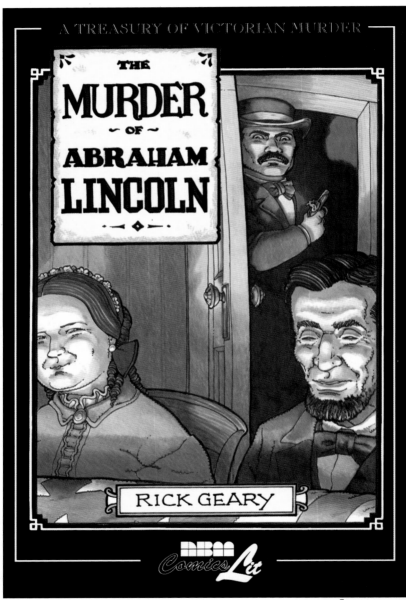

Look for the entire series of "Victorian Murder" graphic novels from Rick Geary
at booksellers everywhere.

CLASSICS ILLUSTRATED GRAPHIC NOVELS AVAILABLE FROM PAPERCUTZ

CLASSICS ILLUSTRATED DELUXE:

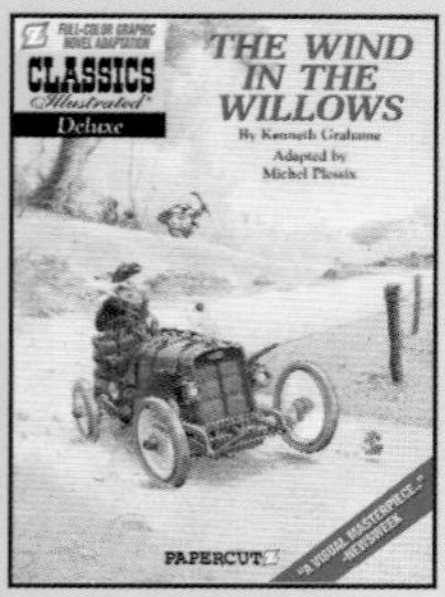
FULL-COLOR GRAPHIC NOVEL ADAPTATION
CLASSICS Illustrated Deluxe
THE WIND IN THE WILLOWS
By Kenneth Grahame
Adapted by Michel Plessix
"A VISUAL MASTERPIECE..." –NEWSWEEK
PAPERCUTZ

Graphic Novel #1
"The Wind In The Willows"

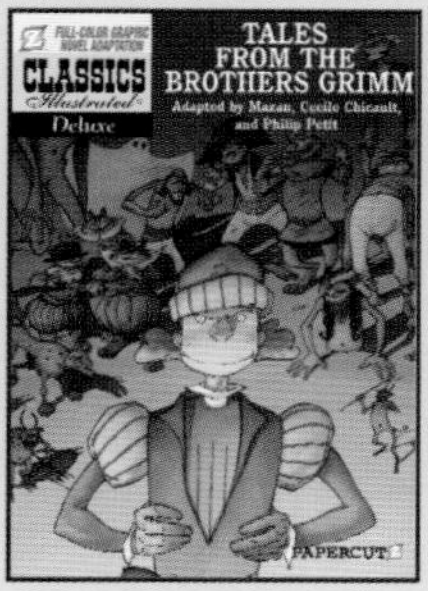
FULL-COLOR GRAPHIC NOVEL ADAPTATION
CLASSICS Illustrated Deluxe
TALES FROM THE BROTHERS GRIMM
PAPERCUTZ

Graphic Novel #2
"Tales From The Brothers Grimm"

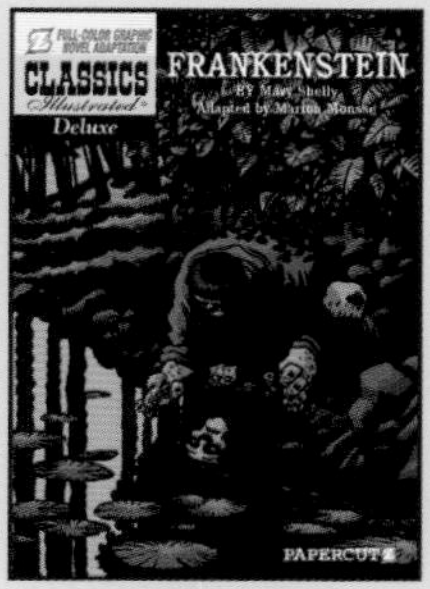
FULL-COLOR GRAPHIC NOVEL ADAPTATION
CLASSICS Illustrated Deluxe
FRANKENSTEIN
PAPERCUTZ

Graphic Novel #3
"Frankenstein"

CLASSICS ILLUSTRATED:

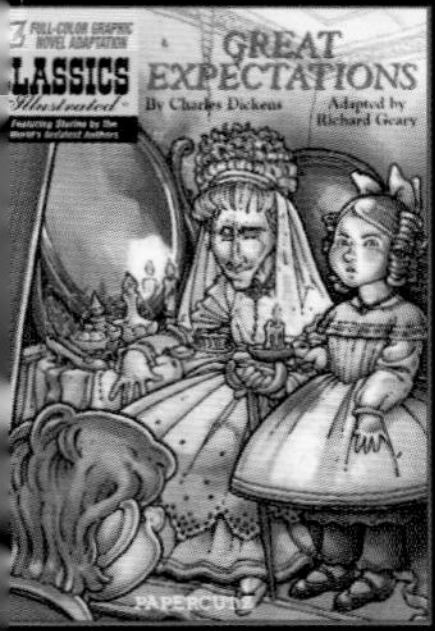
GREAT EXPECTATIONS
By Charles Dickens
Adapted by Richard Geary
PAPERCUTZ

Graphic Novel #1
"Great Expectations"

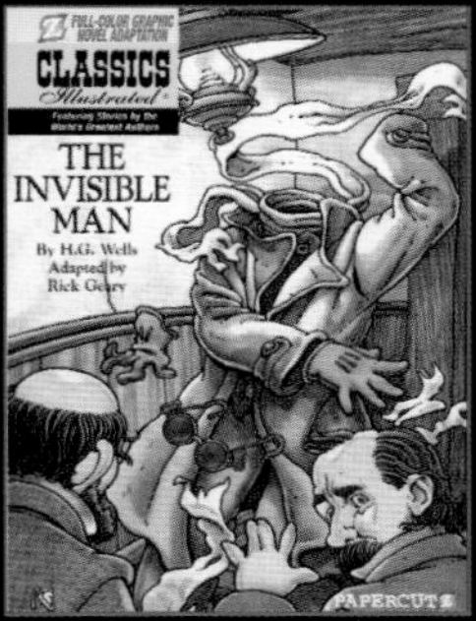
FULL-COLOR GRAPHIC NOVEL ADAPTATION
CLASSICS Illustrated
THE INVISIBLE MAN
By H.G. Wells
Adapted by Rick Geary
PAPERCUTZ

Graphic Novel #2
"The Invisible Man"

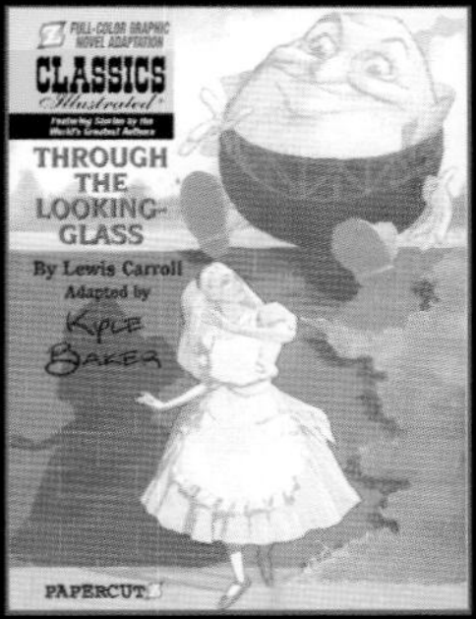
FULL-COLOR GRAPHIC NOVEL ADAPTATION
CLASSICS Illustrated
THROUGH THE LOOKING-GLASS
By Lewis Carroll
Adapted by
KYLE BAKER
PAPERCUTZ

Graphic Novel #3
"Through the Looking-Glass"

Classics Illustrated Deluxe are available for $13.95 each in paperback and $17.95 in hardcover. Classics Illustrated are available only in hardcover for $9.95 each. Please add $4.00 for postage and handling for the first book, add $1.00 for each additional book. Please make check payable to NBM Publishing. Send to:

...cutz, 40 Exchange Pla... Suite 1308, New York, NY 10005 • 1-800-866-1223 • www.papercutz.com

THE HARDY BOYS

A NEW GRAPHIC NOVEL EVERY 3 MONTHS!

#12 "Dude Ranch O' Death"
ISBN - 978-1-59707-088-1
#13 "The Deadliest Stunt"
ISBN - 978-1-59707-102-4
#14 "Haley Danielle's Top Eight!"
ISBN – 978-159707-113-0
#15 "Live Free, Die Hardy!"
ISBN – 978-159707-124-6
NEW! #16 "Shhhhhh!"
ISBN - 978-1-59707-138-3

NEW!

NEW STORY! FULL-COLOR GRAPHIC NOVEL
THE HARDY BOYS
#16
SHHHHHH!
based on the series by Franklin W. Dixon
UNDERCOVER BROTHERS
Scott LOBDELL
Paulo HENRIQUE
PAPERCUTZ

Also available – Hardy Boys #1-11
All: Pocket sized, 96-112 pp., full-color, $7.95
Also available in hardcover! $12.95

THE HARDY BOYS
Graphic Novels #1-4 Box Set
ISBN – 978-1-59707-040-9
THE HARDY BOYS
Graphic Novels #5-8 Box Set
ISBN – 978-1-59707-075-1
THE HARDY BOYS
Graphic Novels #9-12 Box Set
ISBN-978-1-59707-125-3
All: Full-color, $29.95

CLASSICS Illustrated
Featuring Stories by the World's Greatest Authors

#1 "Great Expectations"
ISBN 978-159707-097-3
#2 "The Invisible Man"
ISBN 978-159707-106-2
NEW! #3 "Through the Looking Glass"
ISBN 978-159707-115-4
All: 6 1/2 x 9, 56 pp., full-color, $9.95

FULL-COLOR GRAPHIC NOVEL ADAPTATION
CLASSICS Illustrated
Featuring Stories by the World's Greatest Authors
THROUGH THE LOOKING-GLASS
By Lewis Carroll
Adapted by
KYLE BAKER
PAPERCUTZ

ON SALE NOW!

Please add $4.00 postage and handling. Add $1.00 for each additional item.
Make check payable to NBM publishing.
Send To:
Papercutz, 40 Exchange Place, Suite 1308,
New York, New York 10005, 1-800-886-1223
www.papercutz.com